Daisy Chain

DCI Kath Fortune - Book 1
Julia Vaughan

Cahill Davis

Publishing

Cahill Davis Publishing

First published in Great Britain in 2021 by Cahill Davis Publishing Limited.

First published in paperback in Great Britain in 2021 by Cahill Davis Publishing Limited.

ISBN 978-1-8381820-7-6 (eBook)

ISBN 978-1-8381820-6-9 (Paperback)

Cahill Davis Publishing Limited

www.cahilldavispublishing.co.uk

structions in his head from the call, he
ental bowl from the side table, pulled
nd pushed two fingers into her mouth,
dn't bite down. Her eyes flew open,
:d. Todd removed his fingers from her
 to avoid the flow of puke.
ol smell rose from the vomit pool in the
y back against the cushion.
ave me?' Her voice was hoarse; throat
ing.
eadlights flashed through the window,
o look down at her. 'I don't like people
n.'
iva from his hand down the leg of his
nde man in jogging bottoms and an
he room and crossed to where she lay.
d as he set his medical bag on the table.

now all that stuff's out of her.' Todd ran
s hair, the curls falling back into place

speak for myself.' The woman pushed
position, then fell back, weakened by
ol still in her bloodstream.
opened his bag. 'Coffee would be good,
 penlight and blood pressure cuff in his

e room, Andrew perched next to the
ck you over.' It wasn't a request. The
erself to an examination. He pushed the
dress up to the shoulder and strapped on
e closed her eyes as the band tightened

Thank you to C, T and Z for faith in the story, family and friends for all the support and to Steve for sharing the journey.

Repeating the i
grabbed an ornai
her onto her side
praying she wou
and her body ten
mouth just in tim

A pungent alco
china bowl. She l
'Why did you
raw from the hea
He stood as cai
then turned back
dying in my gare
Todd wiped s
jeans as a tall, b
overcoat entered
He glanced at T
'How is she now
'Seems coherei
a hand through
across his forehe:
'I am here. I c
herself to a sittii
the pills and alco
Andrew Tayle
Todd.' He held
hands and waite
'Right. Coffee
As Todd left
woman. 'Let's c
woman resignee
loose sleeve of h
the black band.

He carried her :
body was limp,
his knees as he
Her hair brush
lolling head cai
open to reveal
on the sofa, cate
floor. Her pulse
He grabbed his
him.

'Andrew, it's '
a…situation.'

Her arm slip
across her chest
shallowest of bre

'I've got a wor
seen the empty l
to her body as he
the voice on the
do. 'Yes, okay. Ji

He tossed the |
head, placing a c
he muttered. 'Jus

and the gauge hissed. Satisfied that her pressure was okay, Andrew shone the light into her eyes. She pushed his hand away.

'I'm okay.'

Andrew pursed his lips. 'I'm guessing 'unfortunately' lies at the end of that statement.' He glanced down at the Meissen bowl and the pale amber bile peppered with white sediment.

'Whisky and pills? Must have been serious.'

She wiped her mouth with the back of her hand. 'It wasn't a cry for help.'

Andrew packed his bag and pushed his hands into his coat pockets. 'Do you want to talk about it?'

She shook her head and closed her eyes.

'Okay. Rest here. I'll be back.'

He found Todd in the kitchen, three steaming mugs of coffee on the work surface. The steam fogged the lower panes of the window as he stared into the darkness. He saw Andrew reflected behind him and turned to face him. 'How is she?'

Andrew perched on the edge of the pine table and faced his friend of many years. 'You found her in time. I don't think there'll be any lasting damage… physically anyway. She'll be fine. Weak but fine.'

Todd sighed. 'Lost one, saved one.'

Both men let the statement hang between them.

'It's the anniversary today.'

Andrew nodded, rising and reaching past his friend to push a mug towards him. 'You want to tell me exactly what happened?' He sipped his own coffee and waited.

Todd shrugged. 'I was upstairs, and I heard Samson meowing.' At the sound of his name, a ginger cat appeared, rubbing round Andrew's legs and leaving a furry reminder of his presence on his jogging bottoms. Andrew provided the required stroking as Todd continued. 'I thought he must have caught something, so I came down to have a look. It seemed like he wanted me to follow him into the garden, so I walked across the lawn, to the shrubs at the bottom. And there she was.'

Andrew smiled. 'Obviously fed up with rabbits and mice, aren't you, mate?' The cat's purr was amplified in the stillness of the hour.

'God, Andrew… she was just lying there. I wouldn't even have known if it hadn't been for him.'

Samson was now sitting between the two men, looking from face to face.

Todd continued, 'I felt for a pulse—first thing I did. Then I brought her in here and called you and stuck my fingers down a strange woman's throat. The whisky bottle is still outside.' He knew the words came out as a witness statement, echoing the last time.

'An average Saturday night for an ex-rock star, then?'

Todd's laugh was small but genuine. 'I'm glad you're here. Thanks for coming.'

'Anytime, my friend. I'm presuming you don't know her?'

'Never seen her before. I can't explain any of this. I need to ask her why—why me? why here?'

Neither of them had been aware of her in the doorway, the lighting making her skin seem even paler. 'Where's my bag?'

'Bag?'

'I had a straw bag with me. Where is it?'

'I don't know. It must still be outside…'

The woman made to walk to the back door but stumbled. Andrew dropped his mug and caught her as she

hat. 'I don't sleep much, so if you
ound, don't be scared.' He couldn't
to say. 'Night, then.' He closed the
.

collapsed. She fought him and steadied herself against the table. 'I need it. I need it now.'

Andrew pulled out a chair and motioned for her to sit, glancing at Todd and at the back door.

'Okay, I'll go and check.' Todd disappeared into the night with Samson following.

'I suggest sitting down.' Andrew did not touch the woman again but busied himself picking up the broken mug and mopping the coffee dregs, taking the opportunity to study her in more detail. Her long, blue velvet dress had garden detritus clinging to the nap. A necklace of wooden beads and crystals were hanging down her front, almost perfectly straight, and she had swept her mass of Pre-Raphaelite curls forward to rest over one shoulder like a red corsage. He put the broken china and the cloth in the bin and placed the third mug of now cooled coffee in front of her. He guessed she must be late twenties; maybe older. It was difficult to tell. Her elongated fingers wrapped themselves around the mug, but her gaze remained on the back door.

'Can I call anyone for you?'

Her laughter was unexpected and shrill. 'Yes. Please call God and tell him I'll be a little later than planned.'

Andrew clenched his fists, not a doctor now but a protector of a dear friend who had already had more than enough tragedy in his life. 'If you're planning a repeat performance, don't even think about doing it here. He doesn't need this.'

'And what about what I need? Isn't your solemn promise to serve the good of the patient?'

She shot back in her seat as Andrew lurched towards her, his face now inches from hers.

'Listen to me…' His angry breath sprayed saliva into her eyes, and she blinked to clear her vision.

'Andrew. It's okay.' Todd was stood in the doorway, the straw shopping bag an incongruous accessory for a six-foot-two man.

She crossed the room before either man registered her movement, grabbing the bag and retreating into the safety of the house, the return of the bag somehow giving her extra strength.

'I'll take care of her tonight,' Todd said.

'I can sort this, Todd. Take her to hospital…'

Todd placed a hand on his friend's arm. 'Really, it's okay, Andrew. I feel I should.'

'No, Todd. Don't you dare say you feel responsible for her. I don't want to hear that crap from you.'

Todd held his hands up. 'Okay, okay. Let me get your bag.' Todd disappeared into the lounge, leaving Andrew to make his way to his Range Rover.

The woman was sitting back on the sofa, stroking Samson who was happy to have found a comfortable lap and soft hands to massage his chunky body. She didn't acknowledge Todd but stared straight ahead at the fireplace. He picked up Andrew's bag and went outside.

'Look, I know it's nearly 2a.m. but if you need me, just call.' Andrew threw his bag into the back of his car and climbed in. Todd smiled and stepped back, the gravel under the tyres filling the quiet of the early morning as Andrew drove away. He watched the taillights until they disappeared, then made his way back inside, suddenly tired to his bones.

She looked up as he settled himself into one of the overstuffed chairs.

'How are you feeling?'

Sh

'I h   her but didn't know

and m   hear me wandering a

straw   think of anything else

you?'   door, and her tears fe

'No.'

up the b

He list

the oppo

envelope.

for pryin

the envelc

inside. He

the envelop

as she enter

'This way.

She took th

an oak-panell

and soft silk

was sparsely fu

drawers and wa

'The bathroo.

out for you.'

She placed her

'Feel free to ha

so I'll put it in the

or drink?'

'No, thank you.

kind.' Her voice wa

curls.

'Well, help your

across the landing.' I

looking. He felt he s

| 2 |

Her face creased into astonishment. 'What? You can't be serious.'

'But I am, Detective Chief Inspector Fortune.'

She leaned forward, placing her hands on the polished walnut veneer of his desk. 'No. This is a wind up, right?'

'Sweetheart...'

'No. No. Don't do that. You lost that right forty years ago.' She stopped, lost in the amazing clarity of the moment when she discovered the boy she loved was inside the knickers of Donna Partington. Donna—she of the almost boyish figure, no tits, long blonde hair and an attitude that told the world she could have any boy she wanted.

Chief Superintendent Lenny Howard knew the look on her face. He felt a brief flash of shame at the reminder of his decades-old indiscretion. 'You should have married me and stayed at home having our babies and making my tea.' He grinned at the way her thin lips formed into a cavern of disbelief at his words, then enjoyed the moment as she relented and gave in to his charm, knowing it was useless to fight it. 'Take the weight off that arse of yours, and let's talk details. You can thank me later.'

Kath Fortune wedged herself into the chair as directed. 'Let's start again.' She smiled. 'I really do appreciate you looking into my request for scaled-down duties but this can't be right. And where the hell is the money coming from for all this?'

Lenny leaned forward. 'I've been given some money to spend. It's been ring-fenced for five years. I have to do it before the next budgets are announced. If I don't use it, I really will lose it. So, this is perfect.'

'But a cold case unit? Please explain to me why we need one and why you want me to head it up. I'm a damn good officer, Lenny. Working cases is what I do best, what I enjoy best, and you seem to want to stick me in a back office or basement with no daylight—'

'Shut up, woman, and let me get a word in.' Lenny sighed, but he had rehearsed his speech in anticipation of this exact reaction. 'You wanted less demands on your time; not to be on call to get hauled out of bed by your sergeants at 4a.m. to stand in the cold and look at a body on a piece of waste ground.'

'Yes, I know all this, but—'

He held up his hand. 'Let me finish. Please.' He undid his jacket and sat back again, arms open—a relaxed pose that Kath knew meant he was going to get his own way. 'You can't be a part-timer, Kath. I know you. As much as you've come to hate the demands of this job, you would be mad as hell if you thought you were missing out.'

She tucked some stray strands of hair behind her ear.

'This way, you get to head up a brand-new squad which you can handpick...'

Her head tilted slightly. She rolled her hand, indicating to him to elaborate further.

'It will make our figures look good if we can clear up some of the mess left behind from the last twenty or thirty years, and it raises our profile.'

'Let's go back to the bit about picking my own team.' Kath smiled, and he knew exactly what was coming.

'No, no way. That is not going to happen.'

'You can't just say these things and then go back on them. Sir.'

Lenny sighed and wagged a finger at her. 'You know how I feel about having that damn psychic in here.'

Kath stood and smoothed down her skirt over her rotund waistline. 'Then I guess we have nothing more to talk about.' The slightly shambolic but damn fine police officer he should have held onto when he had the chance walked out of his office.

Back in the squad room, Kath sat back in her chair, sipping coffee and picking at a loose piece of wood veneer on the front of her desk. Her brain was in overdrive. She glanced around at the people at the other desks. She had been through so much with her team: DCS Marvin Henshall, Kerry Harris and David Broome; DS Shirley Thompson and Ruth Goodwin; civilian administrator Jodie James. Corpses violated beyond comprehension, evidence examination, crowded courtrooms, nights out involving good wine and good food, nights in comforting each other. Did she really want to give all that up to be stuck in the past, raking over old bodies and old evidence? But she had to confess to becoming stuck; frustrated with the image of the police being constantly tarnished by the media when cases dragged on with no result in sight. Damn Lenny for knowing her too well. He knew that merely reducing her hours would not satisfy her, even if it was possible. He saw her spark being smothered by paperwork and regulations, new governments bringing ever more changes. Kath was good with change; had always been ready to accept a challenge.

This new idea was way out of her comfort zone. But there had been a tingle in her gut since she had walked out of Lenny's office. The idea of putting together a new team had awakened something in her. She recognised it as excitement and anticipation. But that contrasted with a tinge of fear at the unknown. Lenny obviously thought she could take on the role but he was biased. He had loved her for so long.

She shook her head, memories of the past threatening to flood her brain. Lenny was pragmatic even against all his feelings towards her. He had never given her special treatment, but he had always had her back. And she loved that about him. He would not have thrown this cold case idea at just anyone. She tossed her empty coffee container into the waste bin as a text came through on her phone.

Okay. You win.

She grinned but refrained from replying. She needed more details now, especially in respect of her team. She wanted to know who exactly would be replacing her. She needed to know her team would be okay. She already had an idea of who she wanted to join her. Those who did not know her often took her arrogant, matter-of-fact manner as a slight against them, not realising abrupt and pragmatic was the mask she used for caring deeply about her team and her work.

She scribbled questions and ideas onto her pad of paper, doodling in the margins between thoughts. She threw down the pen after ten minutes and looked over to see what Shirley was doing. Kath took her cigarettes and lighter from her bag.

'Shirl. You and me. Fag break?'

'Okay, Boss.' Shirley grabbed her packet and followed Kath out of the office and onto the roof. The day was deliciously warm, a slight breeze playing with Shirley's blonde fringe. They stood together, hanging over the rail, smoke chasing smoke into the air and across the view of Telford town centre with its myriad of shops and cafés. Shirley knew there was something coming but waited for Kath to speak.

'Lenny has a proposition for me.'

Shirley looked at Kath. 'That's not news.'

Kath smiled. 'I mean a work proposition. A new team. Cold case squad.'

Shirley, being a similar age to Kath, had always been a sounding board for her thoughts and ideas. 'Okay. How do you feel about that?'

Kath flicked at her cigarette filter. 'I'm considering it. Need more info first.'

'Like who will replace you as our great leader?' Shirley threw her cigarette butt over the parapet. 'We'll miss you but we'll survive without you. It sounds like a good move. New challenge.'

'I'm afraid of missing out.' Kath sighed and bit her lip. The forty-eight-year-old detective sergeant was a steadying influence in the team, and in Kath's life. Kath had pushed her to move up to inspector level for several years but Shirley was happy exactly where she was. And she was a valuable and necessary cog in the division.

'Afraid you'll miss the buzz but secretly could be very glad handing over the reins to someone else?'

Kath flicked her cigarette butt towards the car park below and watched the breeze guide it towards the rear entrance door. 'You and Lenny seem to know me too well.

I need to start keeping stuff to myself.' She rubbed the back of her calf with the front of her other foot. The breeze was now definitely turning into a wind, and her bare legs were feeling chilly in the August morning. She hadn't meant to turn up bare-legged, but ripped holes in four pairs of tights in succession proved she needed to file her nails down or buy a bigger size. Not that she liked wearing them. Tights were so unflattering to the fuller female figure. Coupled with big pants and an ample support bra, the look of a fifty-something copper hauling her hosiery over her belly and feeling her finger run another hole in them had not been a great start to the morning. Any morning really. She had resigned herself long ago to the fact she was never going to be a skinny minny again. At five foot four, she knew damn well she was carrying more weight than her GP wanted. That, of course, was deliberate. But no one needed to know that.

'Let's have one more.' Kath offered her pack to Shirley, and they hooked their hands around her lighter.

'So... new team. Can you have anyone you like?' Shirley knew exactly who Kath's first choice would be: Lane Petreus—a psychic who had helped them out on previous cases. Not that the public knew. Or at least they weren't supposed to know. A local hack working for the local paper had done some digging and put in some extra-curricular time trailing the team on more than one occasion. It had fallen to Lenny to dispute the intervention of a psychic because the team had no leads.

Kath shrugged. 'I don't know. I just gave Lenny the impression to wind him up.' She took a long drag. 'But it was worth it to see his face.' They both exhaled smoke and laughter. This was what Kath would miss. But then she thought that maybe it was viable. Her team, her choice.

Lane and Shirley got on well, as did Lane and Ruth. She crushed her half-finished cigarette underfoot and followed Shirl back to the office.

3

There was no clock in her room. Hunger had roused her from sleep; those magical few hours where her brain was silent. She stood at the window and looked down on the huge garden—a tumble of overgrown shrubs and unpruned trees. It was a garden that TV design teams would smother with gravel and decking and weighty stone ornaments. Fields lay beyond, and she could just make out cattle grazing.

She meant to go straight downstairs but his bedroom door was slightly open. She stood in the doorway, then crossed to his bed. He lay sprawled, facedown, his tumbled curls spread across the pillow. Limbs and an expanse of hairless back had fought loose from the duvet. His clothes were draped haphazardly across the small Chesterfield. Other than that, the room was tidy; devoid of, bric-a-brac and unnecessary clutter. One large silver photo frame graced the mantelpiece. From the picture, a blonde woman smiled as she clutched a small blonde girl to her chest. They were sharing a hug of love; of devotion. The child was laughing.

'Daisy,' the woman whispered, fingering the glass. 'I'm so sorry.'

The woman went downstairs. The kitchen seemed larger in the morning sunlight. She flicked on the kettle and started at the noise coming from the utility room. Samson appeared, a small rabbit hanging from his jaws. He dropped his prize at her feet and meowed.

'What have you got there, big guy?' She bent to pick up the corpse, its body still warm. Samson rubbed around her legs as the limp rabbit lay in her hand, a small stain of blood around its throat. She scanned the shelves for a box or bin liner, finding a stash of used carrier bags. She took one and placed the body inside, then deposited it in the wheelie bin outside the back door. She washed her hands and proceeded to make coffee and look for cat food. She tipped a handful of multi-coloured pellets into the empty bowl on the floor and wondered how cats managed to purr and eat at the same time.

He's a tidy man, she thought as she looked around at the gleaming surfaces and shiny appliances. *Or he's got a very good cleaner.* Mug in hand, she unlocked the back door and stepped onto the flagged patio. Dandelions and islands of grass pushed their way between the flags. This domain was very different from the house; unkempt, uncared for. The lawn—shaggy and in need of a haircut—spilled over into beds of tight, bright foliage, wet from the dew of an unseasonably cool August night. Two large sheds and a greenhouse nestled against a fence, all in need of a little care and attention. Miranda had successfully evaded Todd's questions, but now, wandering around the crazed patio, she had to seriously think about her next move while he was out of range in the shower. She'd heard the water running and the panic had risen in her. She craved his company and yet a part of her still did not want to face him. She wanted to give him the bag and the envelopes.

That was why she was here. To give up her life and her secret. But his kindness and concern had overwhelmed her. She knew what she should do. Yet, his company was now something she needed, and she did not want to leave him just yet. She hugged herself as she wandered around the exterior of the house. Maybe he wouldn't actually want her here. After all, why would he? She was a stranger to him, yet she knew their horrifying connection. She could not tell him. Not yet.

Warmed by the coffee and sunshine, she wandered down to the spot where Todd had found her, her thin pumps absorbing moisture and memory.

Todd watched her from the window in the room where she had slept. It made no more sense to him now than it had done a few hours before. As a precaution, he had removed all prescription and over-the-counter drugs from the bathroom cabinet. He had checked her pink straw bag again, but all it contained were the envelopes. He wandered back to his room, hoping she would feel a little more like talking today. He pulled on jeans and a T-shirt and went downstairs.

Samson had joined the woman in the garden but turned and trotted back towards the kitchen as soon as he heard Todd. She followed the cat and stood opposite Todd on the patio as he sipped his coffee and lit a cigarette.

'Want one?'

She nodded and took one from the proffered packet. They stood in an amiable silence, wreaths of smoke curling around their heads. 'My name is Miranda.'

'Interesting coincidence.'

She feigned a puzzled expression.

'My name is Prospero, Todd Prospero.'

She smiled. 'Is that like Bond, James Bond?'

He smiled back.

He has such a warm face, she thought, guilt coursing through her. A face that had adorned magazine covers and newspapers in his heyday as rock god and frontman of the biggest rock band to hit the scene at the end of the '90s. Of course, she had seen his face many times but now it was so close and so personal. Everything about him was big but it all fitted together. Big hands enveloped his mug, long-lashed hazel eyes gazed at her.

'So'—he exhaled a plume of smoke and aimed his cigarette butt at the grass—'I'll make us more coffee and then you can tell me why you chose to die in my garden.'

As he moved to the kitchen and busied himself with the coffee, Miranda pushed down the huge wave of panic that threatened to send her running.

She heard another voice in the kitchen and angled herself so she could see through the open door. An elderly woman put a wicker basket on the table and lifted out a shallow dish. Her white hair sat in curls around her harsh face. She stared back at Miranda. Todd was talking and pointing to the garden. Miranda tried a smile, but the woman turned away from her and busied herself taking off her jacket and putting on an apron from the basket. Todd came to the door and beckoned her inside.

'Miranda, this is Mrs Tinkerson, my housekeeper and all-round guardian angel.'

'Hello.' Miranda held out her hand.

Mrs Tinkerson stared at her outstretched hand and gave a small noise like a snuffling dog. She looked at Todd. 'You'll have to be careful with that lasagne then if it's for more than one.'

Miranda, eager to get on the woman's good side, bent down and sniffed the dish. 'That smells amazing. I bet it tastes great, too.'

'Food critic, are you?' Mrs Tinkerson went into the utility room and came out with her cleaning caddy.

Todd sighed and smiled at Miranda. 'It will be wonderful as usual, Mrs T. Thank you.'

The woman made her way into the hallway. 'You'll have to let me know if I'm cooking for an army now. I require plenty of notice.' She made her way up the stairs.

Todd moved the lasagne into the fridge to protect it from Samson, who had been known to also be an admirer of Mrs T's cooking.

'Well, she hates me.' Miranda grabbed the fresh mug of coffee and went back outside. Todd joined her.

'Don't take offense. She doesn't know you. She treats everyone like that. Even me.' He smiled and sipped his coffee. 'When I first advertised for someone to come and take care of the house, it was like she was interviewing me!'

Miranda smiled.

'Oh yes,' Todd went on, 'she laid down exactly what she would do and what she expected of me. She gives the air of a sergeant major but she's just really protective of me, I guess.'

'How long has she been with you?'

'Ten years, just about.'

Miranda's stomach went into spasm. *Around six months or so after it all happened,* she thought. *It's nice that he's had somebody all this time. And now I have someone else to avoid or get to know. It has all got suddenly so much more complicated.*

| 4 |

'Where the bloody hell do we start?' DS Ruth Goodwin was stood in the middle of the upstairs room with its high ceiling and double windows overlooking the car park. She stared at the boxes of documents stacked against the walls. The property had previously been used by social services and housed the community mental health team. They had inhabited the ground floor rooms, the upstairs rooms being used as storage. The police cold case files had been stored there for years, and Kath had been given the task of arranging the transportation of them to their new home across Madeley, in the small police station outpost.

Kath was stood next to Ruth, arms crossed, and playfully kicked her ankle. 'You're the organiser, feng shui queen. Off you go.'

At five foot eleven, Ruth towered over Kath and quite a few of her other female colleagues in the force, along with some of the men. A West Bromwich lass, she had worked with Kath for many years, and they worked well together. Her forte was making sense of chaos—both physical and within evidence files. But even she was feeling a little daunted.

'The truck's coming in two hours, and we have to get this lot downstairs. We'll sort through exactly what we're

going to need when we get to the other end.' Kath walked
to one of the windows. Three days into her new role as
Cold Case team leader and she had chosen her officers
and civilian staff, and agreed to set up base at the Madeley
station.

'Life and death, Ruth,' Kath said quietly. 'Each box holds
a person and everything about them.' She turned back to
face Ruth. 'I've done the right thing, haven't I?' She had
been looking to her colleagues for reassurance since her
meeting with Lenny a week ago. He was right, and she
hated to admit it. Active murder investigations had taken
their toll on her over the last few years; late nights and even
earlier mornings, bad diet and bad sleep patterns had all
added lines to her smooth, rounded face. But she loved the
end results, and that was what had kept her going through
each case. Justice for the dead and their families. That was
all that mattered at the end of the day. That was what they
all strived for: results and closure.

Ruth sat on the only chair in the room and leaned
forward, elbows resting on her knees, and looked at Kath.
'Don't start doubting yourself now. You are the best
person for this new squad and you know it. It'll just be a
different way of working but still getting to the same end
results.'

'I know, I know.' Kath walked around the boxes, lifting
lids and peering inside at the masses of paperwork. 'But
where do we actually start? How do we decide which cases
get priority? Do we work in date order, oldest first, or pick
one at random? So many questions and I don't seem to
have any answers.'

'Christ, Kath.' Ruth folded her arms.' It's been less than
a week since this all happened. Don't run before you can
walk. We'll sort it out when we get to our new home.' No

sooner were the words out of her mouth than they heard the transport pulling up outside.

Two male civilian staff from Malinsgate, the main Telford police station, entered the room.

'You're early.'

'Sorry, ma'am. What's the plan, ma'am?'

Kath narrowed her small eyes. 'The plan is for you not to call me ma'am, otherwise you may find yourself in one of these boxes.'

The two men laughed and then stopped suddenly, fearing Detective Chief Inspector Fortune might actually be serious.

Ruth moved forward. 'Ignore her and just grab a box. There's coffee and sandwiches at the end of this.' She grabbed a box and followed them down the stairs.

Kath tested a few for weight, picked the lightest one she could find and went to move onto the landing, only for guilt to get the better of her. She sighed and went back to find a heavier box.

|5|

Todd carried two bottles of cold beer into the lounge. Andrew smiled and took his bottle, slouching in the armchair. He loosened his tie and savoured the first mouthful as Todd sat across from him on the sofa.

'Come on then, out with it. I've had a long day.'

Todd grinned. 'Okay, it's just knowing where to start.'

'Just let it pour out, and we'll make sense of it later.'

Todd took a pull of his beer and sighed. 'Christ, this is so weird. This girl has come into my life under the craziest of circumstances, and it feels good.' He shook his head, not quite believing he was admitting it out loud. 'What is it they say—you save a life and you're responsible for it forever.'

Andrew pulled himself upright and leaned forward, arms resting on his thighs. 'Don't be a martyr, mate. You don't owe her anything.' Todd opened his mouth to speak but Andrew had the bit between his teeth now, ready to spew forth exactly what he had been holding back ever since Miranda had appeared. 'No, no, I'm serious. This has been huge for you and... where is she, by the way?'

'Lying down in her room. You can speak freely. I trust you, Andrew, you know that. You're my oldest friend.'

That much was certainly true. They had met in school aged thirteen and continued a healthy and loving friendship even when Todd and the band had become globally famous. Two good-looking boys; Andrew the blonde academic who had always known he would go into medicine in some way, and Todd the curly-haired brunette who'd messed around in class and yet was still adored by the teachers, and who had picked up a guitar aged eleven and knew he wanted music in his life.

'I'm just looking out for you. I remember only too well how lost and vulnerable you were after Daisy's death and then losing Zoe.'

Todd sipped his beer, nodding. They let the memories hang between them; the tragic murder of a daughter and the equally tragic death of a wife in such swift succession. It had seemed impossible at the time to process the act of his wife taking her own life; giving in to the pain, unable to fight her way out of the grip of it. Todd had felt madness slowly envelop him to a point of inertia. But Andrew had been his saviour—comforted him, held him as he'd cried and taught him coping mechanisms to get through each day, hour by hour.

'But I'm not back there, Andrew. I'm done with all that. I've moved on; got past it. I still have days when it's bad but it doesn't last the whole day anymore. A few hours maybe, and I can get myself out of that now, thanks to you and the things you taught me I could do to cope when things become unbearable. I feel a connection with Miranda. I like having her around.'

Andrew sat back. 'Oh God, you're not in love with her, are you?'

Todd shook his head. 'No, no, nothing like that. I can't explain it.'

'Look, I've never tried to tell you how to live your life or behave or dress...' He raised an eyebrow at Todd's tie-dye shirt and ripped jeans, and Todd threw a cushion at him. They laughed, and Andrew hugged the cushion, taking another swig of his beer. 'I just can't help thinking something feels...hinky.'

'Hinky? Really? The preppy Brideshead doctor comes out with hinky?'

Andrew threw the cushion back. 'I can't help being tall, blonde and beautiful.'

'And that could be why you have three divorces behind you.' Todd stood and waved his empty bottle at Andrew. Andrew nodded, and Todd left for the kitchen to get fresh supplies.

Andrew let his head fall back and sighed. His friend had become a hermit following the deaths of his wife and child, but a relaxed and at peace with himself hermit. He was still in touch with his old bandmates but had no desire to jumpstart his career. The local villagers acknowledged him but left him alone, and he had found an angel of a housekeeper in Mrs Tinkerson, who fussed over him, cleaned his house and made amazing meals for him. She had reluctantly agreed to search the bedrooms regularly for mouse corpses, as Samson was an accomplished killer. She feigned dislike of the feline but Todd and Andrew had caught her on more than one occasion stroking him and talking in a baby sing-song voice that made the two men chuckle quietly.

Todd returned and handed Andrew a new bottle.

'How is Tink taking to your new houseguest?'

'Surprisingly well, actually. I haven't told her the circumstances of Miranda being here, just that she's the

daughter of a friend, who needs somewhere to stay for a while.'

'And her Miss Marple antennae was happy with that? I don't even want to think about what she'll do if she finds out you've been lying to her.' Andrew exaggerated a shudder, and Todd smiled.

'She was her usual dismissive self, but I think she'll be okay for the moment. As is her way, she'll just carry on and make sense of any chaos I may bring to the party. By the way, I'm going to cook for Miranda and me tonight. Do you want to join us?'

Andrew drained his second bottle of beer and shook his head. 'You're alright, mate. I'm off home for something unhealthy and a stint of Call of Duty. I don't think I'm mentally prepared to play nice with your new houseguest yet.' He stood and made his way to the front door. Todd followed.

'You know, for a dedicated health professional, your diet is pretty crap. And you don't exercise. And your alcohol intake is above what is nationally considered acceptable.'

'It is very much a case of do as I say, not as I do.'

Todd put a hand on Andrew's shoulder. 'Thank you. Again. Now, give me a big old man hug.'

They embraced and slapped backs.

'Anytime, mate. You know that. Just... be careful.'

Todd waved from the doorway as Andrew got into his Range Rover. Maybe in a more relaxed setting, Miranda would finally open up. Todd went into the kitchen, deliberately making kitchen sounds, hoping Miranda would finally come down.

Miranda sat at the pine table with Samson on her lap as Todd moved around the kitchen, collecting ingredients.

She had heard the kitchen noises, just as Todd had wanted, and had wandered downstairs.

'I can cook,' he explained as he gathered mushrooms, onions and garlic from the fridge, his large hands easily encompassing everything required. 'It's just that it's normally...well, just me, you know, so I'm a big fan of the microwave.'

She smiled. 'Mrs Tinkerson is an amazing cook. That lasagne she brought over a couple days ago was fab.'

Todd started chopping the onions. 'Yes, she's so good to me; a real find. It was actually Andrew's suggestion that I get a...well, housekeeper, I suppose you could call her... so, I put a card up at the Post Office in the village and there she was.'

Miranda stopped stroking the cat, who meowed and pawed at her hand. He had found in her a regular go-to human for constant strokes and ear kisses, and he wasn't about to give it up. She began the rhythmic movement again, and he purred his satisfaction. 'I believe people come into our lives for a reason.' She closed her eyes.

Todd stopped chopping and turned to her, eyes moist with onion tears. 'So, why are you here, then?'

She rose quickly, tipping Samson off her lap. He protested with a catty yelp and moved quickly towards the back door. 'Don't ask me.' She spat the words, heart racing, heat rising through her body. 'You promised you wouldn't ask yet.' She hurried past him to the back door, but he stopped her, the large kitchen knife still in his hand. She looked down and tried to control her breathing. *Damn him, it's too soon. I don't want this to end yet. It can't end yet because then it really will be the end of everything.*

Todd put the knife down. 'Sorry. I'm sorry.' He put his hands up in surrender. 'Please sit down.'

She moved back to the table but remained standing, pushing her hands into the pockets of her jeans. She had been relaxed and peaceful in his company. Now, she was fighting the urge to run, which would undo all her work in beginning to heal and repair the damage she had done. The damage he was unaware of and would despise her for.

'I'm just going to carry on cooking my fantastic spag bol, and we are going to talk about anything you want. Anything at all. Or nothing,' he added, picking up the knife and continuing the process.

He busied himself as the onions sizzled in the hot oil, fighting the urge to turn and see the look on her face, and her manner. He opened cupboards, getting out the spaghetti and herbs, regretting his mouth running away with him.

'Have you tried on all the clothes you bought? Everything fits?' Todd asked.

She removed her hands from her pockets and picked at the sleeves of her fluffy lilac jumper. At his insistence, he had taken her into Bridgnorth with its wealth of charity shops and bespoke new-age dress shops he thought she might like. He'd given her money to get herself everything she needed, having turned up in his garden with just the dress and the underwear she'd been wearing underneath it. As she had pointed out, she hadn't been planning on living, so why bring clothing with her to his garden?

He had enjoyed their afternoon together watching her pick items of clothing from the rails as she'd held up one or two and asked his opinion. He had felt a calm joy envelop him—something he had not experienced for a long time. They'd bought ice cream cones and wandered along the High Town walls, looking down over Low Town at the river, the swans, people enjoying the various beer gardens. She had been relaxed in his company, and it had felt natural, her guilt pushed way down as they'd laughed at two pigeons trying to mate on a delicate tree branch.

Shame flooded her thin body as his kindness swept through her. She swallowed her urge to flee and tried to continue a normal conversation between two people who enjoyed each other's company.

'Yes, everything's fine. Thank you again.'

He stirred the bubbling sauce. 'Good, I'm glad. You have a really good eye for colour. I had a really nice afternoon.' He paused. 'I'm enjoying your company.' He heard her sit back down at the table, and relief swept through him. Crisis averted, for now. He was afraid to face her and break the mood again, but she saved him by speaking.

'Do you cook for Andrew?'

He filled a saucepan with water for the pasta and set it on the hob to boil. 'I do, actually. It's usually the same meals, though. I have a very small repertoire.'

Grey clouds filled the early evening sky. Todd dropped the pasta into the water and stared out the window, his back still to his guest. 'I saw you in the garden earlier. Gardening isn't one of the things I'm good at, I'm afraid.'

She smiled. 'No judgement from me. I like that it's natural. It blends in with the fields beyond, into the horizon.'

'That's poetic.' He turned to face her. 'But I think Alan Titchmarsh might disagree with you. He'd probably put decking everywhere with a yucca plant in the middle or something.'

'Alan who?'

Todd laughed as he gathered cutlery and placemats from a drawer. 'Never mind. Hope you're hungry. I think I'm subconsciously trying to fatten you up.'

She clasped her arms around herself. 'I've always been skinny. Get it from my mum.' She pressed her lips together, willing words to stay inside her body. She did not want to reveal anything more. She had said too much already, and once words were out, they could not be bundled back inside.

Todd started laying the table around her, wanting to ask about her background, searching for any scrap of information on this waif that had arrived in his life. 'My big hands and feet are from my mum, believe it or not. She was nearly six feet tall, size eleven shoes. A real amazon. Dad gave me the impossibly annoying curly hair and the toothy grin.' With that, he gave her a toothy grin and pushed his hands through his hair. It sprang back as if not touched, and she laughed. 'Do you want to talk about your mum? It's okay if you don't,' he added, hurriedly.

'She's dead.'

Todd grasped the back of one of the pine chairs and looked at her. 'I'm sorry. My parents are both dead now. Cancer. Two years apart. Mum first. Andrew tended to both of them, getting them into the local hospice when the time was right. He said a strange thing to me about Dad.' He lowered his head, the memory flooding his brain and churning his gut. 'He said although the cancer was going to kill him, he felt that Dad's heart was almost broken from Mum's passing, like he just couldn't bear her not being there.' As soon as the words were out, the memory of his wife galloped back across his emotions, and he turned to the sink and grasped the edge, forcing the bile down.

Miranda sensed the tension in him. 'I'm sorry, too. Let's not talk about it anymore. The food smells great. Can I do anything?' She stood and approached his back, wanting to reach out and put a hand on his shoulder, the middle of his back, anywhere she could have a closer connection to him. She knew that, when the time eventually came, she would have to confess, and her words would break him.

|6|

'Why does Lenny hate Lane so much?'

Shirley and Kath were sat on the bench at the back of their new office, enjoying the sunshine and keeping out of Ruth's way. The three of them had spent the morning moving desks and getting the IT equipment arranged and set up with the help of Simon and Neil from the IT department. Ruth was now cleaning, organising cables and taking four years of dust off the venetian blinds that covered the entire wall of windows overlooking the road down to the Ironbridge Gorge.

Kath lit a cigarette. 'He doesn't like what he can't understand. Doesn't get the whole psychic woo-woo stuff. Also, doesn't get women. Hence, double whammy. Female woo-woo.'

'Yeah, I get that,' Shirley said, taking a drag of her own cigarette. 'But she gets results, she's proven that, and that is the only thing that matters at the end of the day. It doesn't matter how we get to the solution—within the confines of the law, usually—but we put the bad people away and let families heal.'

Kath nodded and squinted up at the sun. 'You're preaching to the converted, mate. But he's got no choice. He said I could have anyone—and I want her.'

'If she'll come.'

'I did some checking, made some calls. She'll be with us in a few days. I haven't spoken to her for a while but she remembered me like we'd been speaking yesterday. Guess it's the energy thing. I don't pretend to even get a handle on what she does but I'm open to it all, and I guess she picks up on that. We get on really well, or at least, we did last time.'

Lane Petreus had worked with many of the police forces around the UK and the USA, helping with murder cases and aiding the officers to get results. Most forces in the UK still had a tight rein on information given to the press regarding the use of psychics, and with good reason. There had been two cases, one in Yorkshire back in the '80s and one in Lincolnshire only a couple of years ago, where so-called psychics had inserted themselves into the investigations of two murders, only to be revealed as complete charlatans. They'd compromised both cases to the point the CPS were unable to prosecute. The investigations were held out as examples of how not to conduct an investigation, and although a couple of forces had worked with reputable people in the 'woo-woo' business, it had been completely hushed up even though the results were watertight and did indeed result in convictions and viable sentencing.

'She's going to stay with me, actually. I quite like the idea of company for a change.' Kath's three-bedroom cottage was nestled on the edge of woodland in a village close to Bridgnorth, with barely a hint of passing traffic, except for when the main road was flooded and the commuters and locals alike used it as a way into the town. The main noise came from the rookery in the woods beyond. It had annoyed the hell out of her at first, but after a couple of weeks, she had made her peace with the birds, and the vixens screaming into the night, and now considered her home a safe haven from the evil that she had to deal with every day.

'So, we have a couple of days to pick our first case from those boxes.' Shirley stubbed out her cigarette, wondering where to throw it, then decided it didn't matter and threw it under the bench.

'How are we doing this, then?' Kath joined her, and they entered the building, nodding to the PCSO behind the desk.

'Well, I have an idea on that, but I need to speak to everyone first.'

They found Ruth slumped in an office chair, her standard uniform of blue polo shirt and jeans now grey with dust and clumps of fluff.

'I'll get the hoover in a minute, but I need tea and cake first. Need to get my headspace back.'

The office now looked like a workable space with four desks and their requisite IT equipment in a line down the centre of the room, facing the windows as per Ruth's instructions, for good energy flow and productivity. The boxes of files were stacked against the wall where the room expanded into a large alcove. Three spare desks were lined up in front of the windows for laying out files and evidence. Although there was a kitchen downstairs, Ruth had managed to set up a small 'beverage area', as she called it, behind the door with a kettle and coffee maker, biscuit tin and assorted mugs and cups.

'Aren't there cleaners that come in and do all this?' Shirl asked, rattling the biscuit tin to check for content.

Ruth gave a grunt. 'Not to my standards.'

Kath and Shirl exchanged smiles.

'And I think we ought to limit the amount of people that come into here,' Ruth added. 'I'll get extra keys cut, as there happens to be a workable lock on the door.'

'That's a great idea, Ruth,' Kath said. Shirl sat down at the desk farthest from the door and gazed out at the view of the trees beyond and the roof of the Foresters Arms pub—a handy addition to the office move.

'You're not there,' Ruth barked and pointed to the desk nearest the door. 'That's you. Kath should be sitting there.'

Shirl was about to protest but Kath jumped in. 'I think Ruth has been very considerate in her arrangement of the flow of energy for the room'—she had her back to Ruth and raised an eyebrow at Shirl, who stood up, trying not to make a crass remark—'as you'll be closest to the kettle and you are the one who needs the most hydration.'

Ruth put her hands on her hips as Shirl made her way down to the other end of the room. 'I know you're making faces, Kath. I can tell by the way the back of your head moves.'

The three of them spat out girly giggles as Shirl sat at her confirmed new desk.

'Thank you, Ruthie. I am very grateful for your consideration to my needs.'

'Don't call me that, mouthy cow. You know I hate it.'

'And that is why I do it,' mouthy cow acknowledged.

'Why don't you pop to Tesco to get some supplies? I can't drink this bloody cheap tea that I stole from downstairs.' Ruth reached into her pocket and pulled out a twenty, passing it to Kath to pass to Shirley who was about to protest when she remembered there was a Greggs opposite.

'I know. Yorkshire tea all the way.' She picked up her handbag and left the building, a new burst of energy bubbling inside her. She had been relieved that Kath had wanted her on the new team. They had worked well together for many years now. Shirley loved her job, was passionate about it and damn good at it. But it was never going to consume her the way it had done with other colleagues who had just wanted to work their way up the ranks. Shirl had a solid marriage which she worked at to keep kind, fresh and vibrant, never taking her husband, Dave, for granted. He worked within the agricultural farming machinery industry and had done since he'd left school forty-two years ago. They had raised four amazing sons together. She was a big fan of stability and safety outside the world of work where chaos and confusion reigned. Everyone on the job had their safety net outside the job, to be kept completely away from what they had to do every day; what they had to face. Yet, never once had Shirl regretted her decision to join the police. Except maybe when Ruth was on a mission to rearrange the office to 'facilitate the energy flow and improve productivity and harmony'. Which she did regularly. Her favourite saying was, 'The only constant thing is change'. And Shirl now appreciated that as she got into her car and decided she would have a steak slice for a change, instead of her usual sausage roll. Yes, change was good.

'Fuck me—is that him?' Ruth was stood at the office window, her Espresso coffee cup halted on its way to her lips, when she saw a thin, young lad crossing the road towards the station.

Kath joined her. 'Yep, that's the newest member of the team. There's more to him, trust me.'

Ruth grunted and took a sip of her coffee. It was all for show. She knew Kath would have chosen the perfect person to complement the team. Plus, it would balance out the feminine energy and give DC Marvin Henshall an ally. Kath had received many applications for the civilian position within the squad, and Byron had ticked all the boxes and then some. She also had a good feeling when she was in his company and within their interactions so far. And that counted for a hell of a lot in Kath's book. Ruth would continue to rib her about him, probably for many months to come, but that was Ruth's job. And she did it well.

He appeared in the open doorway and gave a polite but needless knock. Kath ushered him in and pointed to a chair.

'Byron, welcome. This is Ruth Goodwin, Detective Sergeant.'

Ruth moved towards him and offered her hand. They shook—a good firm grip, Ruth noted—and she sat next to him. 'So, I have to ask the obvious question… is that your real name?'

Byron smiled. 'It's okay, I get that a lot. Mum is really into the romantic poets, and with a surname like Lord, she couldn't resist.' His hair hung past the waist of his jeans, a straight centre parting. Trainers and an AC/DC T-shirt completed the outfit. 'I hated it when I was younger,' he went on, 'but I've kind of grown into it now.'

'Good chat-up line with the girls, I bet,' Ruth said, smiling. 'Or boys,' she added hurriedly. 'or… whatever. I can't keep up with this bloody gender stuff.' She held up one hand. 'Don't mean to offend but I can't be PC all the bloody time; it does my head in.'

Kath shook her head, her eyebrows raised in apology. 'Sorry about her, but you do get used to her, I promise.'

Byron's small eyes crinkled at the edges as he returned the smile. 'It's all good. Actually, it would be a great talking point if any of them *girls* had even heard of Lord Byron.'

'Well, that's youngsters for you.' Ruth was off again. 'I don't know what the bloody hell they're teaching in school these days, except how to take a picture and put in on your Instagrapple or Whatamiat.'

Kath stopped her. 'She knows exactly how to utilise technology, Byron, she just likes to pretend she's a Luddite.'

Ruth sighed. 'God, I sound like my mother.'

'That's not a bad thing,' said Kath. Ruth's mother was a sprightly seventy-five-year-old who still knew her own mind, and usually everyone else's as well. And she was more than happy to put them right about the many things wrong with the current age in which they all lived.

'Fair point well made,' said Ruth. 'So, Byron, what's Kath told you about us, and why do you want to work with us?'

'It's not another interview, Ruth. I have already given him the job.' Kath pointed a finger at Ruth. 'And he has accepted.' She turned to Byron. 'Please don't change your mind.'

Byron sat back, relaxed, with a confident air that belied his twenty-three years. 'I've not always fitted into environments. People still judge me by the way I look, and that's okay because they don't know me and what I can do; what makes me...me.'

Ruth had the good grace to squirm under Kath's gaze at her previous comment on seeing Byron.

'I have nine GCSEs, five A levels and a degree in Computer Sciences & Technology. I like computers and data and facts, and I can function well within a small team of people that accept me. I like results and I enjoy the processes of getting them. I think this team is really interesting and it's helping people. That's all that matters.'

'Can't argue with any of that,' said Ruth.

'And he volunteers for a local homeless charity and a food bank. And he helped an internet investigation team shut down a puppy farm in Church Stretton.'

Ruth laughed. 'Okay, enough already. You're a boy genius on your way to a Peace Prize, even though you like AC/DC.'

Byron picked at the T-shirt. 'This isn't mine. It's my mum's. I just like the fit. I prefer Celtic folk and rock.'

'Fair enough. As long as you can make a decent cup of tea—when Shirl returns with decent tea bags—and work the coffee machine, you'll fit in great. And I hope you don't mind foul language, otherwise you're in for a fucking shock.'

Byron got up and moved towards the kettle. 'No judgement here. And I do make a mean brew.'

'See what you can do with that shite then. Christ, you do realise we'll all want to adopt him by the end of the month,' said Ruth, waving her empty cup at Kath.

'Shirl will definitely mother you to death,' Kath said, getting the milk from the small fridge. 'You'll meet her later. She has four grown-up sons and is always on the lookout for a new addition.'

'Where's Marvin, by the way?' Ruth asked.

'He's in court finishing up the Phillips case so the official handover of teams can go ahead. Should be with us by the end of the week. He'll be glad to have some male energy around him.'

'You think?'

Detective Constable Marvin Henshall was an eager twenty-eight-year-old who saw himself galloping up the ranks as soon as the next Sergeants exam was available, then a few more solid years under his belt and into Inspector big boy clothes. He knew exactly where he was going and what he needed to do to get there. Kath was his biggest supporter and had pushed him through situations he had struggled with; his first murder case was a teenager and Marvin had become emotionally attached to the family, spending more and more hours at the station, poring over evidence and witness statements. It had paid off, although to the detriment of his home life. His wife of a few months had left him. She had always known what she was getting into with his job but was unprepared for the reality. Babies were on her mind—her single driving force. She needed Marvin on a regular basis for his end of that particular job but his energy was constantly directed into his work and she had finally seen the writing on the wall—a future of lonely nights, and if there ever was a baby or two on the scene, she would effectively be a lone parent. She had not wanted that for her future. Surprisingly to everyone at work, and Marvin himself, the decision for his new bride to leave had not been such an emotional disaster, and it made Marvin realise that if there was going to be a female in his future, she would need to have the same goals and ideals as him. Kardashians, baby clothes and nail extensions might work for some. He wanted different. For now, he was a single guy again, the divorce proceedings trickling along without any force or push from either side. It was to be an organic process, and he was happy to have work back completely as his main focus.

Kath watched as Byron manipulated kettle, mugs and spoons. 'We'll have a full meeting in a couple of days when the final member of the team gets here. Her name is Lane and she'll be'—she looked over at Ruth who held out her hands—'consulting on the cases with us.'

Byron stopped what he was doing. 'That's an unusual name. It wouldn't be Lane Petreus, would it?'

'And he's heard of Lane.' Ruth shook her head. 'I am liking you a lot, Byron.'

He smiled. 'There's a little bit of Fox Mulder in me, I guess.'

Ruth pursed her lips, getting up and adding milk to the disgusting brew that passed for tea in the station. 'I could have done with a little bit of Fox Mulder in me a few years ago.'

<u>May 12, 2009</u>

'Are we really going to do this?' The girl pulled her beanie hat down to cover more of her face, trying to push all her hair inside.

'Yes. Right here, right now. I've been dreaming about it for so long. It will be perfect. Look, here they come.'

The school bell sounded the end of the day, and the children began filing out of the main door, into the May sunshine. The boy and girl hung back from the other people at the school gates. The school only had forty-three pupils from the surrounding villages. When the teacher gave the signal, the children broke from their lines and surged forward towards their mums and dads, aunts and cousins, nominated adults. As the adults split off and went their separate ways with waves and nods and smiles, back to vehicles with excited five and six year olds still chattering, still full of energy after their full day of learning, the boy peered from behind the oak tree to the side of the one-storey building, waiting for the last child.

The teacher smiled and waved, shielding her eyes with her hands, looking around for the last expected adult.

Daisy Prospero pushed her hand into the cardigan pocket of the teacher. 'Is Mummy coming?'

The teacher watched the vehicles edge their way down the narrow road. 'I'm sure she will be here really soon.' She patted Daisy on the head and frowned. There was now only the two of them left at the gate. The teacher looked at her watch.

'Okay, let's go.' The boy adjusted his baseball cap and moved forward, the girl tagging along behind, bile threatening to force its way up from her stomach. The teacher felt a fluttering of uncertainty as the boy smiled and waved.

'Hey, Daisy. Ready to go?' He held out his hand. Daisy looked up at the teacher and removed her tiny hand from the pocket.

'Hello, have you come to take Daisy home? I don't believe we've met before.'

'Yes, her mum's running late, so she asked me to come by and get her. I'm Daisy's cousin, Jack. This is my sister.' He cocked a thumb at the girl standing behind him who gave no smile or gesture of greeting.

Daisy squinted as she looked up. 'Hello, Jack. Are we going to play?'

The teacher relaxed. Obviously, Daisy knew him. 'You go straight home with Jack then, and I will see you tomorrow.'

The teacher looked at the girl again as Daisy stepped forward. There was something not quite right about her; something off. She seemed uncomfortable; like she didn't want to be there. The teacher pushed down her unease. Maybe she just didn't like kids much. Not everyone did.

Daisy pushed her headband further into her blonde hair and thrust her bag at Jack. 'Here, you carry this.'

'Okay, no problem. Off we go then.'

The teacher watched the three of them as they turned right, out of the school gates, onto the lane leading into the woods. Daisy's house was the other way, but maybe they were going to his house—wherever that was. She strolled back to the main door. As she grabbed the handle, she turned for a final look. The girl, skinny little thing, was behind Daisy, looking at the dirt road. A random thought popped into her head: *her head is big...bunchy, misshapen...* As she pulled open the door, she decided she would give Daisy's mother a quick call, but suddenly, there was a shout from inside the building; something about the toilets and flooding. She headed towards the emergency, all thoughts of a phone call lost.

It was a decision she would regret for the rest of her life.

|7|

Average was a word no one would ever use to describe Lane Petreus. She was a composite of beautiful pieces; the body of Heidi Klum, the attitude of Xena Warrior Princess, the lustrous black hair of a shampoo ad model, the dark eyes of a Disney princess. Throw in a rich Northern Irish accent and a powerful psychic ability, and you had a woman that other women wanted to be and anybody with a pulse wanted.

Kath watched her get out of her car with a feline grace she could only dream about. Lane walked towards Kath standing among the lavender bushes that lined the pathway to the front door. 'You found me okay, then?'

'The satnav, as you rightly said, did want to take me down a very different route. Thanks for putting me up.' She glanced around the front garden, then up at the cottage. She shook her shoulders and flicked her fingers.

'Oh God,' said Kath, moving towards her, 'don't tell me somebody died here.' Kath had done her research on the cottage before purchasing it. It had been in the history of a local family since the 1870s and, to her knowledge and investigation, nothing untoward had happened, although she suspected there were some animal bones in the back garden, as it backed onto fields where cattle and sheep grazed.

'Your house is fine,' Lane said. 'Now, give me a hug and a beer, in that order.'

They embraced, Kath's shoulder barely reaching Lane's collarbone, and at that moment, Lane knew. And Kath knew that she knew. They released.

'So, beer it is.' Kath tried to keep her voice steady as she moved through the doorway, already regretting her decision to have Lane stay with her, knowing the damage had been done. Now, it was all down to damage control. But there were bigger things to get to grips with. The case was the most important thing. Her own issue had to be put on the back burner, and she prayed that Lane would not speak of it. But Kath knew she would open up, if pressed; if it needed to be in the open. She had chosen not to tell anyone, thereby not involving anyone else, but she had, at times, wished there had been someone to share it with. She had thought about telephoning the Samaritans one night after too many beers and a horrible day at work. But she felt she could not burden another soul. So, it had stayed within her. And now she had found the one person that could see into her head. Maybe that was what this was about all along; she knew she had wanted Lane for the new team, but what if it was also for her own selfish means?

They moved through to the kitchen, chatting about nothing in particular, but Kath's mind was working in a frenzy. They had never been physically that close before. When Lane had been previously called to assist on a case, they had touched hands briefly and just gotten on with the case in hand. Lane had been calm, accurate, emotions in check, all about facts, little snippets they could work with, and it had all produced results. A killer was caught.

Evidence had been sufficient and the CPS had made a case. Jury convicted. Twelve years handed down. The right result. But Lane's input was kept quiet. It was becoming more fashionable, even acceptable now, to use psychics on cases but it was still frowned upon in some circles. And the people at the top had to be placated.

Now, she was going to be a real asset. Trails gone cold, evidence looked at with new eyes, new feelings or whatever emanated from items and locations and people. Kath still didn't know how Lane did what she did; in truth, she was probably what would be described as a healthy sceptic. But that was a good thing. Ask the questions—is it evidence? Can it be proved beyond a reasonable doubt in a court of law?

They progressed through beer to microwave meals and coffee, curled up on sofas in the front room with table lamps casting warm glows across the windows.

'I'm real pleased to be working with you again, Kath.' Lane raised her coffee mug in a toast. Kath acknowledged her with a nod.

'It will be good for everyone to get a result for the first case. And I am confident we will get a result with you on board. You know the team—Shirl, Ruth and Marvin—and I have a new boy, Byron Lord.' Kath waited. And there it was.

'Are you frickin' kidding me?' Lane wiped her mouth and nose where coffee had splattered.

'I kid you not. He's great and bloody good at data shit. You know I can't be doing with all that. Anyway, you'll meet with them all tomorrow.'

'Can you tell me any details now?' Lane settled back into the cushions and stretched her legs along the length of the sofa.

'Well, I need to confirm with the team they are happy but...it's the Daisy Prospero murder. Do you remember it?'

'Aye, I do. Of course I do. Rock star's daughter abducted and murdered? Yeah, I reckon everyone remembers where they were the day that happened. What's the plan?'

Kath sat forward, elbows resting on her thighs—her work position. 'Visit the schoolteacher...me and Ruth will probably do that. Byron can do a data timeline or whatever stuff he does; he knows what I want anyway. You can go to the woods where she was found and over to Todd Prospero's house, and just... do whatever it is you do in whatever way you want to do it. Just get me some answers.' She paused to drain her mug. 'Those two kids are adults now. Assuming they're still alive, I want them found. We just hit a bloody fat dead end last time. We had nowhere to go and we were all miserable about it. It stayed with us. But then more murders and fucking evil stuff took over and... we didn't forget but we got into the zone of the next case and then the next case. Now, it's time to get the job done. We've moved on forensically and in many other ways. Byron worryingly knows his way around the dark web and that may be useful to us. So, there we are.'

Kath smiled but it didn't reach her eyes. Lane was looking at her intently, and Kath was uncomfortable enough to get up and start tidying. 'Anyway, my house, your house etc. Feel free to go to bed whenever. You have to pull the toilet chain quite hard. People have been trying to force me to do over the place—new bathroom and kitchen—but I kind of like it the way it is. We'll leave at 8:30a.m. but I'm usually up quite early. I'll try not to wake you. Anything you need, just ask.' She turned to take the mugs into the kitchen.

'I've always had a good feeling around you, Kath. I like you. I respect you and I think you are a damn fine detective with a fine set of morals and a tenacity to get to the truth of any matter.'

Kath stopped in the doorway but did not turn to face her. Couldn't. She knew what was coming and tried to steady her hands as the china threatened to tremble and tumble to the quarry-tiled floor.

'And I know what you did. I will trust that you had a damn fine reason for doing it. I will never speak of it again unless you wish to talk about it. And it does not in any way change my opinion of you or your ability to do the amazing job you do.'

All the breath seemed to leave Kath's body as the tight brick of fear dissipated from her belly. The tick of the inherited grandfather clock seemed to fill the room. 'Thank you, Lane. Goodnight,' Kath whispered.

| 8 |

'So, are we ready then? Everyone have their required beverage?' Kath looked around the new office space at her team, all together and ready to start. Byron had set up in a back corner with barely anymore room on his desk for equipment. Kath was perched on the edge of a desk as Shirl, Ruth, Marvin and Lane moved their chairs so they could all see her and each other. They all nodded and raised their mugs.

Kath held up a fat manila file. 'This is our first case, and I know that most of you are familiar with it but we are starting from scratch. Pretend you know nothing. Treat everything in here with caution and suspicion. I'll tell you the bare facts. Then we start. Daisy Prospero was the five-year-old daughter of Todd Prospero—rock singer, as I'm sure you all know—and his wife Zoe. Daisy was taken from her infant school near Much Wenlock on the 12th of May, 2009, by a young lad and a young girl. Her body was found in woodland approximately one mile away, four hours later. She had been manually strangled. No sexual aspect, thank Christ.'

Kath took a deep breath, the memories of the case flooding back in. 'I was SIO on the case, and I guess that's why I wanted it as our first. But I am a fair boss, I hope, and if any of you feel we should start with another case or select them differently, I am happy to hear arguments accordingly.'

'I think I can speak for the majority,' said Shirl, looking at all the others, 'when I say we're happy to start with this one and get the bastards that did this.'

'Yep,' said Ruth.

'Me too,' agreed Marvin.

Lane held up her hands. 'I am the outsider here but happy with this decision, nonetheless.'

'Good. Thank you. Byron has already started data analysis, and I think it will be a real asset to have someone on the team that does not work like we do. It's easy to rely on our own reputations and our own ways of working. Byron can look at making us more proficient and he can bring a new perspective, along with Lane's... abilities.'

Ruth waved her hands in the air. 'Gotta love the woo-woo.' They all laughed.

'Call it whatever you like; I have a thick skin.' Lane smiled and lifted her mug.

'So'—Kath smacked the folder down on the desk—'as if this case was not tragic enough, Zoe Prospero, eaten up with guilt at not being at the school gates to pick up her daughter, took her own life three months after the murder of her child.'

'Fuck,' said Byron under his breath.

'Following the overdose that caused his wife's death, Todd quit music, quit life really, and holed himself up in the family home for two years. The teacher that let Daisy go with the couple was about to telephone Zoe to tell her where Daisy had gone but there was a situation in the school and it went out of her head. She quit teaching, left her husband and the area. She's our first contact, if she's still alive and not plagued by dementia or similar. Ruth, I'd like you to drive to Pangbourne with me to see her.'

Ruth nodded and scribbled on the notepad on her lap.

'Lane, I would like you to visit the scene where she was found. See what you get, do whatever it is you do.' The team all smiled, and Lane smiled back.

'Happy to do that, Kath.'

'Okay.' Kath's eyes scanned her checklist at the notes she had made, usually in the middle of the night when she awoke with an idea; a tiny piece of something that might be useful to follow up, retest, re-examine.

'Byron, I'm leaving you with the DNA sample that was pulled off Daisy.' She shifted against the desk, uncomfortable, but that was the nature of their jobs and had been for a long time for most of them. It just felt unpleasant and somehow disrespectful to a five-year-old girl to describe the state of her still body, its position, its temperature. All of her reduced to samples and fluids and lab results.

'We got a saliva sample from her cheek. Could be he sprayed her, exhaling with the force of his... action.' Kath glanced at Byron, who was trying to keep a neutral face, but Kath could tell he was struggling with the details. As he should, she thought. Otherwise, he would not be human.

She went on, 'The hyoid bone was broken, so we know she was strangled full frontal with the thumbs doing the damage. The DNA from her cheek was run through the databases at the time but we didn't get any hits. Either this lad had never been in trouble, or he had and just never seen the inside of a police station. Byron, you'll be looking at that aspect. The teacher said in her statement that she thought the boy and the girl were young but she couldn't put them any closer than between thirteen and twenty. But they are ten years older now. They are either functioning in society, in the systems of social care, prison or mental health facilities, or dead. I want to know which, and I want them found.'

She looked across the faces. 'I think we are looking at him doing the killing and her watching. I get the impression, from what the teacher said, that the girl didn't really want to be there. I think the teacher had a normal gut instinct reaction to what was happening and she just pushed it down and ignored it, like so many people do. So, we find him, we find her—or at least get to know who she is.

'Shirl, check again on the missing persons reports for the time and the area. In fact, expand the search. Let's not take anything for granted. They may well have been local. If so, nobody missed them at the time. Noone rang after the appeal went out in the media. There were a shit load of calls, some people just trying to help, some cranks—obviously, goes without saying—but look at grabbing CCTV footage from a wider area. They took this child, they didn't go far, they—he—killed her. Then what happened to them? Where did they go? They either disappeared into a hole in the ground or they came out of the woods and went somewhere. People must have seen them and thought nothing of it. Did someone see them, know them, say hello and went on their way? A 'nice' lad, maybe? A 'good' girl? Youngsters who raised no suspicion; no red flags. Maybe these two were so fucking ordinary that no one would in any way suspect them of doing something like this.

'Shirl, look at the call logs again. Byron, help her with that. And draw me up a minute-by-minute timeline, if you can, from the moment Daisy came out of those double doors at the school.' Kath stopped to draw breath. She was getting angry now and itching to get things moving.

Lane put up her hand. 'If it's okay, I'd like to visit the school, too. And her house. Meet Todd Prospero.'

'Yep, whatever you need, whatever you want. Probably best if one of us is with you—Marvin, maybe that's something you can do with Lane.'

Marvin nodded. 'Sure. No problem, Boss.'

Kath felt a pang of guilt. This was tough on him; still a youngster himself. Although, Kath thought anyone under thirty-seven was still classed as that. He hadn't been around in the force at the time of the crime. His only experience had been what the media had put out—garish newspaper red-top headlines, sensational stories resurrected again three months later when Zoe Prospero took an overdose of her prescribed sleeping pills, unable to live without her daughter or the guilt of her actions on that May day. He didn't even know yet whether being a father was in his future, even in his mind's eye ever, but this would taint him. Kath also knew, given his desire to proceed up the ladder, this was be a case to make him. He would be noticed further up the chain; heads would nod when he passed by. This was big for all of them for all sorts of reasons.

'Okay, so there's a starting point for all of us. Remember, it's business as usual in some respects: don't discount the little things, the throwaway comments, the things people might have seen or thought they might have had an idea about. We don't dismiss them; we have the time now to properly follow up on the little things we may have missed or bypassed the first time around.'

Everyone nodded and muttered agreements.

Lane stood. 'Can I visit Todd now, at home?' She looked to Marvin, then back at Kath.

'Fine by me. Marvin, make the call, see if he's okay with that.' As Marvin searched in the file for Todd's number, Kath moved over to Ruth. 'Shall we set off for the schoolteacher first thing tomorrow?'

Ruth nodded. 'Should be nearly three hours down to Pangbourne. I've checked the route. We should allow four there and four back. Do you want to stay over?'

As the rest of the team mingled around them, putting chairs back and chatting, Kath wondered whether a night away would do her good. Away from the scene, from the usual surroundings. She shrugged. 'Can we pack a bag just in case and play it by ear? We can share the driving if we come back same day.'

'Fine by me.' Ruth stood by her desk, pointing. 'Coasters, people. Who left the little ring on my desk? God invented coasters for people with dribbly cups. It's right there.' She grabbed a disinfectant wipe from her desk drawer and erased the offensive ring. Marvin reddened.

'Shocking, Ruth. People should be ashamed. Lane, you ready?' He waved his mobile at her and made a swift exit.

Todd's house was a couple of miles outside Much Wenlock, nestled in the hamlet of Stretton Westwood. The walls at the front of the house left a gap to enter onto the gravelled driveway. The Edwardian property, with a wild trail of roses around the front doorway, was impressive but not ostentatious. Beds of shrubs scrambled for attention at the sides of the house leading round to the back garden. It wasn't that Todd hated being outdoors or tending to the plants and almost meadow-like lawn areas; it was what he couldn't say to Miranda during their evening over dinner. It was Daisy's domain. His daughter had loved playing outside, getting her hands mucky, learning from her mum all about how things grew, the bees and ladybirds, slugs and tiny flies. Zoe had been at home in nature, and their daughter had been showing all the same signs. For Todd, it was still that reminder, and he had chosen to do the bare minimum to keep it from looking like an abandoned house in the wilderness. Mrs Tinkerson constantly badgered him about getting a gardener if he didn't want to do the jobs himself, but Todd had managed to fend her off.

Lane took in the odd balance of the exterior; the sparkling windows and polished door knocker on the cobweb-free wooden front door, clean paintwork and pristine doormat with a picture of a cat on it fighting against the undergrowth and tangled plant life. Marvin knocked at the door, and Todd appeared, holding out his hand and welcoming them inside. The wood-panelled hallway gave way to an impressive staircase with a huge arched window throwing in a good amount of light. All the doors off the hallway were open. Marvin spotted the kitchen but waited for Todd to direct them where they should go. Lane and Marvin followed Todd into the lounge which spread from front to back, giving a view of the back garden and the front driveway.

'As I explained on the phone,' Marvin said, sitting on one of the sofas,' I would like to introduce Lane Petreus who is assisting us.' Lane remained standing, staring at Todd. She had followed the men in body but her senses were all over the place, picking up vibrations, feeling the energy in her, eyes darting from wood panelling to flowers to paintings on the walls, noting every detail of what was there and what was not.

'I'm very happy to be here, Todd.' Her accent and the pitch of her voice was soothing, mellow, and Todd felt drawn towards her. 'I'm also sorry we're meeting under these circumstances.' Todd offered his hand and Lane took it between both of hers. His skin was warm and soft.

'I appreciate that. Thank you.' He wanted to pull away but felt he had to stay connected to her.

'It's okay, Todd. Just be with me, here. Talk.'

Todd's emotions were all over the place. 'I feel like I want to tell you my whole life story.' He grinned, feeling incredibly foolish but also thankful for her presence. Marvin looked at both of them, not knowing quite what to do. He was, after all, the officer in charge of this visit. But he didn't feel very in charge of anything and decided to let Lane lead. He would make notes, he decided, and got out his notebook.

'Erm... can I get you coffee or something?'

Lane released Todd, and he pushed his hands into his pockets. She sat down next to Marvin.

'I'm fine, thank you.' Marvin said, looking at Lane.

'Maybe later.' She smiled and indicated that he should sit in the chair opposite.

Marvin didn't want to break the look Lane was giving Todd but he did feel he needed to move things forward. Patience was not a virtue of his; he was eager to get his teeth into this investigation. Kath had already contacted Todd and told him about the new team and that Daisy's case was to be their first. Todd's reaction was a mess of relief, anxiety at the reliving of the events and gratitude that his little girl had not been forgotten by the world.

'Okay then.' Todd sat and opened his hands. 'Where do you want to begin?'

Lane stood suddenly, alarming the two men. 'Can I take a walk around the house?'

'Go wherever you like,' Todd said.

She left the room, and Marvin gave what he hoped was a professional yet friendly smile.

'I...er... well, I have to confess that I'm a bit starstruck.' Marvin felt the blush rise to his cheeks but he couldn't seem to help himself. 'I grew up listening to you. Loved your band so much.'

Todd gave a gracious grin. 'Thank you, but please just treat me like you would anyone else under these circumstances.'

'Okay, no problem.' Marvin centred himself and fleetingly thought about the phone call he would have with his best mate later about his meeting with the lead singer of Hark—bigger than Bon Jovi, Guns N' Roses and Aerosmith put together.

'I wasn't here,' Todd said softly. 'I was at the recording studio in Buckinghamshire. Russell, our manager, drove me home as soon as Zoe called. Worst journey of my life.' He rubbed his hand across his eyes. 'I don't really think I can tell you anything different than I did when I was first interviewed.'

Todd looked up as he heard the floorboards creak. 'I know who she is; her reputation. Do you really think she can help find who did this? Please, tell me what you think, and not as a policeman.'

Marvin sat forward. 'Todd, I have no bloody idea what she does or how she does it. None of us do. But she has found things before that officers have overlooked. And she asks questions that sometimes we just don't think of. That's what makes her valuable, and we are so glad to have her on our team. We are giving a hundred percent. Not that we didn't the first time around.' He mentally kicked himself.

'It's okay,' Todd said, 'I know what you mean. I expect other stuff got in the way back then. This team, DCI Fortune said, was a new direction; new focus. No stopping until the end.'

They both heard the back door open and Samson meowing. 'Cat's got another bloody admirer,' said Todd, rising and moving towards the kitchen. 'I'm putting some coffee on now. Come on.'

Lane stood in the middle of the shaggy lawn, Samson winding himself around her legs, begging for more attention. She wrapped her arms around her body and faced the August sun, which would have been unbearable but for the clouds that chased it across the sky and gave relief every few minutes. She was trying to process her feelings from the house. She had wandered around Todd's bedroom, noting the absence of fuss and frill—a man's room but not bleak. Just homely and functional. She'd picked up the photo frame on the mantelpiece showing Zoe and Daisy smiling, Zoe's arms around the little body in front of her. Lane had felt the love and devotion and Zoe's heartbreak at the loss. Lane found the bedroom where Daisy had spent her few years on earth, glad to see it hadn't become a shrine. So many parents left the room exactly as it was after the loss of a child. A snapshot. The last time they had inhabited the space. Lane had been into bedrooms where the plates and dishes and cups were still harbouring the last remnants of food and drink, congealed and almost transparent after years of not being touched, the bedclothes flung back as if someone was going to return, the smell of unwashed items almost aligning itself to the smell of death.

This room, though, was a healthy sign; the small bed still held the neatly draped floral patchwork quilt, the wardrobe doors were shut, the chest of drawers neat with no overflow of items. A shelf along one wall held two stuffed animals: an elephant and a cat. It was clear that more would have been there but it seemed that Todd had decided too much was indeed too much. Lane had stood in the middle of the room, feeling the joy and finding no clues.

She'd moved across the hallway, poked her nose into two rooms that looked like functional guest bedrooms with the minimum amount of furniture to just fend off the sense of them being hotel rooms. Another room was sparse—a wooden gateleg table and easy wingback armchair being the only items. One wall had wallpaper on it, rips appearing at the sides and on seams. A room in progress, Lane had said to herself. The last room she'd entered was the guest room where Miranda was sleeping, and the hairs on her body had prickled. A new person, a different energy. She'd opened the old wardrobe and touched the velvet dress, and the visions had come to her—tears, cold and damp earth, a yellow and white striped dress. Flashes, impressions. Her heartbeat had raised. She'd shut the wardrobe door and made her way downstairs to the garden.

Now, she wandered through the long grass to the side fence that backed onto woodland, felt the stares of the cattle in the field at the bottom of the garden. She stopped and noticed the hole—a child-sized hole in the fence. She stood up quickly from her crouched position, holding on to the wooden frame that housed the swing, the seat covered in small clumps of a plant that Lane did not know existed, tiny mushrooms sprouting from the side of the wood.

And she knew it was here, knew she would go back to the house at some point, maybe not today but some time with news Todd would not want to hear.

|9|

'Bloody hell. Genesis. *And Then There Were Three.*' Lenny turned over the CD cover, looking at the tracks, remembering.

Kath was seated on one of her sofas, legs up, wine glass nestled in her hand, watching him, remembering.

He waved the CD at her. 'Our song's on here.'

'Yep,' she said. 'Our slow dance at the end-of-year disco.'

'Mind if I put it on?' He didn't want to presume but he wanted to hear it; wanted to feel that emotion again.

'Go ahead.' She drained her glass, feeling content and warm.

He had turned up on her doorstep an hour after she'd left the Madeley station, finding her in her favourite jogging bottoms and baggy T-shirt. He'd been alarmed to see another car in the driveway but then Kath had told him Lane was staying with her. He had hesitated in the doorway, wine bottle in hand. Lane Petreus had been a thorn in his side for many years, and he was not comfortable around her. But the need to be with Kath was too strong and he was prepared to share space with the psychic. He needn't have worried, as Lane had grabbed a sandwich and headed for her room early, and Kath had assured him they wouldn't be disturbed.

He'd been to her cottage before, had dinner, talked about work. He was different tonight. He hummed as he found the track he wanted: "Follow You, Follow Me". The irony was not lost on either of them. They had, indeed, followed each other into the force, coincidentally, no deliberate act on either part. But the thing Kath never knew, and even as a good detective had never found out, was that Lenny had followed her; engineered a move to West Mercia to be close to her. He'd built up a lot of favours over the years and had been respected early on for his work ethic and ability to get the job done. He and Kath had lost contact after he'd moved to Derbyshire and she was still in the outer reaches of the West Midlands. But he had watched and waited. And suddenly, the time had been right and there he was, there they were, together again. Kath had joked about him stalking her, and in a way he had. But not in a bad way. Only because he truly loved her and wished to be nearby. At least, that's the story he told himself.

The strains of Phil Collins' voice filled the lounge, and Lenny stood, arms open. 'Dance with me?'

He'd taken off his jacket as soon as he'd arrived, rolled up his shirt sleeves, chopped vegetables as he'd invited himself to stay for dinner. There had been no resistance on Kath's part. She enjoyed his company; still saw the fourteen-year-old that had stolen her heart. His cheeks had become rounder now like his belly. But his grey eyes were still the same, dirty blonde hair showing no signs of receding and fingernails still bitten.

She put her glass on the floor and stood, swaying to the music as he folded himself around her. He bent his head so their cheeks were almost touching. 'Our figures don't really allow for this anymore,' she joked.

He snickered like a pony into her ear. 'Yes, true. But our souls are still slender and full of love.' The heat of him was delicious, and she had forgotten how good it was to have that close male touch. She moved her left hand across his broad back and entwined the fingers of her right hand in his.

'Forty-one years ago,' he whispered. 'That was the moment, dancing to this song, surrounded by the whole year in the dim lighting of the assembly hall, the moment that I fell in love with you.'

'I know.' She breathed.

'How? How could you possibly have known? I was a bit of a dick.'

She smiled and she felt him smile, their skin creasing together and fitting like pieces of a jigsaw. 'Because you did exactly what you're doing now. You closed your eyes.'

They were still moving slowly as he pulled back to look at her face. 'How did you know?'

She let go of his hand and touched his face. 'Because I felt your eyelashes on my cheek, and fourteen-year-old boys do not close their eyes when they dance with a girl. Especially when they are a dick.'

His lips moulded themselves into a smile, reaching his eyes, lighting up his face. He took her hand from his face and kissed her palm, and they stayed in that moment for a few seconds.

'Do you still kiss like a fourteen-year-old?' Her blood pulsed a different beat in her ears as a wave of longing she thought was long gone swept through her torso, across her heart and into her brain.

'Let's find out.'

Their warm lips opened and melted, and forty years of absolute love swirled through two bodies. Lenny held the back of Kath's head, and Kath moved both hands around his torso, pressing his body tight against hers as much as breath and breadth would allow. They parted as the track started playing again, and she punched him lightly on the arm.

'You put this track on repeat, you sneaky bastard.'

Lenny shrugged. 'Call me an old romantic, if you will. You can't blame me for wanting to have you in my arms for as long as possible this time.'

Kath pulled away and picked up her wine glass. 'You know you're going home, don't you?' She turned and went into the kitchen, to the fridge to get the rest of the wine. She felt pleasantly warm and fuzzy but still had enough wits about her to not give in if he wanted to push her into letting him stay the night. That was not what she wanted for any of them—Lenny's wife, Susan, included—and she really didn't think Lenny did either. She was well aware of his feelings for her. It was not based on a physical need in the purely sexual sense; they enjoyed being close together. That was what it was all about. The first sexual encounter and then the following few months of frenzy were all very well. But when that died down, when boredom set in and routine threatened the relationship to the point of distance and resentment, well, that was the kiss of death and there was rarely a way back from that. But when a relationship evolved into the easy manner, the shared sense of humour, the cliché of finishing each other's sentences—that was love. In the simplest form. And that was what she and Lenny had. But she had the feeling Lenny had reached that point where he was prepared to walk out on a twenty-eight-year marriage. And she wasn't about to be party to that.

'Put another bloody track on, will you? I'm not dancing anymore.'

She filled his glass to under a third full as he picked out a Blondie CD to pump up the mood, although the volume was softer so as not to disturb the houseguest.

He sat on the sofa next to her, and she swung her legs onto his lap. He angled himself towards her so he could watch her sip her wine. 'I don't know what to do, Kath,' he said quietly. She didn't interrupt. He needed to get this off his chest, and she needed to let him. 'Susan and I... we're rubbing along and we both know it's okay but I still wonder if you and I... if it's not too late?'

'Are you asking or just spiffballing?'

'If I left Susan...' He rubbed a hand over his face.

'If you're waiting for my permission, you'll be waiting a long time,' Kath said, putting her now empty glass on the floor. She pulled her legs from his lap and bunched her knees under her chin. 'I am not going to tell you what to do, and don't use me as an excuse.' She regretted the way in which she'd spoken instantly and laid a hand on his arm. 'Sorry. That came out wrong.'

He looked at her. 'I'm not saying if I leave can I come straight over here and live with you and we'll be happy together forever. Susan is a wonderful person, and she has been a fantastic wife and mother...'

'But?'

'But she's not you.' He stared at her, and she couldn't turn off the feelings; didn't want to. 'And the problem is that Susan has always known she's not you and decided a long time ago to stay with me and love me even though she knew the kind of love I could offer her was a downgrade. And sometimes that makes me feel shitty.'

'It's all down to timing, Lenny. And mine has always been shite.' She levered herself up from her uncomfortable position and turned Debbie Harry off, keeping her back to him. 'You do what you want to do but for you. Not for me or because of me. If you don't want to share a life with Susan anymore then leave. Otherwise, stay.'

She turned to face him. He looked like a schoolkid again, lost in a deep sofa, hands over his eyes. She went to him and pulled his hands away, pulled his body up towards hers. 'Now, it's time for you to go.'

They wrapped their bodies around each other again. Lenny picked up his jacket from the back of the sofa and went to the front door, still the faintest light on the horizon but a clear summer night and another night he would spend without her. He had some thinking to do. He put the car into gear as the engine purred, and he waved to his love standing in the doorway.

Kath watched him pull away and closed the door, facing the grandfather clock that seemed to tick away her life at every opportunity. Each metallic thud signified a moment lately where she was having life decisions thrown at her. She locked the door and passed by the clock, into the kitchen.

'One of these days, you will be firewood,' she muttered.

| 10 |

According to the file, Helen Tranter was forty-two years old. The woman who answered the door looked closer to sixty-two. And a hard sixty-two at that. Kath showed her warrant card, Ruth did the same.

'I told you on the phone I do not want to do this.' Helen Tranter pulled her thick knit cardigan tightly around her spectral frame, her lips set in a thin line, eyes defiant and wary.

Kath gave what she hoped was a reassuring smile. 'And we really appreciate you seeing us, Helen. Can I call you Helen?'

The woman in the doorway nodded and looked back over her shoulder into the darkness of the downstairs flat as if wrestling with the decision of whether or not to allow the two officers in.

Ruth cleared her throat to get the woman's attention again and smiled as she turned. 'We really feel you have valuable information that will help us get the people that hurt Daisy.' She was going to say murdered but the woman looked delicate and Ruth didn't want to spook her. They needed her onside, having travelled to the outskirts of Reading to go over the original statement Helen had given soon after the taking of Daisy Prospero.

Helen Tranter chewed on a fingernail, letting slip a side of the cardigan that revealed the economy of her body. A baggy T-shirt hung over a pair of large jogging bottoms complete with frayed cuffs and two holes near the kneecap of one leg. Shoulder-length blonde hair hung straight, and she pushed the unkempt fringe from her eyes, the hair immediately returning.

'Come on then.' She turned, and Kath and Ruth followed her into the first room. She pointed to a shabby two-seater sofa for Kath and Ruth. Helen sank into an armchair that seemed to swallow her. Kath and Ruth perched on the edge of the sagging sofa cushions.

'Thank you, Helen.' Kath placed the file on her knees, knowing she had to tread carefully with this woman who had let the guilt of her actions consume her, sucking all joy out of her frame, leaving only a haunted look and bad breath. 'As I said on the phone, we have the new team now. Fresh eyes and a fresh perspective—'

'But I told you everything at the time. Everything. This is all just a waste of my time.'

Ruth glanced around the room. The few houseplants on the bay windowsill were on their last legs. A layer of dust covered every surface—coffee table, mantelpiece, fake coal effect electric fire, a small bookcase which held slumped books of varying sizes at different angles. A TV guide sat on the arm of the chair where Helen huddled, the remote on the top, some programmes circled in black felt pen. *Yes,* thought Ruth, *we are interrupting your busy schedule of not having a fucking life, you poor cow.*

Ruth and Kath shared a look, and Ruth took her cue.

'Mind if I put the kettle on, Helen? Through here, is it?' Ruth was already out of the door before Helen could utter a word. She sank back even further, unable or unwilling to fight them anymore.

Kath had read Helen's statement so many times she knew it off by heart and had rehearsed some phrases she hoped didn't sound trite, hoping they would somehow help and reassure the ex-teacher. Helen Tranter had given herself a very hard time over Daisy's death. Apart from the killer, she was the last person to see Daisy alive. Zoe, Daisy's mother, had turned up at the school, anxious and aware that her tardiness may have caused alarm. But she was completely unprepared for the news that stumbled from Helen Tranter's lips—her cousin Jack and his friend had come to collect her. Both women had held onto door and walls as Zoe had told her there was no Cousin Jack and Zoe would never have allowed anyone else to pick up her daughter. She had struck Helen Tranter across the face as the shock of what was happening had sunk its teeth into her reality. The police had been called at once as Zoe ran towards the direction Daisy had taken with Cousin Jack and his friend in the beanie hat, shouting her daughter's name as the stitch in her side slowed her and made her curse. Dry sobs had come, loud, broken. She'd been found by police officers slumped on the woodland path that led up the hill into the woods, her throat closing up, pockets of breath sitting like stones in her chest.

Kath knew the Helen Tranter interview had taken place within the hour. And there was one detail that bothered her—the one detail that might make a difference.

Ruth returned to the lounge carrying a tray with three mugs, a carton of milk and a bag of sugar. She placed the tray on the coffee table and handed round the mugs. 'Found everything okay. Don't know how you like it, so...' She gestured to the milk and sugar. Helen nodded and leaned forward, putting four sugars into her black tea and barely a splash of milk. Despite the state of the lounge, Ruth had been pleasantly surprised that the kitchen was relatively clean and tidy. Not Ruth tidy and clean. But a kitchen that made Ruth feel she could indeed make a drink and consume it without needing to be hospitalised.

Helen dipped her tongue into her tea like a hummingbird searching for nectar. It was a disturbing sight for the two detectives, and Kath knew she had to get in and out fast or this was going to have been a whole new waste of time.

'There is a phrase in your statement that bothers me, and I just want to go over it again. Can we do that, Helen?' The dipping of the tongue continued, and Helen nodded, staring at the carpet, aware but not really there.

'So, the girl that was with this lad, you said she had on a beanie hat and that her head looked too big for her. Can you remember why you said that? Why you thought that?'

Helen stopped lapping, pulled her arm around her head, pointed to the back of her own head in a circular motion. 'Here,' she said, 'didn't look right here.'

Ruth screwed up her eyes, her brain trying to process the words. 'Like some sort of medical condition, maybe?'

'Shit.' The file slipped off Kath's lap as the realisation came to her. 'Helen'—Kath leaned forward, touching the woman's knee—'could it be she had a lot of hair tucked under that hat? You know, like you do when it's raining or when you want to keep it out of the way...'

Helen stared at her, recognition of the memory settling in her face. 'Yes, yes, exactly like that. I did the same when I was about eleven and I had long hair and it was raining. Yes, yes, that could be it. Is that good? Is that helpful?'

Kath smiled, gathering her papers from the floor and pulling Ruth up. 'I knew you'd remember something, Helen. Thank you so much. We need to get back now.'

Helen followed them to the front door and watched them walk down the path to the car. 'By the way,' she said about to close the door, 'it was red.'

Kath wheeled round. 'What?'

'Her hair,' Helen said. 'It was red.'

They found a Travelodge three miles down the road with a pub next door. They had agreed they would stay overnight; Kath wanted to fully process what Helen had told them and Ruth had agreed. Kath also had an ulterior motive. She needed a sounding board for what had happened between her and Lenny the night before, and being away from home gave her the perfect opportunity to be more objective than she actually felt back on home soil. The August day had been a proper old-time, back in the day hot day for the time of year with the odd cloud scudding here and there, and the evening was turning muggy. Sleep was going to be difficult but Kath felt they were going to be talking into the night. They had showered and changed upper clothing and sunk into the relative cool of the Golden Lamb next door, ordering a large pint of alcohol each, as driving was not going to be a factor.

They ordered food at the bar, took their drinks outside and found a table away from the other late evening diners. The wooden chairs had plush seat covers and the rear garden was a little unimaginative with a few large pots with cordylines and surrounding begonias. But there was an ashtray on the table and Kath pulled out her smokes after taking a long pull of the pear cider.

'So, Marvin's told the others where we're up to with what happened this afternoon.'

Ruth nodded and took a long drink of her lager, not her usual bottled brand but a good enough substitute on a hot evening with a murder enquiry that was also hotting up with every phone call.

Kath continued, 'I told him to wait to brief us in the morning about his visit to Todd's house with Lane. But he's like a bloody puppy with a chew toy. He's really excited about what Lane has said to him, and I'm hyped but exhausted at the same time.'

'Yep.' Ruth took another pull at her beer as Kath lit a cigarette. 'I hear ya. But it feels really good; feels like we are getting somewhere already. I hope we don't come crashing to a standstill.' She tilted her head as smoke wreathed around their heads in the stillness of the night air. 'Can you crash to a standstill?'

Kath closed her eyes. 'Don't know, don't care.' She sipped her drink and smoked her cigarette, enjoying the silence for a moment before taking the plunge. 'Lenny wants to leave Susan.'

Ruth pulled the bottle away from her lips. 'Christ, when did this transpire?'

'Last night. He came to see me, we had dinner, talked...' Kath flicked her thumb against the cigarette butt in repetitive movements against the ashtray. '...Kissed.'

'Shit. Okay. So, how do you feel about it?'

Ruth had known for many years about the love Kath and Lenny shared. Shirl too. A select few knew of the deep relationship that had never interfered with her work or his management of the station whilst he had been there.

'I told him whatever his decision was, it had to be for him, not for me.'

Ruth smiled. 'I asked how you feel about it, not what you said.'

Kath took a last drag and stubbed out her butt with more force than required. 'I feel fifty-five, Ruth. And I'd love nothing more than to come home at night, cook dinner and curl up on the sofa with him to watch bad crime dramas on the TV.' She paused, letting the scenario play out in her head, smiling at the image. 'But I don't want to be the cause of another woman's misery.'

The waitress appeared on the patio with two plates, looking around as Ruth gestured. She walked over and placed their food in front of them, the burgers and salad looking less appetising to Kath now she was back thinking about Lenny.

'If it's his decision and you end up together, surely that wouldn't be your doing?' Ruth scraped the mayonnaise from the small container onto her chips and proceeded to work her way through the first decent meal she'd had for a day or so.

'I hear what you're saying... doesn't make it any easier on my conscience though.' She cut the burger into small pieces and stabbed at them with her fork, pushing them into her mouth but not really tasting anything.

'I guess if Susan's happy with the setup, it really is up to Lenny to decide what to do. He can't just assume he can leave and move in with you.' Ruth laughed as she imagined Lenny in a pokey bedsit on one of the rougher estates dotted around Telford. She realised Kath was talking to her and brought herself back to chips and mayo and listening to her boss and friend.

'...Just a bit of a dream really.' Kath pointed her fork at Ruth, chewing the burger and igniting her appetite again. Maybe a slice of cheesecake to follow would settle her for a night of peaceful sleep, even in the heat.

'I'm just saying, as your mate, you always do right by everybody else. Think about yourself for a change and don't beat yourself up. You are not responsible for what people think of you or how they feel about you. Remember that. Do you want any of these chips before I devour them all?'

Kath shook her head as Ruth proceeded to clear her plate and down the rest of her beer. Ruth was right. All her team were right. She always tried to do the best thing by everyone. What was the point of joining the force in the first place if your morals were going to be positioned on the ethical seesaw? Doing the right thing. *Yeah, that was what it was all about*, she thought, as the memory of her actions of that night in 2004 struggled to surface and sat like a ton of weight across her chest. The action taken all those years ago that Lane saw when she looked into Kath's eyes, when she held her body and saw into her soul. Was that still the right thing to have done? Her burger was on the way back up and Kath fought to level her breathing, turning away from Ruth and standing, stretching, to avoid eye contact with another human being who would surely judge her if she knew... if any of them knew. She lit a cigarette, calmed herself, settled the burger where it belonged and looked out across the pub garden to the houses beyond. Lights on, movement across windows as people went about their evening with no thought of murdered children and moral dilemmas.

| 11 |

The team had gathered early at the office, eager to hear the updates from Lane and Marvin and the results of Ruth and Kath's expedition to Pangbourne to see the teacher. Both visits had produced results, and there was now a resurgence of energy, of expectation verging on excitement. Kath and Ruth had set off just after five in the morning, had gone home to change and make it back in time for the briefing. Now that coffee and tea had been allocated, everyone sat in anticipation.

'He's just so cool,' Marvin was saying, piling sugar into his coffee.

Shirl leaned across and ruffled his dark hair. 'Aw, Marv has got himself a man crush.'

He grinned and pushed her hand away. 'I don't care what you say, the man is a god.' They all laughed.

Lane spoke and the laugher died down. 'The wee boy did a grand job once I discovered Mr Prospero has a houseguest. Marvin, do you want to tell it?'

He nodded, smiled and reached for his notebook. 'Lane found women's clothes in one of the bedrooms. There was no one else in the house when we got there, but she asked Todd who the woman was.' He looked at Lane who nodded her encouragement to continue.

'What he told us has opened a whole new can of worms.' Marvin explained about Todd finding Miranda in the garden, her subsequent 'recovery' back to health under his guidance and his reluctance to see her leave before finding out exactly why she had turned up as she did.

'Christ, as if the man hasn't been through enough,' said Shirl. 'I'd have been mad as hell and thrown her out at the first opportunity.'

Marvin licked his lips. 'That's kind of what I hinted at, but it seems he's formed some sort of attachment to this girl.' He flipped over the page of his notebook. 'Miranda, no last name, no more details than that except Todd has learned her mother is deceased.'

'But where the hell has she come from? And why choose to die in Todd's garden? What was that going to achieve? Is she some kind of groupie?' Shirl asked, trying to get her head around the accumulated misery of the man who had lost so much.

'I think Lane can tell you about that better than I can.' Marvin shut his book.

Lane picked up the story. 'There is a connection here I don't think Todd is even aware of, although he does feel something for her.'

Ruth interrupted. 'Like a love thing? Obsession?'

Lane shook her head. 'No, he says not, was actually very quick to stress he was not having those kinds of feelings for her.'

'How old is this girl?' Kath asked.

'Todd estimates early twenties; difficult to tell.'

'Is it a surrogate daughter thing he's going through?' Byron had been quiet so far, still tapping away at his keyboard in the corner of the room but felt confident enough to offer input.

'Well... I really don't know. I don't have all the answers, despite what you may be expecting.' Lane wanted to stress this point. What she did wasn't concrete, more ethereal, and people found it difficult sometimes to put their logic and reasoning on the back burner and just accept things they could not understand. But Kath knew, as she looked around the room, that these people had been chosen by her because of their open minds, their need to question but also accept what they couldn't necessarily understand.

'Believe me,' Lane continued, 'Todd is anxious to know more about her but told me his eagerness to discover more just seems to send her fleeing to the door. Literally. He wants answers before she disappears from his life, maybe for good, maybe to try her suicide again. He freely admits she has brought joy to his life, a new spark he is enjoying even if the circumstances are bizarre.' Lane paused and looked at each of the team. 'But I fear there is a more sinister twist to this event, this appearance in Todd's garden. And I think I'll know more when I've visited the place where Daisy died. By the way, remind me again, what was Daisy wearing when she was found?'

Ruth was quick to remember and answer. 'School dress. Yellow and white stripes.'

Now Lane knew there was a connection, but she needed more before she could present it to the team. This time, faint impressions were not going to be enough. She had to push harder.

Kath nodded, stood from perching on the edge of the desk and stretched. 'That is the next port of call. I think Lane and myself should make that our priority. Shirl, you too.'

Shirl nodded and drained her cup.

'Byron, Marvin—go over the call log information that Shirl has managed to get...'

Byron interrupted. 'I'm working on an algorithm to—'

Kath held up her hand. 'Whoa there, boy genius. You're here to do all that computer shit in the way only you can do. Don't even try to explain it to me. I accept that you are fabulous, just don't make my ears bleed with what essentially sounds like Ruth's husband talking about Manchester United statistics or the history of the Peugeot headlight.'

Everyone laughed, and Ruth sighed. 'That is indeed my life, mock it if you will. What do want me to do, Kath?'

They had regaled the team with the information provided by Helen Tranter; they now felt confident they were looking for a girl from 2009 with a lot of red hair. They had all tossed around the idea she may look different now—weren't youngsters just obsessed with dyeing their hair? But was that the reason for the hat? Her hair was distinctive, and if it was the case, that would surely narrow down their search through the previous witness statements and telephone calls.'

'We track back, people. Go through it all again, as was the original plan. Something will come to light. I can feel it.' Her phone indicated a new text message. She glanced at her phone on the desk, saw it was from Lenny and turned the phone over. Ruth looked at her and raised her eyebrow. Kath gave a slight nod, then turned her attention back to the room.

'Lane, Shirl—when you're ready, let's head out. I'll drive.' She grabbed her keys and read her message while the bustle went on around her. Ruth gathered cups to wash but glanced every few seconds at Kath as she read the message.

Need to see you. Can I come over later?

Kath felt a flutter of excitement as she read Lenny's words. Christ, had he done it? Had Susan said something?

After 8. No dinner.

He responded immediately with a smiley face emoji and a heart.

'Busy later, then?' Ruth passed by without stopping on her way to the kitchen.

'Looks like it.'

The temperature was getting hotter, and a fierce wind bent trees and blew pollen, dander and petals through the air. Kath pulled her Audi Quattro alongside the school gates where Daisy was last seen, opting for the three of them to walk up to the woods where the murder had been committed. Lane looked like a windswept goddess as her black curls fanned out behind her and her long summer dress billowed as wind found its way underneath. Kath had opted for cargo pants and a sleeveless blouse in shades of green, attempting the 'summer day, carefree look' but failing miserably, as puddles of sweat formed under her bra strap and the waistband of her trousers folded over, burdened by the fat around her middle. Shirl pulled a straw hat from the back of the car before Kath locked it, then realised the wind was not hat-friendly and opted to carry it instead. She regretted the decision of jeans and linen top which had creased under the weight of her breasts while sitting in the car and now looked like a forty-two pounds ninety-nine pence piece of cleaning rag.

Lane stood for a moment, looking at the school doors, caressing the double gates where Daisy had passed through with Cousin Jack. She turned back to the woods in front, noting the incline as Shirl was already starting to complain about the decision to walk up a hill in this weather.

'Jack and Jill,' she sang to herself. 'Jack and Jill went up the hill.' She felt the anxiety of that moment in her own body and followed the two detectives, humming to herself.

The twenty-minute slow climb into the woods left two of the three women swearing and fighting for breath, although Kath would have preferred a cigarette and a sit down despite the heat and what seemed to her an altitude she was unaccustomed to. As they caught their breaths, Kath moved over, avoiding hawthorn branches and other trees she recognised but could not name, and came to a clearing. Lane and Shirl followed her. They stood like Macbeth's three witches staring down at a dehydrated bunch of flowers, tied with string. Not a florist's bouquet or something from a garage shop or supermarket but a hand-picked selection of wildflowers. Including daisies. They were propped up against a fallen tree branch.

Lane nodded. 'Yes, I know.'

Shirl and Kath looked at each other, unsure whether Lane was talking to them or herself. Kath bobbed her head, and Shirl followed her as they moved a short distance away, giving Lane room to feel the energy.

'Christ, I've not been up here since that day ten years ago,' said Shirl, trying to tuck her hair back into the slide at the back but failing against the strength of the wind.

'I have,' Kath admitted. 'Several times. Just stood, expecting some sort of divine intervention to give me the answers to this fucking tragic event.'

'It is what we think but not what was meant.'

'What?' Kath moved towards Lane. 'Say that again?'

Lane knelt in front of the flowers shrivelling fast in the heat, petals and fronds from grasses turning aerial acrobatics as they spun off every time a gust blew through the clearing. 'The act of killing was designed and intended but did not serve its purpose.'

Shirl shrugged. 'I'm hearing the words but I'm really not getting it.'

Kath patted her hand down at Shirl. 'Lane,' she said softly, 'Lane, can you explain this to me—what you're feeling right now?'

Lane ran her hand through the leaves at her side. 'It didn't work, and it was too late.' Lane turned to Kath and grabbed her arm. 'He did not mean to do it as it happened.'

Kath let out a breath as Lane let go and stood from her crouched position, knees groaning, twigs scratching at her ankles.

'Okay, okay.' Kath moved around, talking to herself, thinking, reasoning, trying to make sense of and redirect the thoughts racing through her head. Shirl stayed back, looking through the trees, dodging the thinnest branches as they threatened to whip her face, looking back and just making out the school building.

Lane stood, putting on her sandals. Neither of the other two had even seen her take them off. Kath was feeling the strangeness of the atmosphere but put it down to Lane's presence.

'I need to leave now.' Lane walked past them in the direction of the car, starting down the hill.

'Okay, we'll catch you up,' Kath shouted after her.

Shirl came to stand next to her. 'Okay, well, we know... what we know from that, but that still leaves the mystery; the one question we have never been able to answer.' Shirl looked at Kath and then did a three-hundred-and-sixty-degree turn, taking in the remoteness of the woodland with fields all around and only one road going past from the school back into the village.

'You mean, where the bloody hell did they go?'

<u>May 12, 2009</u>

Danny ran through the woods, down, down, brushing past the branches, trampling the remnants of bluebells and wild garlic, tears in his eyes and breath ragged, sobs coming out of him in waves.

Miranda tried to keep up but the shock of what had just happened made her sluggish, legs leaden, breath too short to provide the oxygen she needed. 'Danny, wait for me.'

He wasn't listening, legs pumping, threatening a fall at any moment down the hill. It had all gone wrong, and now he was unable to do anything except carry out the next phase—the escape. He knew she was behind him. She had to follow because that was what had been discussed and planned. He reached the bottom of the hill where the woods melded into the meadow that backed onto Westwood Hall. He stopped, letting her catch up, wiping his arm across his eyes, squeezing his eyes shut so tight to try and block out the image of Daisy. But she was there now. She was always going to be there in his head; when he was finally able to sleep, he would dream about her. Awake, she would haunt him. He was supposed to feel different. And he did. But it was totally the wrong kind of different. Not a good different. Not the right different. Miranda fell into him, gasping, clutching her chest, beanie hat pushed back now from her face, red curls escaping their prison. They stood together, breathing, trying to silence the noise that filled both of their heads.

'Danny?' She grabbed his arm, and he turned to her, face full of anguish. They hugged.

'We have to carry on. Do you understand? It has to be as I said. We can't go back now.'

She nodded as he pulled away.

'This way.'

She turned away, feeling her mouth fill with saliva, then vomited brackish water and the remains of an early-morning cup of tea. Danny stood and watched, ashamed of what he had asked her to do. They had been through so much together, and she was the only one that had been forced to bear witness to his shame from the past. And now again, to his new shame. She wiped her mouth on a handful of leaves and spat one last time. She nodded at him; she would be okay.

He took her hand and they moved towards the Hall, skirting the edges of the meadow, still just within the tree cover. They walked as quickly as the terrain allowed until Danny took a sharp left turn back into the woods. They came to a mound in the earth covered in brambles and fallen branches. Danny was glad of his long sleeves as he bent forward and shielded his face, hand searching for the handle of the passageway that led through to the icehouse. He pulled hard and he gained purchase, but the undergrowth was not going to give up its treasure so easily. Miranda watched him, unable to help, trying to keep herself still by wrapping her arms tight around her thin body. A final hard pull gave enough of an opening to allow them to pass through into the underground vault, and Danny paused to get the torch from his pocket. It gave enough of a beam for them to be able to see a few feet ahead, and he gestured for her to move forward as he pulled the door shut, grabbing a handful of foliage to pull with him to try and disguise the opening he had just made. He barely felt the scrape of thorns and the coarse fronds of sticky weed that entwined itself around everything it touched as the darkness closed in on them. And then the silence enveloped them.

He had told her what was going to happen. He had planned everything to do with their departure, and she had agreed to it all. A new start for both of them, apart but forever joined by the act of taking a life. She walked close behind him, a hand on his back as the torch beam led them along the passage. She didn't know whether they were under the woodland or the meadow as they seemed to turn on a slight downward trail, on and on, further into the darkness. She shivered, her thin top enough for the May sunshine above but barely providing any comfort underground. Danny pressed ahead, knowing the timing was essential for the next stage and hoping nothing had gone wrong that was out of his control. He hadn't made a plan B. He moved spiderwebs and tendrils of plants from his face. He was calmer now. Maybe he was expecting too much too soon. He was reasoned now. Yes, maybe it just took time to settle into his body from her body. He was being too impatient.

He stopped suddenly and she ran into him. They were in the larger chamber now—the icehouse. Low shelves formed by stacks of bricks sat around the walls, and light filtered through the two-hundred-year-old wooden doorway that led out into the gardens of Westwood Hall. Danny handed her the bags he had put there two days before. He had told her they needed only the bare essentials; just what they could easily carry. She didn't have that much anyway: favourite clothes, two pairs of shoes, a couple of necklaces and some old photos of her mother with various people she did not know and had not had the chance to ask her about, as a brain aneurysm had snapped the life out of her six months earlier. Danny walked up the four steps and turned off the torch. He lifted the latch of the door, and they crouched to emerge in the sunshine again, dragging his rucksack and her holdall with the galloping horses pattern. Off to the right was the walled garden and the greenhouses and the impressive potting shed where Fred the head gardener at the Hall for the last twelve years had taken Danny under his wing and shown him how things grew, how seeds became plants and plants became more plants. How life gave new life. Danny smiled. Yes, patience was required now. Life giving new life.

'...Where Sir Mortimer Langley liked to sit and admire the many paintings he had acquired on his Grand Tours.' Ida Costain swept her hand around the room, and the gaggle of tourists made noises of admiration and awe. She checked her watch. 'Please, have a look at the marvellous paintings; we have ten minutes before boarding the coach, and you can purchase any postcards, handbooks, mugs and all manner of memorabilia at the gift shop adjacent to the tearoom. I shall meet you at the coach.'

Ida smiled and patted the arm of the nearest Japanese tourist who was interpreting for the group, duly relaying the message about timings. The group nodded at Ida, smiled and began walking around the drawing room as instructed.

Ida made her way outside the main house in search of Peter the coach driver who was sitting on a bench down the side of the conservatory-style tearoom. He was stuffing tobacco into his pipe, a mug of coffee next to his feet.

'Nearly done, are they?' He pulled out his lighter, and smoke swirled around his bearded face as Ida sat next to him, enjoying the smell.

'Yes, be out in about fifteen minutes after they've hopefully cleared us out of gift items. Have you seen my two yet?'

She scanned the car park and shielded her eyes against the afternoon sun, looking over to the sheds leading through to the walled garden, flanked by hollyhocks and lavatera with red hot pokers lording it over the smaller bedding plants below them.

Peter shook his head. 'They're kids, Ida. No sense of timing or urgency.' He patted his belly which threatened to push the buttons off his company shirt like the Hulk in angry mode. 'Might have time to have my flapjack before we set off.'

'And what exactly did the doctor say about your cholesterol?'

Peter huffed. 'She's twelve and knows nothing about the nutritional goodness of the humble flapjack.'

Ida laughed and checked her watch again. 'I'm sure they'll be here any minute. They know what time you have to leave. Thank you again for doing this.' She patted his hand and stood as she saw Danny and Miranda hurrying towards them, dodging the visitors getting ready to leave, closing time for the gardens nearly upon them.

'I was wondering where you were...' Ida stopped mid flow as she saw Danny's pale face and his blonde fringe sticking to his forehead. 'Goodness me, you are pale, my sweet. Are you feeling okay?' She lay her hand on his forehead, feeling for a temperature or signs of illness. He pushed her hand away as kindly as he could and gave a weak smile.

'I'm good. Really. Just want to get going.'

Peter nodded towards the coach. 'Get yourselves in there, and we'll be off in a few minutes.' He drained his mug and tapped out his pipe. 'Here they come now.'

The coach party from the house emerged into the sunshine, talking and showing each other their purchases from the gift shop. Ida marshalled them forward onto the coach as Danny and Miranda climbed aboard and sat themselves at the back, clutching their bags on their laps, looking for all the world like kids going on a school trip. But this was more than that for them both. A fresh start in a new place; a new county. Ida waved at them, her small frame only just allowing her to see the tops of their heads. She was going to miss them. They had been with her for so many years now, coming to her when they were just five years old. But that was the nature of fostering. You looked after them for as long as it took and then they were gone, either to other families as adopted children or back to their own families who now felt able to cope with them and begin building new relationships.

These two were definitely different. They had come to her together from a very unpleasant woman, and she had worked hard, alongside her husband, to encourage them and guide them into being the best people they could be. And she felt they had done a good job with these two; good grades at school, a few friends but they pretty much kept their own company. They were polite and respectful but now were embarking on a new journey. School had become a distant memory and they were drifting.

Danny, Ida noticed, was becoming increasingly unsettled and taken to taking himself off for hours at a time. She was happy to let him have his secrets but she'd begun to worry and had talked long into the night many times with her husband Jim about what might be best. The one thing she couldn't ignore was the fact that, the year before, Danny had been involved in an unfortunate incident which had seen him spiral into moodiness; an unsettled demeanour he couldn't seem to shake. Ida's husband had come up with the idea of them going to live with Ida's brother in Worcestershire. Stanley had a small nursery and was a widower who had said he could offer Danny work, as he had shown a natural aptitude with plants. Ida had been a tour guide at Westwood Hall for nineteen years, and Fred, the gardener, had had nothing but praise for the enthusiasm Danny had shown when Ida had introduced them to each other. And Danny had shown a real interest as he had grown into a teenager.

Miranda had also spent time at the Hall with Ida, learning about the history and doing odd jobs of tidying and polishing when the Hall was closed to the public in the off-season winter months. It seemed a good idea all round, all parties seeming to embrace the idea and the move away. Miranda, Stanley said, could be a kind of housekeeper, if that's what she fancied, until she found something she might like to do for a job. Ida had agreed to send money to help support them, as Stanley was getting by quite nicely but wasn't exactly sure how it was all going to pan out.

And now the day was here. Ida felt a swell in her heart as Peter patted her head like she was a dog patiently waiting by the coach doors.

'They'll be fine, Ida. I'll drop them at the bus station, and they can catch the bus from there to Stan's place.'

Ida nodded, pulling a handkerchief from her cardigan pocket. It was always hard saying goodbye, but they said they would keep in touch and Stan would give her regular updates. The kids were seventeen now; just shy of legal adults. They needed to expand and grow like the plants in the nursery, to forget the pain of the past and move forward. The incident had not reared its head but she didn't want to tempt fate and it was just, it seemed to Ida, the right time for them to leave before any more suggestions of improper behaviour could be cast. Peter started the engine and the doors closed with a soft hiss. Ida stepped back, and the coach rolled along the driveway, unaware of a sobbing woman not two miles away and a dead child that was never destined to move forward.

| 12 |

'It's as if the act of killing Daisy was not for the sole purpose of ending her life,' she said.

Marvin shook his head. 'But why else do you take a child and take her into the woods, for Christ's sake, if you don't intend... bad stuff.'

Kath held up her hands. 'Okay, back to basics. Why do people kill? What prompts them to take another life?'

'Sometimes it's a spur of the moment; crime of passion, man catches wife with another man—or woman—whatever, and they snap. Boom,' said Marvin.

'Yes, but there is a reason—jealousy... and revenge. It serves a purpose, however 'spur of the moment' it is,' Shirl said. She held up her hand with outstretched fingers, ready to tick off all the reasons she had in her head, but Ruth beat her to it.

'It's usually sex and money. That's the two main reasons, surely? And this was definitely neither of those.'

'He wanted something from her,' said Lane, twisting a black curl around her finger. 'It wasn't a kidnap for ransom money. It wasn't to fulfil a sexual desire—I'm certain of that and the evidence would support it. But it was about desire. He was in control; it was planned, and he felt that small child could give him something he had been looking for.' Lane sighed. 'Find the motive, find the killer.'

'Great,' muttered Marvin under his breath.

The mood in the office was flagging, so Kath pointed at Byron. 'Anything remotely interesting from your afternoon?'

Byron sat back. 'I have been through the CCTV footage from Telford train station for six hours after the time of the murder. Lots of "young people"'—he made quotation signs with his fingers—'getting on various trains. I've isolated some that may be viable but I just don't get the feel of them.' Byron took a deep breath as they all waited for him to continue. 'I know I'm not really one of you and I haven't been here that long but I don't think this is what they did. I don't get the vibe from the tapes. I'm going to stick my neck out and say I don't believe this was the route they took. They were either still in the area or they left some other way.'

Lane, still playing with her curl, smiled. 'I think what the boy is trying to say is he feels it isn't right. And we know that we all trust our instincts, right?'

Everyone nodded.

'Okay.' Kath stood, needing to pace and move her own energy around to be able to think clearly. 'I'm happy to go with that, Byron. Thank you. What about a car? Did they have a vehicle?'

'But why take her to local woods if they had a car? Wouldn't they have driven somewhere even more remote with an easier escape route to... wherever?'

'Good point, Marvin. And also, are they old enough to drive? Although, you don't have to be legally old enough to take and drive away a vehicle. Isn't that right, Shirl?'

'In my defence, I was a quick learner and had watched my dad operate the tractor on many an occasion, Your Honour.'

'What's this?' asked Marvin.

Shirl swivelled her chair round to face him. 'I was very advanced for ten, and I was confident I could drive the tractor down to the bottom field...'

'Oh my days, you mad woman,' Marvin said, shaking his head.

Shirl spread her hands. 'Noone got hurt, except my arse where my dad thrashed me, and I never did it again. But I am an excellent driver, am I not?' She looked at Kath who had been in a car with Shirl on many occasions and had lived to tell the tale, meals still residing in her stomach and not splashed against the car doors.

Kath rolled her hand. 'And we are back in the room. Vehicle. Yes? No?'

Ruth had been spreading sheets of paper across one of the desks under the window as the laughter had spread behind her with Shirley's tale of vehicular theft. 'There's nothing here about any rogue vehicles at the scene.' She held up a report, two pages long. 'All cars were accounted for in terms of parents etc. picking up their children. There were no sightings of different or strange cars; they were all the usual vehicles that picked up the kids.'

'So,' said Kath, getting into her stride now, 'they got to the school on foot, they knew they were taking Daisy to the woods, and they knew... well, thought they knew what was going to happen. And then what? They must have had an escape plan. Must have done. Everything else had gone to order. Helen Tranter said the boy was smiling; confident. He had an easy manner, and Daisy knew him. She was happy to go with him. Wait...' She grabbed the file from her desk where she had made notes from the visit with the teacher and flicked paper quickly. 'Here it is. Helen Tranter said Daisy said something about playing with Jack.' She snapped the manila file shut. 'They'd had contact before, so where was it? Daisy was a five-year-old who had only been at school a few months. She hadn't been to nursery, as Zoe had looked after her at home and taken her through some pre-school learning...' Kath caught her breath as she imagined how loved that little girl was by her mother who'd played with her and tried to teach her the alphabet and writing and drawing.

'We go back to Todd's house,' said Marvin. 'Although he wasn't around much of Daisy's life because the band had just finished a tour and he was off in Buckinghamshire recording the new album, he might remember somebody coming to the house. Maybe Zoe said something about a new friend?'

Kath pointed at him. 'Good, yes. Let's go with that. And yes, you can go back and see the rock god again.'

Marvin blushed and grinned.

'I'll go with him this time, shall I?' Ruth stepped forward, and Lane nodded.

'I will go back again, but you'll have a different view; a different feel. Go keep an eye on wee Marvin. Make sure he doesn't steal any souvenirs.'

Kath left the room, Marvin protesting, Byron typing and staring again at his two computer monitors, the team ribbing Marvin about his crush.

Lane came down the stairs and poked her head around the kitchen door. 'I'm off to Ruth's. Don't wait up.'

'Lane, are you sure this is okay?' Kath paused, cleaning cloth soaked with antibacterial spray in one hand. She had been cleaning the work surface for ten minutes as much to soothe her anxiety as an actual part of her cleaning regime. Ruth had given Lane the heads up that Lenny was going to be round at the cottage and invited her to dine with her and her husband. There was also the offer to stay over, and Lane had nodded sagely.

'It's fine, honey. I know Lenny will be... unsettled with me here. Seems you two have a lot to talk about, and I don't want to be in the way. You know I always travel with an overnight bag in the boot. I'll see you at the office in the morning.'

Kath threw the cloth into the sink. She put the kettle on for a coffee as she looked at the clock with chickens on it above the brick fireplace. Another half an hour and Lenny would be here. Again. She poured the water into her favourite coffee cup. As she walked to her back garden, she reflected on the afternoon's events. She had driven them back from the woods after Lane's visit to the crime scene, the three of them unsettled, sweaty and feeling no further forward. Lane was mumbling in the back seat and all Kath and Shirley could do was exchange glances and shrug.

Kath was so busy in her own thoughts, she didn't realise half an hour had passed until Lenny's car pulled into her driveway at exactly eight o'clock. She was still in the back garden with a coffee now gone cold and the remnants of a cigarette almost burnt down to the filter. She rounded the side of the cottage and grinned at him trying to look cool in the August heat in his green chinos and short-sleeved shirt she was sure was new. He had a small gift bag in one hand and a bunch of flowers appeared from the rear seat as he slammed the door. She threw the butt into the begonias.

'Better get these inside quick.' He held up the presents and proceeded through the slightly open front door and into the kitchen. Kath followed and smiled.

'What's the occasion?' she gestured at the fresh bouquet as he glanced around for a suitable receptacle.

'Life, my dearest. Life is the occasion.'

She opened a cupboard and handed him a ceramic vase; another relic that had come with the house that she hadn't the heart to discard. She never bought herself flowers and certainly no admirer, of which there had only been a handful, had ever done it.

Lenny grimaced as he filled the vase with water. 'God, that's ugly.'

He set about opening drawers until he found a pair of scissors and started to release the blooms from their cellophane and sellotaped prison, carefully cutting stems to size and removing lower leaves.

'Bloody hell, you've done this before, haven't you?' Kath squirmed with pleasure as she moved around the kitchen, past the pine table, arranging placemats and the cruet set for something to occupy her hands; she desperately wanted to hug him and feel him in her arms.

'Put the bag in the fridge; I don't know how it's fared in this heat.' He gestured to the small gift bag.

'Can I look?' She had already peered inside as he agreed. She pulled out a box of After Eights. A fit of giggles swelled inside her. 'I didn't mean it fucking literally, you arse.'

'All part of my charm, dear. We may have to eat them with spoons, so... actually, chuck them in the freezer. Where's my drink, woman?' He was still busy with the flowers, fussing and turning the vase to look at the display from every angle. 'I always thought I'd quite like to be a florist if I had my time again,' he muttered, pleased with his efforts as he stood back and admired his handiwork.

Kath poured them both a white wine from the bottle in the fridge door and carried the glasses through to the lounge where the sun had relented and moved away, leaving a slightly cooler atmosphere. 'Lane's out for the night, so you've no need to worry about running into her on your way to the loo.'

Lenny placed the vase on the table in the window and sank onto the sofa next to Kath. 'Can't believe she's staying with you, but, hey.' He held up his hands. 'None of my business, I know.'

Kath was regretting her decision for Lane staying with her but couldn't admit it to Lenny of all people. She knew Kath's secret—at least, she had one of her feelings about it. But it was still dangerous territory, and Kath had enough to think about with work, without dredging up the private hell she fought on a daily basis to keep hidden.

'So...' Kath sipped her wine, afraid to ask but knowing it was better out the way at the front of the evening. 'Why are you here?'

Lenny swirled his wine and cleared his throat. 'Susan and I are officially separating. I'll be moving out, and she will stay in the house until she's decided otherwise.' He didn't look at Kath; couldn't look at her.

'Okay... I guess I should say I'm sorry?' She raised her eyebrows at him, and he smiled weakly.

'It was a joint decision, and there were a few tears on both our parts.' He sighed, remembering the conversation of last night. 'We managed to joke that we are both having a midlife crisis and, realistically, we both have a lot of years left to spend alone or... with someone else.' He let the suggestion hang in the air, and Kath felt the fluttering of excitement in her belly.

'Where are you going to live, then? Staying around Shrewsbury?'

He laid his head against the sofa, wine glass nestled in his lap. 'You know Steve from the Fraud Division?'

Kath creased her brow, trying to place him and failing but nodding anyway, not wanting to break the conversation.

'He's got that one-bed cottage in Bomere Heath he does as a holiday let, and he's said I can have it for as long as I want. Regular income for him for a while, so it's all good. Susan's looking at maybe going back to the Bristol area to be closer to her parents. There are plenty of jobs.' Susan had been a nurse within the NHS for many years and currently worked within the Oncology unit at the Royal Shrewsbury Hospital.

'Do the girls know?' Kath wanted to top up her glass but was afraid to move, so sank back next to Lenny, their elbows touching. Lenny and Susan had twin daughters, aged twenty-five. Candice worked for HMRC and Bethany had her own accountancy business.

'Yep. Susan phoned them both. Candice was fine but Bethany has mixed feelings. Not sure she wants to talk to me at the moment, but it is what it is.'

They sat in companionable silence for a minute, then Lenny took Kath's glass from her and put them both on the floor. He turned on the sofa and pulled her towards him. 'We'll do this however you want, if you want. But I can't say it in any other way except I love you. I've always loved you, and I would be so happy if you and I could see the future together in some way.'

Kath's breath caught in her throat, and she suddenly realised she didn't want to pretend anymore. She loved her work but it was hard on the emotions and she had been given a window into what her life could be like from now on. And it looked fine indeed.

Lenny stared at her. 'Bloody hell. Not often you're lost for words. Don't cry, my love.'

'Happy tears.' She gulped. 'Very happy tears. I love you, Lenny. Always have, always will.' She traced her fingers across his eyebrows, to his high forehead and then pushed her hands into his hair and kissed him with a soft passion.

| 13 |

'Do you fancy doing something today? Going out somewhere, I mean?' Todd tipped scrambled eggs onto toast and placed the plate in front of Miranda. He ran water into the saucepan and decided, shamefully, he would leave it for Mrs Tinkerson to clean.

She began to eat, chewing the food slowly as her brain was trying to race ahead. Was that what she wanted? Another trip out with him? 'Er... yes, I guess. That would be nice.'

Maybe today's the day, she thought, *today's the day he is going to ask me again why I'm here, and maybe today's the day I can tell him and we can all find peace.* She was fighting the two sides every day now; the burning desire to tell him the whole story and watch the destruction of their worlds come tumbling down against the urge to keep this wonderful dream alive. For she knew, in her heart, it was a dream that could only be sustained for so long.

In truth, when Todd had told her about the police visit, Miranda had freaked and hid away in her room for the evening, feigning a headache. She had seen Lane and Marvin arrive and hurried out the back door, ducking under windows and making her way into the woods. She didn't know who they were but the guy certainly looked official in his suit and tie. And if it had been police, as she'd later found out it was, she wanted no meeting with them. She had walked down the lane and up into the woods. Every day that passed brought her closer to Todd, and she was surprised at herself and her feelings towards him. There was a safety she had not felt since she'd left Stanbrook Abbey and the nuns at Callow End. That episode of her life seemed a million miles away now.

Living with Stanley and Danny had been okay for a few months. But she and Danny had both changed so much because of what they had done that she couldn't see herself with him any longer. She needed another sanctuary, and it had arrived in the shape of Sister Mary Mathilde. The nun was a regular visitor to Stan's nursery. She and two of her fellow sisters were in charge of the garden at the abbey, the growing of their own fruit and vegetables and the law of companion planting of flowers to keep the pests at bay. She and Stan would spend hours over cups of tea wandering around Stan's grounds and through his greenhouses, deciding on the next planting rotation, poring over seed catalogues and new water butts. And Sister Mathilde had taken a shine to Miranda, could see she was troubled and offered her a new life. The abbey needed help in the kitchen and with some domestic chores, as they had taken the decision to turn some of the cells in the west wing into hotel-type rooms for retreats. Paying guests that would help with the upkeep of the ancient building and spread the word of the work they did. Miranda literally saw it as a sign from God that she could now seek redemption. She could not undo what had been done but she could seek forgiveness and give herself over to the work of God and the nuns that so readily took her under their wings. She had been almost happy. Almost repaired. Trying every day to love the Lord and feel his succour. And then it hit. Without warning. There it was. What they had done. A life gone at their hands. She did not feel God's love and forgiveness, although she had fought for those two things for ten years and they had been just out of reach. And there was the hole again inside her. She knew then what she had to do; the only answer: sin or no sin.

Now here she was, eating humble food he had made for her, caring for her well-being, and she did not want it to stop.

Ruth parked the car just down the lane from Todd's house. Marvin pulled down the passenger side flap and checked his hair in the mirror.

'Fuck me, you have it bad, boy.' Ruth dug him in the side with her elbow.

'Like to look my best when I'm visiting,' Marvin said, refusing to give her the satisfaction of a cheap jibe. He flipped the visor back up and was sorely tempted to have a go back at Ruth's daily uniform of blue polo shirt and jeans but, as always, she'd argue that it saved time, effort and energy not wondering what to wear every day. And she had a point. There was a regularity and order many envied even though they often took the piss. But Ruth had got her morning routine down to military precision and timing. Less stress; more time for the real work.

After what Lane had told them about Todd's visitor and Lane's sneaking suspicion the girl had made herself scarce on the last visit, Ruth had decided on a pre-emptive approach. She looked at the car clock. It was just after seven-thirty. Todd had already told Marvin he was an early riser on his last encounter with him, and Ruth wanted to catch them both on the hop in the same place;

see how the dynamics played out. She pulled out her phone and called Todd's number.

'Good morning, this is Detective Sergeant Ruth Goodwin with the cold case unit. Yes, you did meet my colleagues the other day. We would like to come back and see you, have a look around.' There was a pause, and Ruth looked over at Marvin. 'Something has... come to light and we would just like to investigate a little further which involves another visit to your property.' She nodded at Marvin and started the engine. 'Well, we're not that far away. Okay, see you shortly and thank you.'

The engine idled for a moment. 'Er, do I get out and walk or what?' Marvin grabbed the door handle.

Ruth pulled him back. 'Nope, just want to wait and see if the mysterious visitor is going to make a run for it again after he tells her we're coming. If he tells her,' she added. She gave it another thirty seconds, Marvin itching to get going, and then swung into Todd's driveway to see the front door open and Miranda standing there in the morning sunlight.

'Hail Mary, full of grace, the Lord is with Thee,' Miranda whispered.

'Fucking Bingo,' said Ruth.

| 14 |

Kath and Shirl sat outside the station on the bench at the back, looking out at the woodland separating them from the Sutton Hill estate. A Springer Spaniel snuffled at the chain link fence in front of them, tail frantically wagging, eager to get fuss from the two women. The owner carried on walking through the long grass, gesturing a wave in their direction and calling the dog to heel. He galloped off and the man and his dog went on their way. Kath blew out a plume of smoke and sipped her coffee.

'Lenny wants us to have a dog when he retires.'

Shirley laughed, lay back on the bench and stretched her legs in front of her, hands curled around her mug. 'Bloody hell, this is really happening, isn't it?' She put a hand on Kath's arm. 'I'm so pleased for you.'

Kath's cheeks were beginning to ache, as she'd been smiling since she had woken up with Lenny three hours ago. They had both known he would spend the night in her bed without either of them having to speak the words. There had been no frantic fumbling of clothes, no tearing of buttons from shirts or saliva mishaps from passionate kissing. Kath had watched from the doorway of her bedroom, unseen, as Lenny had automatically gone to her side of the bed and then, realising it was indeed her side, moved around to the other side and started to remove his clothing, placing it on the chair next to the bed. It was the simple gesture of giving up his regular side of the bed he had probably slept on for most of his adult life that had filled her heart up. And they had laughed and kissed and made love, the forty-year-old memory of teenage sex transitioning to an ease of body against body, no awkward shyness, bedside lamp still glowing so that they could see their bodies with extra hair, more creases, age spots and scars. None of it had mattered, and that's what had made it so right.

Kath stubbed out her cigarette butt and stood, stretching her body that had suddenly needed to get used to sharing its space with another body.

'Christ, was that your hip clicking, old girl?' Shirl got up, smirking. 'Sex is for young people, you know.'

'It's not the sex,' Kath explained, 'it's the actual sleeping together. I like my own space. It's Lenny that likes to cuddle. Remember Ross and Rachel in *Friends*? She was a "cuddly sleeper" and Ross liked his own side of the bed. I'm officially Ross but Lenny is cool with that.'

They walked up to the office to find Byron at his desk. He nodded but continued looking at his monitors. Shirl sat at her desk as Kath poked her.

'For your information... actually, I'm not going to tell you and that is your punishment for mocking me... us... me and my man.'

Shirl scrolled through emails singing under her breath, 'I think he loves you; he wants to kisssss you...'

Kath was only half listening as she found a note from Ruth explaining the early visit to Todd's. It was a good plan that would hopefully give them something. The time for smiling had passed. Lenny was moving to his new place the following day and she had to focus now on what little they had so far in this case and dig further to find what they were not seeing.

Lane suddenly appeared in the doorway, holding a box from Greggs. 'Sugar rush for everyone, if you fancy.' She set the box down in the beverage area. Kath was certain Lane's body had never seen a doughnut in its life but she would partake, needing to keep that layer of fat; that layer of protection. But the thought flashed through her mind—could she let that go now? It had been fifteen years. There had been no comeback; not even a sniff of suspicion. And if she kept it going now, Lenny was just another person in her life she had to shield from the truth of what she'd done. It was easy when he was at arm's length, and she had managed a veneer when she was around her team that was solid and would not crack. But could she let that go now and forget?

'Thanks. What's your next plan of action?' Kath knew she was in charge but it seemed natural for Lane to dictate her own movements, as she obviously couldn't force what Lane had going on inside her.

'Well, I thought I'd go back...' She looked around. 'Have Ruth and Marvin left already?'

Kath nodded and handed her the note.

'That's a good idea. I was going to say that I feel I want to go back to the house but approach through the woods, from the other side of the garden. Not announce myself, you know?

'Whatever you need.' She looked Lane up and down. 'I'm loving the G.I. Jane look, by the way. You're such a chameleon.' She tried not to sound envious and hoped she wasn't coming across as bitchy. Lane's hair was loosely tied back in a messy ponytail. She had on combat style casual trousers with a plain black T-shirt and not a scrap of make-up, and Kath knew she would still get a Vogue fashion shoot if required. Lane smiled and looked at her as if she were reading her thoughts, and Kath looked away, unnerved and thinking how great it would be if she could be halfway to looking like that again.

Byron held up his hand and peered over the top of a monitor. 'Er... I think I may have something.'

The energy suddenly shifted, and the three women perched themselves on desks in front of Byron.

'I've been designing an algorithm, as I explained to Kath...' Kath tilted her head, and Byron knew he needed to skip the technical stuff and get to the good part. 'Since we dismissed the idea that the two left via the train station in Telford or by car, I mapped the terrain around the school, the woods and Todd's house using a... sorry. Can't help myself; I'm used to explaining everything.'

'It's fine, Byron,' Kath said. 'We trust in whatever you do, that's why you're here, but we don't need to know how you do it, just if it will get us results.'

He nodded, his curtain of hair falling forward as he hit some more keys. The printer burst into life, making the three women jump. Lane was nearest and grabbed the paper coming out of the printer. The three of them crowded round.

'Okay... it's a map,' said Shirley. 'I can see what... Oh, Holy shit.'

Byron nodded and gave a hopeful grin. 'I think it answers the question of where they went after they killed Daisy.'

Kath pointed to the building that lay to the east of the woods. 'They went to Westwood Hall.'

| 15 |

Miranda had only a few seconds to decide what to do as Ruth and Marvin got out of the car and walked towards the house. Her feet seemed glued to the tiled hallway. She wanted to run but it would look wrong and yet here, perhaps, was her chance to confess. But did she want to do it with just her and Todd, to have that moment together, alone?

Ruth's hand was advancing. 'Detective Sergeant Goodwin. And you are...?'

'I am just about to leave actually.' she said with a half-smile. There. It was out of her mouth now. All she had to do was to move past the two police officers and try to appear as if that had been her plan all along. She didn't want to appear rude, so she shook Ruth's hand as briefly as she could and stepped past her, into the sunshine.

'Actually, we could do with having a word with you as well as Mr Prospero, if you don't mind.' Ruth was closing in, not wanting to let this girl get away a second time. If Lane had a feeling about her, that was good enough for Ruth, and she was going to get to the bottom of where exactly she had come from and what she was doing here in the first place.

Fight or flight. Miranda only had the two choices.

She ran.

Kath grabbed her car keys and made to follow Shirl out the door. She turned and looked at Byron. 'That was inspired. Really great, Byron. Thank you.'

He nodded.

'Will you be okay here on your own?' Lane had already left for Todd's house and she and Shirl were going to the Hall.

'Yes. I'll be fine. I'm about to go somewhere in Computer Land that I don't want to go but feel there may be more answers, and I think I want to be alone when I do it.'

'Okay.' Kath felt a twinge of concern but was confident he knew exactly what he was doing and could handle whatever came his way. He was one of what Lenny called 'good people', and she was glad her choice had paid off.

Fifteen minutes later, Kath brought her car to a stop in the car park of Westwood Hall. It was an impressive eighteenth-century stately home just outside Much Wenlock that was reputed to have its fair share of ghostly goings on. The TV programme *Most Haunted* had put it on the map a few years back with an overnight investigation. Visitor numbers had jumped after the show had aired, along with the regular coach trips of tourists. Paranormal investigation teams from around the country were still paying good money to spend the night and publish their findings.

'I've lived in Shropshire all my life and I've never been here.' Shirl looked up at the red brick turrets on the east wing.

'We always miss what's on our doorstep,' said Kath, trying the main wooden door at the entrance and finding it locked. She pulled her phone from the pocket of her summer jacket and, seeing it was only still eight forty, pulled up the website. 'It doesn't open until ten.'

Shirl peered through the conservatory windows of the tearoom and spotted a woman setting up the counter with a cake stand of scones. She gestured to the side door. The woman shook her head, pointed to the clock above the counter and held up both hands, fingers outstretched.

'I know.' Shirl was nodding at the woman. She pulled her warrant card from her jeans pocket and slammed it against the glass. The woman moved forward to look at the black wallet, gasped and turned the lock on the double-glazed door.

'Has something happened? What's going on?' The woman's hands fluttered across her apron pockets.

'Nothing to be alarmed about. We were just hoping to talk to the...' Shirl hesitated for the right words. Was it a house that was 'owned' or 'run'? Did they need the lady of the manor?

Kath jumped in. 'Can we talk to someone that can tell us a bit about the layout of the Hall and grounds?' Kath also held up her warrant card. 'Detective Chief Inspector Fortune. Yourself, perhaps, Mrs...' Kath glanced at the woman's hand to check for a wedding ring, hoping there was no offence to be taken. It was all too easy these days.

The woman stopped fluttering and pushed her hands into her apron pockets. 'Mrs Bryant. I run the tearoom.' Her dark eyes flicked from one detective to the other. She was used to dealing with cakes and cups of tea; this was way outside her comfort zone. She gestured to the gardens. 'Try Fred. He should be in the potting shed round about now.' She turned to go back inside. 'Would you like some tea or something? It's no trouble.' She was torn between wanting to get rid of them and offering hospitality by way of gleaning more information about just what they were doing there.

'Thank you but no. We'll just have a chat with Fred. Sorry to have disturbed you.'

'It's Ida you want,' the woman shouted as Kath and Shirl made their way down the driveway, across to the walled gardens.

Shirl turned back. 'Ida?'

'Yes, Ida Costain. She's been the main tour guide here since forever. She knows everything that goes on and all about this place. She should be here in about ten minutes.' She closed the door.

Shirl approached the shed. The door was open, but the shed was empty. 'Potting shed? I could live in here quite happily.' Shirl muttered. She poked her head through the doorway, taking in the neat arrangement of tools hanging on the one wall and the mismatched terracotta pots waiting to be filled with all manner of new life.

'Let's take in the view, so to speak, until Fred or Ida show their faces.' Kath said. She turned towards the woods.

'There.' Kath pointed, getting her bearings now from the road and the position of the wooded areas across the pastureland. 'That's where it happened. They could have come here. Look, skirting the meadow, keeping in the tree line or...' Kath's brain was in gear now, imagining, putting herself in the shoes of the perpetrators. 'Maybe just straight across the grass. No animals in the way. Wouldn't look unusual, would it?' She was talking more to herself now as Shirl moved away at the sight of an elderly man coming towards them wearing a brown overall–type coat.

His rheumy eyes took in the two officers, and he smiled, running a hand over his white hair.

'And what can I do for you ladies? Do you wish a guided tour of the potting shed while you wait for the main house to open?' He held out his hand to Shirl. 'Fred—head gardener.'

'Shirley. Detective Sergeant.'

He shook her hand in slow motion, trying to push his brain into operational mode. 'Police? What's this all about then?' He cocked his head at Kath, who smiled. 'I never found the treasure buried under the statue of Athena in the west garden. Vicious rumour.' He nudged Shirley, and she rolled her eyes.

'You don't strike me as a jewel thief, Fred.' Kath moved in front of him and waved her hand across the expanse of woodland. 'We are re-opening the investigation into the Daisy Prospero murder.' The way the smile fell from his face told Kath all she needed to know. He pulled himself up straight.

'It was a Tuesday afternoon, May 12, 2009. Never forget it. Worst thing to happen in these parts since... well, the year before, I suppose, when...' He looked towards where Kath had pointed, to the woods where it had happened, suddenly aware he was talking far too much. No time for showing off now; no time to be sharing information that didn't need sharing.

They all turned as a car drove through the gates and pulled up next to Kath's Quattro. Ida grabbed her handbag from the passenger seat and got out, all smiles and ready for the new day. As she approached the group, Ida noticed the look in Fred's eyes. He was standing slightly behind Kath and put his finger to his lips.

'Morning, Fred. Who do we have here?' Ida already knew. She remembered Kath's face from the original investigation when she had done the television appeal for information regarding Daisy's murder.

'Police, Ida. Fancy that, eh?'

Ida pulled her handbag closer to her body, willing her bowels to hold themselves steady. It was happening now. It was finally happening. 'Oh right. Do we need to answer some questions, Officers?'

'Yeah,' said Shirl, standing away from them next to a small wooden door. She tapped on the mottled wood. 'What's in here?'

Ida's mouth filled with saliva. 'The ice house. It's the ice house.'

| 16 |

Marvin was startled by the sudden movement of Miranda's body rushing past him. He looked back at Ruth standing in the doorway. 'Do I go after her?'

Ruth looked back into the house to see Todd, a puzzled look on his face.

'Has Miranda gone? She was just here...'

'Don't worry. I've got it covered. Detective Sergeant Ruth Goodwin.' They shook hands, and Marvin followed her into the house. 'Marvin. I believe you've met before.' They nodded greetings to each other, and Todd walked to the kitchen. He filled the coffee machine with water and set about putting a new filter in.

Ruth stayed in the hallway, texting Kath about Miranda's sudden flight of fancy, and Marvin joined Todd in the kitchen.

'Coffee. Great idea. Thanks,' Marvin said. He wandered to the back door, staring out at the garden.

Todd was trying to pull together his thoughts as the water filtered through, becoming rich brown liquid. He had wrestled with a new coffee machine but found himself attached to his old one and still preferred the taste of good strong filter coffee. He had given the new machine to Andrew who already had two but smiled and took it anyway. There was always an ex-wife with a birthday on the horizon or a new lady in his life that he could lavish with gifts.

Ruth joined them and sat at the kitchen table. 'Thank you for meeting with us again. It can't be easy, but we have just a few more questions, if you feel it's okay...' She let it hang as Todd nodded.

'I appreciate your concern. And I have to say it actually feels more encouraging than upsetting at the moment. It feels like I'm doing something positive, and I can't express how grateful I am that you've decided to open this up again.'

'I'll be straight with you... can I call you Todd?' He nodded and she continued. 'I'm not unsympathetic to the nature of what has gone on and how things are progressing and how this is affecting you but my way is less softly, softly and more direct. It's how I work. I'll apologise now if that is in any way upsetting or offensive.'

Todd cut her off with one hand held up and a determined look on his tired face. 'That's quite refreshing. I still get the tilt of the head sympathy looks when I go into the village.' His big hands scooped three mugs from the back of the marble work surface.

'Did you ever think of selling up and going somewhere else?' Marvin asked.

'Somewhere with less memories?'

Marvin nodded. It was a question he had always asked himself. What would he do in Todd's situation? He had the feeling, if faced with the devastation Todd had lived through, he would want to be far away from the misery.

'There are two sides to the argument; yes, I have to live every day with the door to her room still ajar, catching glimpses of her stuffed elephant, seeing the rocking chair my wife bought to nurse Daisy when she was born and finding her body in that same chair when she downed enough tablets to stop her heart and her pain and her guilt. That's tough but bearable because I fill my mind with the happiness of the previous six years. We moved to this place everyone said would be 'too small' for a rock star family—Zoe was pregnant and we had talked about having lots more kids...' He stopped as that particular memory burned through his brain, but he pushed it down and carried on. 'And then Daisy came to this house and filled it with so much love and so much joy. My only regret, and I try not to dwell on it because it would drive me fucking bat shit crazy if I let it, is that I was on tour and away from this house and I missed months of both my girls. But even if I leave and fly a thousand miles away'—he tapped his head and his curls shook—'it's all still in here, pain and joy, and wherever I go, that will never change.' A sob escaped his body, and before Marvin even had time to rationalise what he was doing, he was holding his rock star god in his arms as Todd sobbed onto his favourite jacket.

Ruth's brain was yelling 'what the Holy fuck?' but her heart softened as she watched young 'wee' Marvin, as Lane called him, cradling the six-foot-two man in his arms, letting him cry out his pain.

A text came through, interrupting her thoughts. The two men parted, and Todd clapped Marvin on the shoulder. 'Sorry, kind of overtook me a bit.'

Marvin's brain was dividing itself into I've had Todd Prospero, the rock god, in my bloody arms and Christ, what will Ruth think?

The text was from Kath: *Lane on her way but you might not see her... she'll deal with the girl, I think. Me and Shirl at Westwood Hall. BIG news. Tell later.*

Westwood Hall? No time to think about what was going to be discussed later. Ruth had to get on now and pick up the momentum lost by Todd's tearful outburst. He was busy getting milk and cream from the fridge and dividing the coffee into the three mugs. He placed them on the table with a sugar bowl after spooning a couple of heaped teaspoons into his own mug. He leaned against the work surface, and Marvin joined Ruth at the table, trying to avoid eye contact.

'So, the first question I have is concerning Daisy and the possibility that she may have met this lad before.'

Todd sipped his coffee. 'Yes, I remember that came up before. Wasn't it the teacher who said she was happy...' Todd left it there. Happy to go off into the woods with him. Happy.

'Did anyone come to the house that you can think of? I know you went all over this before but sometimes things come to light we didn't see or didn't register because we thought of them as unimportant at the time.'

Todd shook his head. 'I've been over this so many times in my head. We didn't have delivery men—the postman was interviewed... most of Much Wenlock seemed to have been interviewed. She didn't play with any of the other children around. Noone really lived near enough and she was just so young and loved being with Zoe.' He turned to look out the window, down to the very end of the garden which seemed such a long way away now that Miranda had swept her way through the long grass, identifying plants he didn't know the name of and had no idea if they should be there or what to do with them. She had said to leave it as it was—the bees and insects would be better for it; nature reclaiming and giving the finger to

Alan Titchmarsh when Todd had finally explained who he was.

Todd suddenly laughed and turned back to Ruth. 'Do imaginary friends count?'

Ruth looked at Marvin, and her brain crackled at the possibility of something just out of reach. 'How so?'

'It's just come back to me. Down there.' He pointed to the swing he couldn't bear to get rid of with its rotting wooden seat. Ruth and Marvin scraped their chairs back and joined him at the window, looking down to where he was pointing. 'She loved being down there, and we would hear her laughing sometimes and chatting away, in her own stilted toddler way, you know? sitting by the swing on the grass...'

Ruth put her hand on his arm. 'Go on, this is good.'

'Well, when we asked her why she was laughing one day, she said Jack had told her a funny story. Jack was her friend...' The mug smashed against the porcelain sink as it slipped from Todd's hands, splashing remnants of dark liquid onto his white shirt. He gripped Ruth's arm, and she fought not to cry out. 'That was his name, wasn't it? The boy who took her. It was Jack.'

Marvin stared at the swing. 'Not imaginary at all,' he whispered. 'And definitely not a fucking friend.'

Miranda ran down the road and turned left onto the footpath into the woods. She stopped to catch her breath, hands on her knees leaving sweaty marks on her flowered skirt that brushed the plants beneath her feet. The trees gave her some shelter from the sun—an August day that weather forecasters were threatening would be the hottest of the year so far. But the heat in her body did not come from the external ball of fire in the sky. No, it was from her own fear and guilt.

She gulped in the dry air and looked across to the house, the chimneys just visible through the branches. This was it now; the end was coming fast. Two visits from the police in two days. It was all closing in.

She was so lost in her panic that she did not see the figure ahead, half hidden behind a tree, and gave a scream as two hands grabbed her arms.

Lane Petreus looked deep into her eyes.

Ruth had made Todd sit at the table, his body almost folding in on her as the realisation of their discovery hit him. She nodded to Marvin who moved forward, ready to give more comfort if required, an excited but dreadful knot forming in his gut.

'Kath, it's me.' She moved into the hallway, her phone to her ear. 'We've got a lead.'

'Me too,' Kath replied. 'Are you still at Todd's?'

'Yep. Do you want to come over? If you're still at the Hall, you're down the road—'

'Yes, I know, but something is kicking off here and Shirl and I need to stay. Can you manage? Do you want to talk about it?'

Ruth looked through the doorway at Todd with Marvin's hand on his shoulder. 'It can wait. I'll meet you back at the office. Text me when you're leaving. Don't quite know where I'm going with this information yet... oh shit. Gotta go.' She ended the call, re-entering the kitchen at a pace as she saw Lane dragging Miranda towards the house from the bottom of the garden, Miranda struggling against her captor, curls flying as she fought to release herself from Lane's grip.

'Red hair.' Ruth grabbed hold of the sink as she watched them approach the back door. 'Red fucking hair.'

Lane pushed her through the doorway, and Miranda shook her hands away.

Todd stood. 'Miranda, what the hell?'

Lane tucked back a loose curl that had come adrift from her ponytail. 'I think we just found the Jill to young Jack.'

| 17 |

Kath stared at her phone as Ruth abruptly ended the call. The desire to know exactly what was transpiring at Todd's was gnawing at her insides, and she would have skipped out in a heartbeat but the small, dark-haired tour guide in front of her had a demeanour that screamed secrets and lies, and Fred the gardener was also doing his best not to look as if he knew anything was going on.

Fred had mentioned the reopening of Daisy's murder to Ida, jumping in before Shirley had a chance to say anything.

'So, Ida'—Shirley threw a look at Fred, and he stepped back a little, pulling some string from his pocket and pretending he was about to do something interesting with it—'do you remember anything at all about the afternoon Daisy was murdered?' Shirl was sick of pussyfooting around everyone now. She was never one to blunder in with both feet and be coarse but people needed to be reminded that a child had been murdered; her life snuffed out by another person. Killed seemed almost a kinder word when detectives were talking to witnesses or canvassing for any leads but now it had to be hammered home to shock people into thinking really damn hard about where they were and what tiny things they might remember that could spark a whole new direction.

'Well'—Ida was still clutching her handbag to her body; a barrier against the barrage she knew was about to come—'like I said at the time, it was a usual Tuesday. It was a Tuesday, wasn't it, Fred?' She looked over to him, and he nodded and disappeared into the shed as Shirl gave him a glare that said, 'step back, please, this is your final warning'.

'So, we probably had the odd coach party and usual regulars—local people, you know, who have an annual pass and come here for tea and cake maybe once a week, buy some of Fred's plants, you know? We do need all the income we can get; a house like this takes a lot of upkeep and, well, you know, the staff have to be paid and the—'

Shirley held up her hand. 'Okay, Ida, I get the picture.' The woman's ramblings were not giving her anything useful, but Shirl felt there was something underneath the surface that she couldn't quite grasp.

Kath had wandered back over to them now having had an ear cocked to the conversation. The rush of words tumbling from Ida's mouth was not giving them anything but a mundane list. Kath looked at Shirl and gave a slight nod. Shirl picked up on the gesture. The woman had more information to give them but now was not the time.

'We need to get back to the station. Thank you both for your time.' She angled her head to look through the door of the shed where Fred was busy with pots and soil. He held up his hand and returned to his work.

Ida was about to pass Kath to get to the main door when Kath pulled at her arm. Ida physically jumped and held a hand to her breasts. 'Gosh, sorry, you scared me. I thought we were all done?'

Kath held out her hand. 'I just wanted to say thank you for your help today, and sorry... you don't strike me as a woman that startles like a frightened rabbit.' Ida looked down and slowly took Kath's hand. Ida did not raise her eyes as they shook but Kath caught the tremor in her lips and the flush of her cheeks and felt the moistness of her palm.

'You just took me by surprise, that's all.' Ida pulled herself up to her full five foot one.

Kath released her hand and fought the urge to wipe her hand down her trouser leg. 'Hopefully the next time we come back, it won't be so surprising.'

Ida watched Kath and Shirl get into the car and drive away. 'The next time,' she muttered.

Todd looked at the four people standing in his kitchen, his brain trying desperately to process what was going on. Miranda stood completely still, knowing there was no escape route now. It was all coming to a head; had all been building to this moment.

'What's happening?' Todd asked. 'Where did you come from?' He turned back to the window, looking down the garden, past the shrubbery where Miranda and Lane had emerged.

Ruth stepped forward to Miranda. 'Come with us, please, back to the station. We have a lot of questions for you.' Ruth was itching to grab the girl who, for all the world, looked like a Pre-Raphaelite damsel in her floaty orange blouse and flowery hippy skirt. Her eyes flickered with defiance but there was a resignation in her stance.

'Down there.' Todd pointed to the bottom of the garden. 'That's where I found you.'

Lane pushed Miranda towards Ruth and stepped to the side of Todd, laying a hand on his arm. 'There's a hole in the green wire fence leading from the garden into the woods,' she said. 'That's how she got in so she could die in your garden.' She half-turned to Miranda. 'Atonement, eh? That's what it was all about, wasn't it? And he had no idea.'

Marvin got it now, all of it slowly fitting together. 'That's where the lad was talking to Daisy, making her laugh, gaining her trust.' His base instinct kicked up a gear, and he pushed his face an inch from Miranda's. 'Were you with him? Were you?' She shrank back as his spittle landed on her cheek, and Ruth pulled him away.

'Not here, Marvin. Let's go.'

They herded Miranda into the hallway, Todd following in body but his brain was trying to catch up, piecing together all the fragments; finding her in the garden, saving her, feeling a purpose to her suddenly appearing in his life.

Lane and Ruth pushed Miranda as forcefully as the law would allow into the back of the car as Marvin turned to Todd in the doorway. 'We will tell you more when we know more,' he promised. They were on the edge of giving this man the closure he needed. Marvin felt a swell in his gut; a mixture of disgust for the woman in the back of the car shifting uncomfortably next to Lane and staring out the side window, avoiding all eyes. But there was also satisfaction he was going to be a part of this solution.

'Marvin'—Todd held out his hand—'thank you.' Marvin nodded, shook Todd's hand and got into the passenger seat. Todd watched them pull away, waiting until they were out of sight, and then threw up over the trailing roses.

'Bloody hell, Byron's away from his desk.' Shirl looked up at the office window as Kath drove into the station car park. Byron waved at them and moved away, mug in hand. When Kath and Shirl arrived upstairs, they found him perched on the edge of the table in front of the window. He looked pale and shaken.

'Are you okay?' Kath sat next to him as Shirl made them both a coffee.

'Yeah.' His posture was slumped, energy levels low. 'I've found out something that might be pertinent but I had to read some pretty disgusting stuff to get there.'

The women settled down in chairs with their drinks, and Kath gestured for him to continue his thread.

'I've been in the world of paedophiles... Christ.' He rubbed a hand across his face and let his hair fall forward, trying to disguise the fact that tears were so close to falling.

'But how's that relevant, Byron?' Shirl looked confused, but Kath glanced at her and she shut up.

Byron took a deep breath. 'I know that's not an aspect of Daisy's murder. But it occurred to me that there may be a discussion board or something similar leading to a possible reason why this child's life was taken if it wasn't to satisfy... those types of urges.' He was finding it difficult to voice what he'd been reading. The level of depravity these people were only too happy to discuss under the sheltered umbrella of anonymity within the deep web was truly terrifying. Their likes, preferences, fantasies and the knowledge that a lot of these people had carried out their personal dreams of hell. He had found threads where discussions had led to admissions of active participation in the most heinous acts Byron had never even considered. He'd found sites where children were actively auctioned off to the highest bidder, assurances made that the 'merchandise' could be procured for the right price and protection was guaranteed. But Byron had continued working through, going back ten years in the hope of finding something to do with Daisy's murder.

'It occurred to me that this Jack might have tried to take a child before.' He was fighting for the right words, trying not to alarm the two women and keep his language professional and focused.

Kath sat up in her chair, her brain working to catch up with him. 'That is genius, Byron. It's something we hadn't even considered. What did you find?'

He put his empty mug on the table beside him. 'There was chatter around eleven years ago about the attempted abduction, although that's not quite the right word, of a toddler in Much Wenlock.' Shirl and Kath looked at each other, trying to recall anything that had come to their attention all those years ago. 'It was so... discreet, uneventful even, that it was never reported,' Byron continued. 'But a young lad got "chatting" to a little blonde girl in the playground round the corner from the church. Mum was apparently setting out a picnic on one of the benches while the child was on the swings. 'Jack' was on the swing next to her, and the next time Mum looked up, this lad was holding the child's hand and leading her off to the churchyard.'

'Christ,' muttered Shirl. 'How did this get onto the dark web if nothing happened? I'm confused.'

'It was the excitement,' Byron explained, and they all grimaced at the thought of people being actively excited at the thought of a young lad taking a child off somewhere and the details that might be revealed about the act.

'Mum ran after them and grabbed the girl, asked the lad what he thought he was doing, but he talked his way out of it—something about taking her to see something in the church.' He paused. 'It seems Mum knew the lad; she wasn't as alarmed as we think she should have been, just surprised he was going somewhere else with the child. It did shake Mum up a bit, child was fine, but Mum had then talked it over with friends, gossip got around the village, as these things do, so the chatter on the web—whoever put it there, and that's a whole other issue I don't even want to think about—was more about the fantasy of what could have happened; what could have been done to the child.'

'So, he is local. That confirms it.' Kath stood and went to the files spread out on the tables where Byron was still perched, although he looked as if he wanted to run away and hide in his room for many days. Kath flicked through papers, searching for something, but she didn't really know what. Just a suggestion; a tiny atom of an idea that was forming.

'And I have another theory,' Byron went on. 'I've been looking at the reasons why a young person, or child even, might be killed if not for all the obvious reasons we've been throwing around.'

Kath stopped shuffling paperwork and sat next to him.

'There's a cult in Papua New Guinea that believes if you extinguish the life from the body of a child, their life force, their spirit, their energy becomes part of you and can heal your soul.' Shirl pulled her cigarettes from her bag discreetly. 'It's called Errimya.' He pushed his fingers into his eyes to stop the moisture. 'If you inhale the dying breath of the child, your soul is forgiven for its sins and you are reborn.' He walked as sedately as he could through the office doorway into the toilet next door. Kath and Shirl exchanged looks at the sound of him retching, and their hearts went out to him.

'What have I done, exposing him to this shit?' Kath went to her bag and also pulled out her cigarettes and lighter.

'I know, I'm feeling pretty crap about it, but God, Kath, this is a real lead here. We can work with this.' Shirl stood. 'Let's give him some space and go for a smoke. I can't wait to see what Ruth's excitement is all about.'

| 18 |

'Can you talk? Sorry to call you at work, but I really need you to come over.'

Andrew watched the door close as his patient left, swapping his mobile to his other ear as he scrunched his shoulder and tried to type a few extra lines onto the patient's notes. 'It's okay... I'm free for a couple of minutes now.'

'Andrew, please come. It's Miranda.'

At the mention of her name, Andrew stopped typing and concentrated on the call. 'What's she done? She hasn't tried it again, has she? Because I'm not rescuing her this time, so call an ambulance—'

'Andrew!' Todd had never raised his voice to him in all the years of their friendship.

Andrew stood. 'Mate... what is it?'

'Please come.' Andrew was alarmed at the tone of Todd's voice and thought he could hear him crying.

'I think I can be there in about forty minutes. Can you hang on 'til then?'

'Yeah.' Todd ended the call, and Andrew was left staring at his phone as if it had just decided to end the call for him.

Andrew sat and pulled up the patient list for the remainder of the morning. There were a couple of repeat prescription check-ups and a pregnancy review. He rang through to reception and asked that the remaining patients be dealt with in a 'timelier' manner than usual, as he really needed to be away from surgery for a private emergency.

Andrew found Todd pacing the front garden, waiting for him. He slammed the door of his car, and Todd almost fell into his arms.

'Oh my God, you're scaring me now.' Andrew pulled Todd away from him and looked at him properly. His eyes were red; Andrew had been right in thinking he had been crying. His shirt was covered in what looked and smelled like coffee, and he could hear Samson wailing from inside the house. 'Come on. Let's go inside, and you can tell me what the hell is going on.'

Todd had already told him about the previous police visit and Lane's walkabout around the house and grounds. Andrew was supportive as ever, glad the case was being investigated again. Like Todd, he didn't just see it as a case. It was part of his life too. He had lived through the pain with Todd and Zoe and then through Todd's spiral into depression and hermit-like existence after Zoe's death. He had been the professional and had tried to keep Todd together, but quietly, a little piece of him had withered and died. He wasn't concerned that the investigation would open the old wounds; he knew Todd would be able to cope. It was the Miranda aspect that riled him, and he was trying hard to be there for his friend who seemed to have found a new interest in life through this random girl. When Todd had mentioned her name on the phone, he'd just known something was about to blow and it would all be to do with her.

Todd pulled Andrew into the kitchen. Miranda's straw bag was on the floor, empty, the contents spilled across the table. Letters and envelopes, all colours, some floral paper, others with a faint geometric design. Some of the envelopes had Todd's name on them. No address, just his name written in the middle. There were a dozen or so piled up addressed and postmarked to Miranda at an abbey in Worcestershire. Unopened. Samson, very pleased to see another human, jumped onto the table among the papers and made a beeline for Andrew for some fuss. Before Andrew could stretch out his hand, Todd grabbed Samson roughly under the belly and threw him onto the floor. He got the message and slunk out the back door.

'So'—Andrew waved a hand across the table, picking up random bits of paper—'what the hell is all this? This is her bag, isn't it? The one you found with her in the garden?'

'Yeah, and guess what? She was playing postie. All this was for me.'

'Make us some coffee and start from the beginning.'

Todd's movements were jerky. He seemed like an uncoordinated puppy, hands filled with water jug and paper filter, and he tried to put them all together. It was normally second nature to him. Now, nothing fitted into its rightful place. Everything was wrong in his world. Everything was suddenly out of place and he didn't know what to do about that.

Andrew took over as Todd told him about the visit a couple of hours ago. They stood at the window as the coffee machine burped and gurgled, Andrew's mouth opening and closing again, no words coming forth, eyebrows raised, eyes wide, astonishment settling into his face and rage in his belly as he wanted to shake Todd so badly and yell, "I told you so".

'And this was what it was all about.' Todd walked back to the table and picked up a piece of delicate violet-coloured paper. 'A confession. Every single one of them. Virtually the same letter, over and over again. The part she played in my daughter's death. And how very sorry she is.' He spat the last sentence out like poison from a wound. The two men stood in silence, looking down at the array of coloured letters. Todd leaned forward in such a swift movement he caught Andrew on his hip and swept everything onto the floor.

'The little bitch watched my daughter die and the poor lamb has had to live with her guilt for ten years. Fuck, Andrew... so she comes to give me the letters and die in my garden... what the fuck was that gonna do? What did she want from me—forgiveness?'

Andrew pulled Todd to him as his tears flowed and his anger strummed through his veins. It was like holding on tight to a tornado that shifted and swayed beneath his fingers. And Andrew was glad the little bitch was not close by.

The machine beeped to alert them to coffee availability. Todd was fighting dry sobs now; involuntary spasms of pain lurching out of his body.

'We are going to have coffee'—Andrew pulled out a chair and pushed Todd onto it—'and we are going to call the police and give them all this stuff as evidence.' Todd didn't acknowledge the words. Andrew pulled his mobile from his pocket and called the surgery, asking them to cancel his afternoon appointments, as he would have to attend the police station. He was sketchy on the details but assured Hannah on reception there was nothing for them, or the surgery, to worry about.

He poured the coffee and set a mug in front of Todd. He wasn't sure Todd could even focus, so he moved around the kitchen to the paper on the floor and began to gather it up. He wanted to look through it all before the police came. He briefly wondered about DNA contamination; he wasn't worried for himself, as his sample had been taken at the time of Daisy's murder to confirm him within the DNA in the house. Apart from Miranda—and now Todd and himself—who else was likely to have touched the letters if they had been sitting in the bag or a drawer? That was not for him to determine, and he had to hope neither of them had destroyed anything useful.

Todd looked at Andrew as he sat opposite him and began to read. 'How could I not have known?' he whispered.

'Todd, don't be stupid. There is no way you could have known anything about this bitch, let alone what she's done.' He glanced down at the straw bag, still lying on its side like a corpse. 'I'm just glad they took her away,' said Andrew quietly.

| 19 |

Danny put down the pen and looked at the words he had spent the last four hours searching for to put into reality and finally tell the story. His beginning, the turning, had been in his head for so long, he did not think he would ever be able to get it out. But his story had flowed easier than he'd thought possible. Only Miranda knew the absolute truth of what had happened because she had been there to witness it. The little blonde boy and the red-haired girl pushed into a home filled with broken ideals and rules that would be followed at all costs. As Danny grew older, he would come to realise the foster system was a minefield; there were good homes filled with good people like Ida and her lovely patient husband and then there were bad homes where a child's distress was ignored and moulded into a new thing that would serve as a solution to the pain of an adult that could not be erased or put right. Ida had been given scant details of Danny and Miranda's early years, and Danny had let forth a little more each year as he'd realised Ida was the good foster mum; the one that would look after him and protect him. Her horror at his treatment under the so-called watchful eye of his first foster mother had been evident in her usually smiley face as he'd revealed what she had done. Ida had not smiled.

Instead, she'd pulled him to her large breasts which smelled of baking and a perfume he did not know the name of but would always associate with her whenever he would smell it in the future. A warm embrace was always going to be there for him and for Miranda, too.

And now, here was his story. He looked at himself in the mirror of the dressing table where he sat, composing his words, his life, his reason for his being. The two side mirrors of the Victorian dresser gave him angles of his beautiful face he could now admire instead of look at with disgust and disdain. His blonde lashes held tight to the black mascara, full lips coloured with an apricot lipstick pursed in an attempt at a kiss blown to himself now he could accept and love himself completely. He could now say, with absolute conviction, he had been given a gift. Why had he tried to fight it for so long? He wondered if he should send it to Miranda for her to read. But she already knew. From his letters. One sent to her at the abbey every year on May 12. No, he would read it again, all the way through, just to make sure he hadn't left anything out...

We found it in an antique shop—one of those ones tucked away down an alley. We never would have found it, me and my new mummy, if it hadn't started raining. Not the gentle autumn rain poets write about where lovers shelter under a big umbrella and share kisses and their dreams. No, this was God slicing open the clouds and letting all the insides fall out. My tweed coat was already smelling like a wet dog as she pushed me into the doorway to shelter from the deluge. I had a friend who had a dog. That's how I knew the smell. Comforting really. I was never to be blessed with a comforting smell such as that in her house.

Mummy pushed so hard that the door opened inwards, and I felt myself falling into the dim interior. But she grabbed me, kept me upright, her thin lips—stained with an apricot hue—folded in so tight they disappeared completely into her powdered wrinkles. She tried to make it look as if we had always meant to enter the shop, keeping hold of my skinny wrist and brushing the rain from her coat, looking around at the stacked shelves and the huge, cluttered table in the centre of the room. Mummy was not a woman at home with incidental moments. Serendipity and coincidence found no truck with my mummy.

A painfully thin man with sleek grey hair appeared from a back room and asked if he could be of assistance. Well, obviously not, as we had not planned to be here. My mummy, loosening the grip on my wrist, told him my birthday was coming up and she was looking for something unusual. The man smiled at me. He seemed a long way up. I was short, even for nearly six. It was a lie, of course. My birthday had been and gone. I had never had a present from Mummy at any time in my short life. But I knew better than to disagree.

He nodded wisely and indicated we should follow him through the archway into a larger back room. As we followed the man, Mummy pushing me ahead of her, I tried to take in all the wonderful objects around me. But it was too much; I didn't know where to look first. So, it all went by as an apparition, nothing solid, items floating just above the shelves. There wasn't any conversing between the man and Mummy. She was a woman of few words as if she had a daily ration and they were not to be squandered on social niceties.

The back room was windowless, airless, like the wardrobe that led to Narnia. This room had three silky fur coats hanging from the walls on deer antlers…monstrous stuffed deer heads with bright eyes that said, 'Here I am, preserved for your viewing pleasure'. My foot kicked something metallic, and Mummy glowered at me. There was even less light in here and the smell seemed different. The items of people long dead closed in on my small frame, inviting me to smell their memories of lives lived.

And suddenly it was gone—that sense of wonder, excitement at this new and strange environment. My tiny insides clenched like I knew I was in a bad place now. I could not appeal to Mummy. That would never do. And it would never work. Children were to be seen and not heard. All I wanted was to put my hand in hers and for her to give it a little squeeze that said everything would be okay. But that was not going to happen. So, I did not attempt it. The rejection would be worse.

The tall man ducked under another archway, thinner this time like it was only made for him. There was a light, brighter than the others, and I could see a desk with lots of papers and books. A kettle, cup and saucer balanced precariously on a stack of magazines on one end, but he moved deftly between the obstacles as if his body had been programmed to avoid all collision. And then he reappeared with the cupboard, held before him like a ventriloquist dummy. He put it down in front of us, and my meagre breakfast forced its way back into my mouth.

It was the most terrifying thing I had ever seen. Between five and six foot tall. The main body was thin, like the man, dark green and black paint flaking around the tiny door handles. The black boots were large, peeking out from the body, no legs, just the body and then the feet. The arms were jointed, hung at each side. But it was the head on top of the cupboard. The clown head. It seemed out of proportion to the rest of the anatomy. White face. Red and black and yellow circles around the eyes. Impossibly big black eyebrows raised as if in surprise. And then there was the mouth. I tried to look elsewhere. I focused on the green hair, painted to seem to curl out from underneath the yellow bowler hat set at that rakish angle that seems playful and cheeky. But the mouth, a wide red grin showing painted off-white teeth like tombstones framing a dark hole, was the most frightening thing. I was aware of Mummy and the man talking as I took a step sideways, trying to avoid the dull eyes and that mad mouth. My cheek brushed one of the fur coats and its arms threatened to enfold me; to hold me still, facing the clown cupboard. The sick was now in my mouth. I couldn't swallow it down… I just couldn't. The clown was laughing at me. What are you gonna do now, little boy?

I wanted to spit it right into his ugly mouth and let him swallow it. My hand gripped a piece of the fur coat and I felt a pocket. I turned, just slightly, and opened my lips a little, letting the bile dribble into the pocket, praying that Mummy and the man wouldn't notice. They didn't. But the clown knew.

The taste was so horrid but I would have to be brave. I was suddenly aware of all eyes on me. Had Mummy asked me a question? Did they just see what I did? Oh no, did I miss something? No, it was as always. Mummy talking at me and not expecting or requiring a response. The man was still talking. I heard odd words... 'naughty little boys'... 'just big enough'...

They shook hands. And I just knew. Just knew that my new mummy had agreed to buy it. For me. My teeth were drowning in saliva and I had to swallow this time. Brackish bile slid slowly down my throat. I heard our address being given by Mummy to the man who couldn't seem to stop smiling at me. She wanted it delivered. Looking back, I almost thought the clown would flip up a jointed arm and raise his hat to me. The yellow wooden bowler hat with a chunk missing from the bowl. Coming home with you, little boy. What do you think of that?

It was positioned on the wall opposite my bed. My room was quite small—'a small child doesn't need a big room,' Mummy had said. So, I couldn't escape the eyes of the clown cupboard. The wallpaper was a very dark green, I seem to remember, with some sort of leaf pattern. It almost made the clown seem part of the room as if it had always been there, waiting to emerge from *the leaves. I had no choice but to walk past it to get out. Unless I rolled across the bed. And that was not acceptable. Once I was out of bed and it had been made and duly inspected, I was not to touch it again until bedtime. So, every day, I had to squeeze past the cupboard.*

Miranda was never put in the clown cupboard. She didn't need to be because she was already a girl. Mummy just sort of tolerated her as if it was just one of things. We had come to her house together purely by chance—two kiddies without homes, needing looking after. I believe Mummy had protested when she saw me but the man and woman that put us in the house had explained it probably wouldn't be for very long, as someone would want to take us and maybe even adopt us and look after us forever. Two years was a long forever. Two years of being dressed in girl clothes and having my blonde hair curled. She said the clown cupboard was magic and would help me become the little girl she always knew I was inside. But the only thing the clown cupboard did was make me wet myself. It would run down my leg and puddle into my pale pink Clarks shoes which, Mummy took great pains to tell me, had been very expensive, and couldn't I see how she was buying me nice things and I was ruining everything?

No, I didn't see it.

Didn't get it, MUMMY.

I.

Did.

Not.

Get.

It.

But Danny got it now. Now he had a new name and proper girl curls and proper girl things. Because he did get it. It was all so obvious, now.

| 20 |

Ruth's demeanour was completely professional; in the car on the way to the station, she did not speak. Once parked, she carefully removed Miranda from the back of the car and escorted her into the station with a swift and sketchy explanation for the PCSO on the desk. She guided her into the only cell and carefully closed the door. Only then, on the other side of that door, did she let her emotions swim to the surface, eyes moist with rage. She let the images come forth of her grabbing Miranda's silky white throat and squeezing until the life drained out of her as she must have watched the boy do to Daisy.

She pressed the heels of her hands into her eyes and went upstairs. She could hear Lane and Marvin telling the others what had transpired and Shirl adding the information gathered on their visit to Westwood Hall. She stood in the doorway, listening.

Kath moved over to her. 'This is turning out to be quite a morning,' she said, manoeuvring Ruth into a chair.

'I'm okay.' I'm just having thoughts that would get me expelled from the force.'

'Amen to that,' muttered Marvin.

'So'—Kath needed to pull the team together now; put all the emotion aside and deal with the information they now had—'we've got one out of two. I will go and interview her when the duty solicitor gets here.' Marvin had said the staff downstairs had begun making the calls to try and get whichever solicitor was available and would call up when they arrived. 'How's she doing?' Kath asked.

Marvin looked at Ruth, and she nodded for him to go on. 'She just kept mumbling in the car. Think it was "I'm sorry" over and over. Seems she was more concerned with Todd than herself.'

'Have we taken all the usual precautions of a suicide watch, seeing as that is how she came to be here in the first place?' Shirl interrupted.

Marvin nodded. 'There's a PCSO outside the cell with the viewing window open. We did search her before she went in.' There was one cell and a small interview room at the substation, usually used for holding drunks so they could cool off or sober up, or for public disturbance offenders. It was a temporary solution until they were moved up to Malinsgate.

'That man's in pieces,' Ruth said quietly, referring to Todd.

'Aye,' said Lane. 'He was all over the place. Couldn't believe what we were telling him.'

'Living under his roof, forming an attachment to her... Christ...' Ruth rubbed her face as Kath's mobile rang.

'It's him,' Kath said, answering the call. 'Todd, are you okay? No, I don't think it's a good idea for you to... what?' The team looked at Kath as she fought to keep her voice steady. 'Okay, have you got someone who can... right...good. Come on in then and bring it all with you. Yes, okay. See you soon.'

Kath put down the phone. 'Todd is coming into the station... with evidence. Seems we are catching breaks all over the place.' Her phone acknowledged a text message. She saw it was from Lenny. He would have to wait. She would need to fill him in later anyway with the events going on. More work to take home. *This job is turning out to be pretty much like my old one,* she thought, turning the phone screen-down on the desk.

'So,' Kath continued, 'We know from our visit to the Hall that that was their escape route. There's more to come, I feel, from the tour guide. Possibly the gardener, too. But that is just the icing on the cake. We have Miranda downstairs, and she will lead us to the boy... man, as he will be now.'

'What if she doesn't know where he is? Maybe he's dead?'

'Marvin, we have been over this. We are having a good run. I just have to believe we can find him, with or without her downstairs.' Kath took a breath. 'Ruth, do you want to take a break? Go... I don't know... have a walk in the woods or something?'

Ruth stood, brushed her hands down her body. She repeated the action a couple of times. Shirl smiled. Ruth would be okay.

'Get all that crap energy off you and run up to Greggs. There's a dear. There's a sausage roll with my name on it,' said Shirl.

Byron smiled from his corner and the mood lifted a little. The intense heat in the small station had been adding to the cranky attitude of some of the team members, but the assortment of desk and floor fans seemed to be helping a little, if only directing the same heat out the door or into the corners.

Ruth grabbed her purse. 'Yes, I will take a break, and yes'—she looked over at Shirl—'I may even get you two sausage rolls.'

She hadn't been gone more than a few minutes when Kath saw a Range Rover pulling into the car park and glimpsed Todd in the passenger seat. She went down to the reception to meet him, anxious to know what he had discovered. She was shocked at his appearance as he followed the blonde man through the door.

'Dr Andrew Taylor.' Andrew held out his hand to Kath, and she took it, acknowledging an uncalled-for and slightly inappropriate fluttering of attraction in her belly.

'Yes, I remember you. Thanks for coming with Todd. Shall we go up?' The two men followed her upstairs, and Kath threw brief introductions around the room. All eyes were on the incongruous straw bag.

'Can I take this, Todd?' She reached forward, and he passed it to her but couldn't seem to let go. She tugged, smiling at him. 'It's okay; I can take it from here. Really.'

'I hope we haven't destroyed any evidence,' Andrew said, a little sheepish although not regretting his decision to handle the papers. 'Only me and Todd have handled them, apart from... her.' He couldn't bring himself to say her name. 'Luckily, it's Mrs Tinkerson's day off, so—'

'Mrs Tinkerson? Oh, yes.' Kath was remembering now that Todd had mentioned her to Lane and Marvin. 'We will be calling her to get a DNA sample, just for elimination purposes, obviously. But that can wait. Please, sit, both of you. Sorry about the heat.' Kath suddenly felt foolish for apologising for the sun being out as if she had arranged it so they could all work in a truly uncomfortable hot space.

Andrew gently pushed Todd into a chair. Todd seemed spacey; his brain firing images he did not want to see, his guts spewing tiny acid drops of hate and anger.

'Is she talking?' Andrew asked.

Kath walked around to one of the tables in front of the window, found a large, fresh paper evidence bag and placed the straw bag neatly inside it, eager to look properly at the contents but knowing she had more pressing things to concern her. 'I'm waiting for the solicitor to arrive before I talk to her. She hasn't said anything to us yet though.' She waited, wondering if Todd was going to offer anything. He wasn't looking at anyone. He was staring down at his shirt.

Lane was filling the coffee machine. It wasn't so much that anyone really needed any more hot liquid on this wretched August day, just that it was something familiar; something to do to keep the hands and mind occupied.

They were suddenly all aware that Byron was standing next to Todd. His curtain of hair was thrown back over his shoulders, and they could all see the T-shirt no one had really taken any notice of when he'd entered the office earlier. It was a Hark T-shirt from Todd's tour in 2002. A black shirt with a red lightning strike logo. Across the top, it read 'HARK' with the words 'Hear My Light Tour' underneath. Todd looked up at Byron, aware of the proximity of the young man, and he gave a faint smile at the T-shirt. He traced the red logo with his finger. Byron stood absolutely still, not wanting to break the spell.

'Don't let the darkness dim the light,' Byron said quietly. 'We will hear your light again, and it will be bright, and it will be strong.'

Marvin teared up, wishing he'd thought of something that profound to say instead of his inane mutterings about coffee. Todd took Byron's hand and held it in an almost romantic and reverent way.

'Thank you,' he said. Byron moved back to his desk and carried on doing whatever it was he did, although Marvin suspected he was just bashing the hell out of the keyboard. And then the idea flooded Kath's brain and she knew it was another turning point.

'Todd.' She almost snapped his name, and he focused on her face. 'I think you should talk to her.'

Andrew jumped to his feet. 'With respect, I don't think that's a good idea.'

Kath pushed her empathy and sympathy into a box inside her and slammed the lid shut. Time to get back in charge and back on track. 'Thank you for your input, Dr Taylor, but I feel this is the best course of action... if you are happy to do that, Todd?'

'Todd, you don't have to do this.' Andrew put a hand on Todd's shoulder, but he shrugged it off.

'I'll do it,' he agreed. 'I want answers.'

'And we need them, too. I think she'll open up to you a whole lot more.'

'Are you going to read the letters?' Todd gestured to the straw bag.

Kath's mind was racing ahead, trying to slot everything that had to be done into place. She just had to switch her brain back to 'previous job' mode, interviewing a witness or suspect in the proper manner, no hiccups, no sloppy work or the CPS would be down on her like a ton of gravel from a dumper trucker. The case had to be made, and justice had to be served. But there was also the striking of the balance; peace and some kind of immediate reparation for Todd.

'Todd, go back home and wait for my call. I need to read these letters before we do anything else.' She went to him and he stood. 'I'll have her transferred to Malinsgate, and we'll do everything there. Solicitor might take another few hours to see her, so I don't want you waiting around.' She turned to Andrew. 'Are you going to stay with him?'

'Well...' Andrew was aware he should get back to the practice but felt he didn't want to leave Todd.

Todd seemed quiet but more resolute now—more together—his world coming back into focus. 'Just take me home, Andrew, then you can leave me to do whatever I have to do next. I'm sure Detective Chief Inspector Fortune will guide me through it.'

Kath nodded and shook his hand—no shakes now, no tremors, a firm grip that told her he was ready to do this and he would be the one to break the case open even wider. 'Thank you. I'll see you out,' she said.

Lane walked over to Marvin and encased him in her arms, her black curls tickling his cheek. He was about to protest but realised this was exactly what he needed. They held each other tight as Lane whispered, 'He's gonna be fine, my wee boy. Just fine.'

| 21 |

She must be all of twelve, Kath thought as she shook the feeble hand of the duty solicitor Miss Bayley. The woman-child had made the best effort possible to look cool and professional but the heat and the intensity of the case she was about to get involved in made her pale blue linen dress cling to her thin frame, circles of sweat just visible when she moved her arms. She put her briefcase down at the side of the interview table and ran her fingers through her fringe, hoping there wasn't too much hair sticking to her forehead as if she had been for a ten-mile run.

Miranda stood behind Kath with a uniformed PC beside her. She had not wanted it to be like this. She felt stupid for letting it get this far. If only she had confessed all to Todd a few days ago. But those few days had been so magical, even with the parameters of the heinous events that had brought her to him. And she had seen the hate flash in his brown eyes and wished, for all the world, she had not seen it. And now she was never going to have the chance to tell him; to explain. She knew he would have found the letters by now. How had he felt as he'd read her words? Had he felt a little of what she had tried to push into the paper with every pen stroke? It didn't matter now. She was sure prison stretched ahead of her. She wasn't even frightened by the prospect. It was her fate now. It was deserved. Just admit everything, purge, let it all tumble free. She sat next to Sarah Bayley—as she'd been introduced to her solicitor—hands in her lap, red hair hanging forward.

Kath sat opposite the two women. 'Miranda, you are under caution and will be interviewed regarding the murder of Daisy Prospero and your involvement, if any, and with knowledge of any information you can reveal to us regarding this crime. You are not under arrest at this moment in time, and your appointed solicitor is here to advise you and guide you through the process as it may occur. Do you understand?'

She had been read her rights when Ruth had escorted her from Todd's house, although Ruth suspected she had not taken much notice.

Miranda carefully placed her hands on the table. 'Can I see Todd. Please? I need to explain.'

Miss Bayley was about to butt in, but Kath held up her hand to silence her. They had spoken in the corridor before Miranda had been brought up from the cells, and Kath had ran her through the plan of having Todd in the room, just the two of them, before proceeding further. Miss Bayley, although young, knew her stuff and further advised Kath that she would need to be in the room and the officers could watch through the two-way mirror.

'Actually, Todd is on his way. He wants to see you and I have agreed.'

Miranda's eyes lit up, and she smiled for the first time in hours. She had sat in the cell at Madeley station, wondering what he was doing, what he must be thinking. She thought she had heard his voice but dismissed it as hopeful imagination. She would confess everything, she had decided. But there burned inside her a small ember of resentment towards Danny. It was the first time she had felt it. She had known what Danny had wanted to do and why he'd felt he needed to do it. Was she really an accomplice? Was that what they would ultimately charge her with? She would go to court as someone who had helped? But she hadn't really helped, had she? She'd tried to reason it out, like she had so many times over the years. She had been with him, had watched what he had done, had disappeared to another county with him. But helped him? She had offered her explanations to God, her reasoning, her excuses. And she'd tried to make herself believe He had listened to her prayers. But she knew, deep down, He had never understood and could therefore never forgive her for the sin. So, there was no other choice but to remove herself from the earth. But she had been saved, so had God finally got it? Had he sent Todd to find her at the bottom of his garden on that night? Had He spared her so she could finally admit her crime of being there and watching and crying and retching and feeling a hand reach inside her and clutch her insides as Daisy's eyelids had fluttered for the last time?

There was a knock on the door. Kath moved to open it to see the duty sergeant who leaned forward to whisper in her ear that Todd had arrived at the station. Kath nodded, and the sergeant opened the connecting door to reception. Todd entered the room. He had showered and changed into a fresh white collarless shirt, his hair still damp from the shower, making him appear youthful, the previously troubled look now gone from his face. Sarah Bayley stood and smoothed down her wrinkled dress. Miranda also stood quickly and went to move towards him before Kath could get between them, her flowered skirt catching around the chair leg. Todd slapped Miranda so hard her hair swept like a red curtain across the face of the solicitor. Miranda's hands went to her face and she let out a keening wail. Before Kath and Sarah Bayley could move, Todd had enfolded Miranda in his strong arms and stood there, rocking her like a child as Kath sighed and wished for her old job back.

| 22 |

'You let her go?' Ruth's question and open-mouthed astonishment seemed to speak for everyone when Kath got back to the office and told them what had transpired. Kath slung her bag on her desk and stood in front of one of the floor fans, holding up her arms and closing her eyes for a moment in the warm wind.

'There'll be a good reason,' said Shirl, wondering what the hell her boss was doing but, ultimately, standing by the statement.

'So, what's the story?' Ruth sat forward in her chair, wanting details.

Kath turned to face everyone. 'She was not under arrest, and I have released her into the custody of Todd. They need to talk to each other and I think Todd is the priority.'

Ruth stood and started to object, but Shirl tugged at her shirt and gave her a look that said she knows what she is doing.

'Aren't you worried she'll do another runner?' asked Marvin.

'Actually, I'm not.' She pointed to the evidence bag with Miranda's straw bag inside. Kath had been through all the letters she had written to Todd but had yet to open the ones from the lad to Miranda. She wanted the team to focus now on finding him. 'Objectively, and by law'—she raised an eyebrow at Ruth—'unless she confesses, we do not have anything to hold her on. The letters… well, it can be proven she wrote them but that's all. She could deny her involvement and say what she wrote was a fantasy. There was no female DNA found on or around Daisy's body. Apart from the fact she was possibly seen and could be identified as the girl who was with the lad that day, we have nothing.'

'I can't believe Todd's reaction.' Marvin shook his head and opened the fridge for another bottle of water.

'Yeah… took me by surprise too, if I'm honest. But his bond with this girl is something none of us can explain or quantify, and I think he will get more from her. She feels safe with him and obviously wants to be with him for whatever reason. Well, I know the reason because I've read the letters. You should all glove up and read them. Then we will open each of the lad's letters to Miranda and go through them methodically. They might give us a clue as to where he is now, and that is the prize we're after: the murderer; the person who killed Daisy. He is the one we want brought to trial, sentenced and put away.'

Shirley moved to the table, snapped on some gloves and began emptying the straw bag, eager to be doing something. Marvin joined her and they began putting each letter and envelope in a separate clear plastic evidence bag, laying them out across the tables.

'Byron.' Kath moved over to his desk. 'We took a voluntary DNA sample from Miranda. I've asked the lab to fast track the results and send them to you. We still don't have a last name or any other details about her, but get your deerstalker on and see what you can come up with.'

He looked up at her. 'I'm not a miracle worker. There's not a lot to go on...' He saw the look on her face. 'But I guess that's why I'm here so, okay.'

She gently squeezed his shoulder. 'Thank you. Anything else you need, or need to have access to, just ask, although I guess you're pretty experienced at getting into systems and gaining information all on your own.' He didn't need to admit to his ability and Kath didn't need to know. She went to move away but he stopped her.

'This may be insignificant—'

'Nothing is insignificant, Byron. Just spit out all the little bits you find and we'll decide if they fit into the puzzle. What you got?'

'Well...' He pulled up a document on his monitor and pointed. It was a historical page about Westwood Hall. 'I've been doing a bit of digging around the history of the Hall and I came across this.' He clicked the mouse and the printer sparked to life. He motioned for her to get the paper coming out. Kath picked it up and started to read.

'What exactly am I looking at?' she asked.

'It's the bit about the ice house. Lots of big houses had them for keeping stuff cool. This one, though, had a dual purpose. It was an escape route.' Kath stopped reading and stared at him, a picture forming in her mind. Byron saw the realisation in her face. 'From the entrance door at the Hall, you can disappear through a tunnel which—'

'Comes out in the woods across the meadow,' Kath finished.

She pushed the paper into her trouser pocket, grabbed her bag and hurried through the door, almost knocking Lane over who had just come back from the local supermarket with cold drinks and cake.

'Lane, you're with me, please.' She didn't stop but threw the request at Lane who shrugged and placed the items on the nearest desk, following Kath out into the heat and into the greenhouse that was Kath's car.

'Where are we going?'

Kath slammed the Quattro into reverse. 'We're going to Westwood Hall.'

Ida was finishing up for the day, walking through all the downstairs rooms and checking for anything out of place. She had been distracted all day after the visit from the detectives but had tried to carry on as normal. But nothing was normal now. She knew the chief inspector would be back, she just didn't know when. She had fixed the smile on her face all day but it was hollow and without sincerity. Fred had come looking for her on her midday break, but she had waved him away, needing to be alone to think and plan out what to do next. She finished straightening curtains that didn't need straightening and cleaning surfaces that were already pristine. Finally, she had to admit she needed to go home, see Jim, tell him what had happened and how they were going to handle the next instalment of this story that was clouding her brain. She wanted desperately to believe Danny and Miranda were safely out of harm's way and clung to a small beacon of hope that they were never involved in the child's death. But deep in her heart, she knew the truth. She just wasn't ready to share it with the police quite yet.

She locked up and got into her car, cranking up the air con, knowing it wasn't just the heat of the day that was making her cheeks burn. She wasn't prone to panic and anxiety but she felt a real crushing need now to be within the sanctuary of her own home. She slammed her foot hard on the accelerator and was about to turn left out of the gates when Kath's Quattro came speeding towards her from the other direction. She fumbled the gear stick as she recognised the car and the person behind the wheel. Kath was close enough now to see Ida's face, and they shared a brief moment of recognition. Kath threw caution to the wind, a feeling burning in her gut that the woman should not be allowed to get away. She pulled her car across the driveway, almost clipping one of the stone gate posts, cutting off Ida's escape route. Kath got out of her car and walked to Ida's window. She buzzed it down and forced a polite smile.

'That was close, wasn't it?'

Kath had decided, as she'd left the station, to dispense with niceties. 'We need to talk to you again. Where are you going?

'Home,' Ida said. She pulled her small frame up as high as she could in the driver's seat.

'I'll follow you. Lead the way.' Kath turned back to her car, got in and pulled back so that Ida could pull out onto the road into Much Wenlock.

'This is going to be interesting,' Lane muttered as Kath tailgated Ida for two miles until they reached a row of cottages on the outskirts of the town. Ida was clearly rattled, as the usually confident driver almost missed her driveway and scraped the car door against the overhanging shrubs and small trees at the side of the cottage. Kath pulled up outside, and she and Lane walked to the front door as Ida, trying to delay the inevitable, pretended to search her car for something unseen, looking in her bag, brushing off the seat covers. Kath and Lane stood and waited.

Ida beckoned them to come round to the back door. Kath and Lane followed her through the side gate. The back door was open, and in the kitchen stood a man at the sink, washing cups and plates. He started to smile then abruptly stopped as Ida entered followed by the two women.

'This is my husband, Jim.' Ida put her bag on the kitchen table. 'Jim, this is Detective Chief Inspector Fortune and...' she fumbled for the name, not yet having been introduced to the other woman.

'Lane Petreus.' Lane moved forward to shake Jim's hand. He hurriedly wiped his damp hands down his legs and shook her hand. He was a big man, tall, solid with a kind face, crow's feet nestled around his eyes. The husband-and-wife team looked like a mismatch but Lane felt the energy from Jim and knew there was a deep love and kindness that flowed between the couple.

'Ida, have you been speeding again?' Jim joked, and Kath felt the sudden unease in the air. *They know something,* Kath thought as she moved towards Ida.

'Don't be daft, love. Put the kettle on and we'll have a cuppa. The chief inspector came to see me earlier at the Hall.' Jim busied himself with the kettle and getting mugs ready as Ida turned to Kath and said, 'I didn't expect to see you again quite so soon.' She averted her eyes and moved around Jim, putting the tea towel on the back of one of the chairs at the table. Lane caught Kath's eye and motioned towards the doorway to the rest of the downstairs of the cottage and Kath gave an imperceptible nod. Her patience was wearing thin. The heat of the day and the emotional scenes she had already witnessed had drained her. She remembered she'd had another two texts from Lenny and reminded herself to text him back when she got in the car. She had a sudden yearning to be in her own home with Lenny fussing around her kitchen and the smell of the lavender wafting through the windows.

'I think you were expecting me, Ida,' Kath said, 'and I think you have something to tell me; something about the murder of Daisy Prospero.' One of the mugs slipped from Jim's big hands and plunged to the quarry tiles as his startled eyes darted between Kath and Ida.

Lane had quietly moved herself into the cosy lounge. A small but tidy room with a leather sofa, shelves either side of the fireplace with a small log burner and decorative vase of dried grasses on the hearth. Lane moved around the room, feeling the energy, feeling something almost tangible—the presence of happiness mingled with shame and tears. She studied the books on the shelves; volumes of wildlife identification, cookery books, craft books on knitting and card making, art history, several books on the local area. She whipped her head around at the sound of the china breaking, then turned back as if something had pulled her attention to a particular shelf. And there it was. A photo frame with a picture of two smiling teenagers. A blonde boy with tight lips who looked for all the world as if he didn't want his picture taken but had given in because someone really wanted to take it. And the girl. The redhead. Miranda.

'I don't know what you mean,' said Ida, flustered now at the mess on the floor and the tiny shards peeking out from beneath the cooker.

'Two kids, Ida. Two kids came out of the woods, leaving behind the corpse of a child. I think they came through the tunnel into the ice house at the Hall. I don't know what happened then, Ida. But I think you do.'

'No, no, no.' Ida picked up the tea towel and twisted the cloth between her fingers. 'I don't know, I don't know—'

'Yeah, she does.' Lane appeared in the doorway, holding the photo frame up for Kath to see. 'Jack and Jill went up the hill to kill a little girl. They opened up an oyster but didn't find the pearl,' Lane said quietly.

Ida let out the sob she had been holding in and collapsed onto a chair as Kath moved towards her, not out of concern but out of determination.

She leaned forward, her hands on the table either side of Ida's body, trapping her in the space. 'You tell me everything. From the beginning. Now.'

| 23 |

Shirl's fingers sweated underneath the latex gloves as she opened each of the letters Danny had sent to Miranda at the abbey. Marvin held clear evidence bags for each of them as she opened each letter carefully and skimmed the contents before setting them inside their plastic prisons. Marvin set them all out on the table in date order. There were ten all together—one for each year Danny and Miranda seemed to have been apart.

'They're all updates,' Shirl muttered as she swatted away another fly that had found its way through one of the open windows. 'He seems to be giving her a progress report on his life each year. I wonder why she never opened them?'

'Well'—Marvin tilted his head, staring at the letters—'we don't know how they know each other, don't know how much time they spent together before the...' He didn't want to speak of the death and searched for a more appropriate word. 'Incident. They could have known each other for years or months. Maybe she didn't want anything more to do with him after they left the area. Or, at least we know she left because the letters are addressed to her at the abbey in Worcestershire. Where was he then? Did he stick around? Did he go to Worcestershire with her?'

'So many questions,' said Shirl. 'I need a fag. Need to think and process what I've been reading. Back in a bit.' She moved to her desk and picked up her cigarettes and lighter, managing to slap a fly on her desk, killing it.

Byron looked up at the sudden noise and smiled. 'Good shot.'

Shirl smiled and wiped her hand down her already dirty blouse. 'It's not my first time.' She grinned and left the two men in the airless room and stood outside, away from the building, under the relative cool of the shade of the many trees that lined the road. As the smoke curled around her head, she tried to process what Danny had written; tried to find the clues she felt were there. They just needed to be teased out. His choice of words had been interesting: becoming, relenting, surrendering, evolving. An image of a butterfly came to mind, starting life as something completely different in a cocoon, preserved, sheltered from the outside world, then a miraculous emergence of a small, wet creature which dried off, shook itself into its new surroundings and unfurled its wings, showing its beauty.

'How can ugly turn into beautiful?' Shirl said to a blackbird that had landed near her feet and was grubbing in the dirt at the base of the tree. She knew they needed Todd to get the information out of Miranda and, not for the first time that day, she wondered how he was doing.

Miranda's tears had dried like flattened pearls upon her face. She had cried all the way back to Todd's house in his car. He had tried to steel himself from the emotion that flowed out of her but was finding it difficult to deflect it.

There was a strange calm inside him that emanated and surrounded him in a cloud. It had rubbed off on Miranda, and by the time they'd pulled up at the house and entered the cool of the lounge, the whimpers had stopped and there was nothing now except quiet resignation. She sat on the sofa where he had first laid her after finding her in the garden. He sat to one side in a softened leather chair. She had not looked at him, turning the material of her skirt through her fingers, picking at imaginary loose threads. He simply watched her, waiting for her to speak. He wanted to say so much and yet couldn't bring himself to start the conversation he knew would wrench at his heart. After a few more minutes, she finally spoke.

'I don't know where to start. All I have to say will hurt you so much and I really don't want that. Honestly. Please believe me when I say that.'

Todd took several deep breaths; Andrew had taught him breathing methods when he lost his daughter and his wife as a means of coping, of calming himself so he could centre, come back to himself and not let his emotions run away with him. 'I think we both have to speak truthfully,' he said carefully. 'I feel it's going to be beneficial to both of us. I haven't the energy anymore for screaming or shouting and I don't think it would do either of us any good.'

She nodded and smoothed her skirt across her knees which were pressed together, forming a tight seal. 'Do you want to ask questions and I'll answer or do you want to just—'

'Did you kill my daughter?'

Miranda looked at him. His face was open, gaze steady, ready to receive the information he so desperately needed. 'No.'

His heart sang at that simple word, and he couldn't explain why he felt that spark of joy again that seemed to rise in him when she was around.

She wasn't sure whether to go on, but she sensed a shift in him; a movement within the skin of him that told her it was going to be okay. 'It was someone called Danny. And I need to get it all out now, and you need to hear it, but don't interrupt me 'cos I might just fall under the weight of all this.'

'Okay,' he said.

She put her hands together as if in prayer and began. 'Danny and I grew up together in the same foster homes. We were thrown together—fate, whatever, we had no say, no control. Our first home was when we were really tiny; I don't know exactly how old we were. The woman was okay at first. We were with her for a couple of years before we had to be moved.' She wanted to stop and take a breath as the memories came flooding back, but she knew she had to go on and tell Todd everything. She'd had years to process the pain and the shame, but the act of actually speaking the words and telling Todd what she had been a part of was a brutal task. She could only try to soften her words, but she feared it would not be enough.

'She was okay to me, actually. She wasn't a loving, attentive woman but we didn't go hungry or dirty, we had toys and books and our own rooms but there was a darkness in her we didn't know about... we didn't know there was a reason for her doing what she did to Danny.' Miranda looked up at the ceiling and knew Todd's eyes were still on her but she couldn't look at him now.

'She had lost a child—a little blonde girl, died when she was about five, run over by a car, I think... anyway, Danny somehow reminded her of the child, and she tried to turn

Danny into a little girl; a replacement.' She gulped as she remembered the clown cupboard and suddenly could not tell Todd about that. Noone else needed to know. Even though she felt no further connection to Danny now, she felt she had to at least protect this aspect of his past.

'She dressed him in girl clothes and tried to curl his hair and even put make-up on him. It was horrible. Danny didn't understand but he wanted to please her. He always got the clothes dirty or he pulled the curls out of his hair and messed it up, and she would get so mad...' She closed her eyes, head still angled towards the ceiling. 'She never hit him, just was... I don't know how to say it, really. There was such disappointment and venom in her eyes and her mouth. Anyway, Danny ran away one day, and some dog walkers found him in the park and called the police because no one knew who he was, and he was dressed in all the girl stuff and people were a bit... um, well, they were confused. The foster agency was contacted and Danny cried and said he hated being there, and they moved us.'

She heard Todd sigh but didn't open her eyes. She just wanted it all out.

'Then we came here, to Much Wenlock, and we were placed with Ida and Jim. They were just the greatest people and we started again, a new life where Danny could be himself and I was happy and... we were all happy. I thought we were all happy anyway... but Danny wasn't. Not deep down. What that woman did to him had made space in his heart for something wrong; something that festered and grew. He talked to me about it but I tried to ignore it, tried to talk him round, telling him we were okay now. We finished school in 2008, both did okay but didn't want to carry on. We talked about going somewhere and getting jobs, you know, normal teenage stuff. Then he was buying books on cults from around the world and dark magic practices, and some of it was kind of interesting but there was something that took hold of Danny and he became different, secretive, even with me. And then he told me about the girl by the swings. He had talked her into going into the churchyard and...' She curled her prayer hands into fists and held them against her heart which was galloping like a startled horse; running to get away from what had frightened it. She heard Todd shift in the chair, the leather giving a quiet squeal as if in astonishment at what it was hearing.

'He didn't do anything because he got caught but it consumed him. Because he thought he had found an answer—the secret to getting out of him everything that woman had done to him, all the crazy thoughts and feelings. And so, he told me he needed my help; he needed to take the life of a child that looked like the woman's dead child, the child she'd tried to turn him into, because the book said when this tribe in... somewhere in Africa, or... I don't know... when they had a troubled soul in the tribe, that person had to extinguish the life of a pure soul—a child—and watch the life disappear from them. They had to inhale that last breath and then their soul would be cleansed.' Miranda's final words came out at such speed and with such force that her eyes flew open, and she felt the room spin and all the breath leave her body. In one movement, Todd was beside her on the sofa, pulling her into him, rocking her as his silent tears fell, crying for himself, for his child and his dead wife and the crushed souls of the two young people who had felt forced into such actions as to render them smothered and unable to breathe their own life.

'But it didn't work.' Her voice was muted, hot breath against his shirt. 'And he felt so horrible for what he had done. It hadn't worked and your child was dead, and it is the most horrible thing I have ever seen and have ever done. I wish to God it had not happened, and I am so, so, so sorry... so sorry, so sorry...'

Todd pushed her back so he could look at her. 'I forgive you, Miranda.' He moved her red curls from her face and stared into her wide eyes, her brain unable to process what she was hearing through ears that thrummed with energy and emotion.

'Thank you. Thank you, God,' she muttered, pressing herself back into his body and letting her tears flow again.

| 24 |

'Don't be too hard on her.' Jim stood propped against the sink as Ida swallowed another glass of water. Lane had removed herself to the lounge to replace the photograph of Danny and Miranda, still very much in the dark about this young man and hoping for real answers now.

Kath's eyes quickly took in papers tacked to a corkboard next to her and spied a bill yet to be paid. 'Mr Costain, Mrs Costain, you clearly have information that can assist us with the investigation into the murder of Daisy Prospero.' At the word murder, Ida's confident, almost defiant, demeanour had disappeared now, and Kath knew that if she pushed her, she would break.

'In fact,' Kath went on, 'if it appears you withheld this information at the time of the murder ten years ago, we are looking at charges and a possible custodial sentence.'

'Now, look here...' Jim took a step towards his wife and put a hand on her shoulder. The colour had drained from Ida's face now, and Kath thought there might be a chance the woman would faint. She was torn between terrier-mode to get the information out of these two as quickly as possible or a gentler approach to tease out the facts. Before she could make a decision, Lane appeared, and Kath knew she could let her take over.

'Tell me about Danny,' Lane said in a smooth, comforting voice that Kath could not hope to emulate. *And who the hell is Danny?* Kath thought and then shut her brain up. This was Lane, leave it, let her go on. In truth, Lane had found a card propped up on another shelf, a pretty card with a fox and a kingfisher, a card you would send for no other reason than you thought the person would like the picture and it was nice to get a card unexpectedly. It was signed by Danny and Miranda.

'Danny and Miranda are our foster children,' said Jim, pulling out a chair and sitting next to his wife. 'We had them from just before they were six. They're not related or anything, just came to us from the same foster home—a nasty place.' Jim placed his big paw of a hand over Ida's, and she smiled at him. She felt ready to speak now.

'They didn't have a good start in life but they had a happy home with us. They were loved... are loved. We haven't seen them for years now, but Miranda wrote every so often—'

'From the abbey?' Kath asked.

Ida's eyes widened. 'How do you know that?'

There was no easy way to do this. The woman's world was going to come crumbling down and Kath felt bad but excited at the same time. It was all coming together.

'Because Miranda is here, down the road, in fact, at Todd Prospero's house. She appeared ten days ago in his garden. She tried to kill herself, but Todd found her. She's been living with him ever since.'

Adrenaline coursed through Ida's small frame, and she stood with such force her chair crashed backwards. 'I have to see her. Is Danny with her?'

Lane gently put a hand on Ida's heaving shoulders. There was not enough air and Ida fought to draw it deep into her body. 'No, he isn't. We were hoping you could help us with that.'

Shirl had texted Kath to say the letters were still a puzzle; Danny had not put an address on his letters to Miranda, only stating Worcester to indicate his whereabouts. It was as if he did not wish for or require a response—the letters were a simple mapping out of his journey. Shirl had said she had a theory and would talk to her when she got back.

'You have to find him. I need to know he's alright. I need to see Miranda. Take me to her, please. I need to see—'

'Love, stop.' Jim stood and held his wife in his arms. Lane moved back and indicated upstairs. Kath nodded and suddenly didn't know how to play this scenario anymore.

'I didn't know,' Ida said quietly, her words lost in the folds of Jim's shirt now damp with sweat and hot breath and saliva.

'What didn't you know?' Kath asked gently.

'We agreed they were going to go to Worcester, to my brother Stan. Much Wenlock is a lovely place but not really for teenagers. They needed to be closer to somewhere more...vibrant. Somewhere new; a change of scenery with more possibilities for them both. Danny helped Stan with his nursery business—he has such green fingers, you know—and Miranda went to the abbey at Callow End to be their housekeeper for a while.'

'Go on, I'm listening,' Kath said.

'On that day, the day it happened, I had arranged for them to get on the coach of one of the parties that came in from Worcester. I'm friends with all the drivers and I thought it was a cheap solution. They stored their bags in the ice house the day before out of the way because they said they were going to have a last look around the woods—Miranda wanted to get some stones she had seen around the pond further on through the meadow.' She stopped, and Jim sat her down in his chair, setting the chair from the floor back upright and sitting next to her.

'It was only sometime later, when the news broke that something had happened in the woods... and then I saw you on the TV making the appeal and...' The sob in her throat caught Ida unaware and she exploded in a fit of coughing. Jim carefully patted her back until the tears stopped clouding her eyes. Kath waited patiently for her to continue, all the time wanting to shake the woman by whatever body part she could grab and squeeze the damn story out of her.

Ida pulled a tissue from the breast pocket of her short-sleeved blouse and blew her nose. 'I didn't know. It was just a feeling that Danny might have done something he couldn't take back.'

'That is the problem with taking a life, Mrs Costain. It cannot be undone. You should have come forward. You know that, don't you? Both of you?'

The husband and wife stared at the detective and nodded submissively.

'I need to see Danny's room now.' Kath brushed past the couple. She wasn't asking permission. She knew Lane was already up there and would be doing her thing. She climbed the stairs and headed for the room with the door ajar—the 'Goldilocks bedroom' as her mother used to call it. 'You know,' she'd say, 'it's not the biggest one or the smallest one... it's the one in the middle and it's just right.' Kath smiled at the memory and entered the room to find Lane sitting on Danny's bed with her eyes closed, holding a book. She opened her eyes and offered the book to Kath.

'This is the book that gave him the idea of taking a life.' She gestured to the small bookcase on the far wall next to the window. Kath moved over to look at the titles. They were all occult-based practices from around the world.

'What are you picking up, Lane?'

'This boy's been conflicted his whole life. I think he felt he had no choice but to do what he did. I'm not defending his actions.' She sighed and stood. 'I think he felt it was the only way to release what was inside… whatever that was.'

Kath spotted a laptop on the small table next to the single bed and picked it up. 'Let's go back to the office, see what Shirl and Marvin have gathered from his letters.'

'What about those two downstairs?' Lane asked.

Kath turned to her from the doorway. 'We'll leave them here for the moment. They can come to the station to make a statement maybe tomorrow. I'll give this to Byron, see if there's anything he can get from it.' She realised her receipt book was in the car but she didn't want to get it and then come back in. They needed to leave these people in peace, relative peace anyway. Because she knew now that Mr and Mrs Costain, loving foster parents and pillars of the local community, would have to come to terms with what their wards had done and find a way to live with it.

| 25 |

There was a buzz in the office now mingled with sweat and stale air. Kath relayed what had just happened at the Costain's as she finished her second bottle of water from the fridge. She was contemplating a coffee and a much-needed cigarette when her phone pinged again.

'Oh fuck...Lenny.' She realised she had not replied to his earlier three texts and he was probably about to send the armed response unit out for her.

Are you ok? Worried now. Hope it's work. See you tonight?

Kath really wanted to see him but didn't fancy going over to his new place. She was tired and fizzing all at the same time, and she knew that once she stopped, she would collapse like a stringed puppet with no one to hold her up.

My place, please. 7. Bring Chinese for 3.

She was going to have a nice evening with Lenny and with Lane, although she hadn't specifically said Lane's name. She was Kath's guest and Lenny would just have to get over himself.

Byron had possession of Danny's laptop and was delving into the information. It had not been hard to get into—not for him anyway—and he was feeling the excitement and the fresh energy even though they were heading towards the end of another day. Ruth was busy, fingers flying over her keyboard. Kath's last instruction as she'd left the Costain house had been for them to furnish her with the last names of the two youngsters. Ida had said there'd been no real talk of adoption; things were good for so many years, they'd just kept things exactly as they were. Miranda's last name was Allendale and Danny's was Halstead. Ida's last plea to Kath had been for her to ask Miranda if she would get in touch. Kath had given a sparse smile and said she would ask. Ruth was doing a preliminary search and would hook up with Byron at some point if and when she hit a dead end. Fostering records could be a nightmare and a lot of children's records were sealed. They knew they might need Byron more than ever now to unpick the glue on those digital envelopes.

Kath felt a surge of pride as she watched Byron. She had picked a good one in him. He was confident but not cocky, affable without insincerity and his knowledge was beyond valuable to the team. Byron suddenly looked up at her as if her thoughts had pushed his head in her direction.

'Did you want to ask me something... or something?'

'No,' said Kath. 'I was just thinking how lucky we are to have you.'

'Oh...thanks. I'm glad to be here. I just had an idea but—'

'Whatever you need, I told you that,' said Kath. 'Tell me what you need and I will make sure you get thanks. I'm you can do that stuff you do outside the confines of our legal system and I will pretend I know nothing about it.' She grinned. Illegal activity had a special frisson with police officers who were bound by so many laws and restrictions. There was breaking the law and then there was bending those rules into impossible yoga positions and doing it with a cheeky grin and a friendly wave.

'No, it's okay, I was just thinking I could run Danny's face through the facial recognition software I managed to...obtain...but I don't have a photo, so—'

'So, it's a good job I have this then.' Lane pulled a photograph from her pocket—the one she had found in the photo frame at the Costain house. She crossed to Byron's desk and gave him the picture of the smiling redhead and the surly blonde boy. Byron took the photo from her and gazed into her deep brown eyes.

'In my head, I'm kissing you in a non-threatening, non-sexual way to show my gratitude.'

Lane put her hand on his shoulder. 'And my cheek accepts your kiss.'

Kath grabbed her cigarettes and nodded to Shirley who joined her at the door. Shirl and Marvin had been talking over the content of the letters with Ruth and Byron and an idea was coalescing in her frazzled brain. Lane walked downstairs with them. She was going back to Kath's cottage to rest and wait for the promised Chinese takeaway and an interesting evening with Lenny. She had always enjoyed winding him up on their previous encounters but she thought she might even be too tired for that kind of sport today.

Kath and Shirl positioned themselves under what Shirl was now calling her tree. It was too hot to smoke and too hot for the coffee in Kath's hand but, then again, it was really too hot for anything. But at least they were alive to moan and complain. Daisy never got to complain about anything. Todd had said she was such a happy child and he felt she would have grown into a happy girl and a happy woman. Kath's guts tried to process the absence of food and sudden onset of hot caffeine and responded with gurgles which Shirl politely chose to ignore.

'So, tell me this theory.' Kath sipped more liquid.

'Well...' Shirl blew a jet of smoke into the tree branches. 'It seems like Danny's trying to tell Miranda about his progression into turning into someone else. I think it's an identity thing. Byron shared some more stuff about this Errimya practice—taking purity into your body to heal whatever bad stuff is inside. But I don't think it worked, like Lane said.' She moved around, almost pacing, under the trees, sorting her thoughts into some sort of coherence. 'He's frustrated, angry but not... I can't seem to put it into words...' She laughed and took another drag of her cigarette. 'It almost feels like I'm taking on his confusion from his letters. It's weird.'

Kath stared at Shirl, an idea forming, not noticing the dead filter in her hand. 'Christ. Do you think he did it again…killed another child? Oh my God, what if we've got a spate of…'

Shirl threw both of their cigarette ends in the dirt. 'Actually, I don't think he did. It did occur to me too, though, so I asked Byron to check on child abductions, murders, accidents even, in the Worcester area. Nothing obvious that points to him having done it again.'

Kath exhaled, put her mug on the ground and lit another cigarette. 'But why?' Shirl raised an eyebrow but let Kath continue. 'Okay, let's put ourselves in his shoes. You've got this shit inside you and you think the only way to get it out is to do what you did. If it didn't work, why wouldn't you just keep doing it until you get a result?'

'I see where you're coming from,' said Shirl, trying to place Kath's words in line with Danny's words, 'but, God help me for saying this, it feels like he has genuine remorse.

He doesn't actually say it in those exact words but it's like he's looking for other answers; other ways to get the result he needs. Oh, I don't know anymore. I think I've had it for today.'

'Let's start again tomorrow,' Kath said, grinding out her cigarette. They made their way back upstairs. Kath needed to round off the day with a plan for tomorrow. And they all needed a good break. Policing was a continuous balancing act; getting the work done, the tedious, the active, the adrenaline, the frustration and the going home, shutting the door, taking a bath, going to a concert, getting away from it so you could come back with fresh eyes and new vigour. She knew her team, like herself, never left it completely in the office. But they all had their mechanisms for coping and now Kath had Lenny for sharing and soothing, and she smiled at the thought of seeing him.

'Byron, go home.' Kath threw him one of her famed mean stares as she grabbed her handbag and stuffed her cigarettes and phone into it.

'Mmmm...yep... in a minute, I'm just going to—' His hair fell in front of his face as he hunched over Danny's laptop.

'Now, Byron. It'll still be here tomorrow.'

He looked up, saw her look and gave in, starting to shut down all his tech.

'Have a good evening, people.' She made for the door as the famous ting ting sound from the TV show *Law & Order* punched into the air. Everyone stopped what they were doing and swung around to the location of the noise. Marvin's face reddened as he turned his mobile phone over and lay it on the desk.

'Er... seems I might have a date.' He squirmed at the glares he was getting, all in good humour, he knew, and felt a ripple of anticipation in his gut.

'Really, Marvin?' Ruth sniggered. 'That's your fucking text alert sound?'

'What?' He stood, pretending to be chastised. He secretly loved the ribbing of his female teammates and often played to the gallery. 'It's a good show. It's my way of relaxing when I get home.'

'Yep, watching crime dramas all night is a great bubble bath for the mind.' Shirl shook her head and burst out laughing. They all joined in, and soon the room was filled with a tension-relieving laughter they all needed, even at the expense of a red-faced colleague.

'Well,' Kath said from the top of the stairs, 'just make sure you practice safe relaxing tonight. Ting ting.'

Lenny set down the bags on the worktop and pulled Kath into his arms. They kissed—the halfway kiss between long, sensual, building up to something more and the kiss of remembrance of hours gone by. Lenny pulled back first as Kath's stomach made more noises.

'Oh yes,' said Lenny, 'I forgot all about the getting to know your partner's intimate noises stage.'

Kath stuck out her tongue and began emptying the bags, wincing as the foil containers still had enough heat to make her fingers smart. 'It's all about the burps, farts, wee dribbles and snoring at our age,' she confirmed, pulling off the lids and steaming her face in the aroma of her mushroom chow mein. She looked back at him as he pulled plates from the cupboard, already familiar with her kitchen layout and what lay in each drawer and cupboard. 'And I can't wait for it all,' she added quietly.

Lenny froze as Kath added a third plate to the two he'd just set out. 'Wait... I forgot. you said dinner for three. Who's the third?'

Lane appeared in the doorway, and Kath felt Lenny's energy change.

'Lenny, Lane is my guest, and we are going to sit down and have a relaxing meal with perhaps a little alcohol, and it will be lovely.' She snapped the last part of the sentence into his face, pulled a spring roll from a container and threw it onto her plate.

'Sweet and sour okay for you, Lane?' Lenny looked at the psychic he had never really got along with at a professional level. But Kath was eager for him to at least make an effort. And he was going to do whatever Kath wanted.

'Sums up my personality perfectly, Lenny,' Lane teased, and Lenny couldn't help but smile.

| 26 |

Kath woke early the next morning. The sun poured
through the window and lay across Lenny's back. She
propped herself on one arm and looked at him. She still had
perfect images of him as a lanky fourteen-year-old passing
notes to her in school classes. But with the good memories
came the bad, and the face of Donna Partington flooded
her brain. She usually pushed them down and busied
herself with something else until she forgot, but this time,
she decided to run with it, to feel all those emotions again
and deal with them once and for all. Kath and Lenny had
had one of those stupid teenage fights about pretty much
nothing. After eighteen glorious months together—when
you are fifteen, every day is glorious with your fabulous
boyfriend—she had spat some horrible words at him, and
Donna Partington had been there with her Farrah Fawcett
hair and lean body to console him. Kath pushed on as she
came to the sequence where she had gone after Lenny
an hour later and found him in their special place in the
barn at the back of his parents' house, literally rolling
round in the hay with her. Kath felt tears coming now
as she remembered looking at the two of them with such
astonishment mixed with horror. Shame had reddened
his face and wilted his penis as Donna had just looked

up at Kath with her small breasts exposed and her hair still artfully arranged. Kath wanted to stop now, stop the remembering, but it was too late. She let the tears flow and a small sob escaped her with a long breadthens, as if in tune with her breathing, opened his eyes and saw her distress.

'Oh, my darling.' He pulled her into his arms, and she wetted his chest with her sorrow. He stroked her hair, not even asking what was wrong. He didn't need to. Whatever she was experiencing, he would just hold her and get her through it. That was his job now. It had always been his job. He had just had to do it from afar for so many years. She pulled away and looked up at him, at the same time reaching behind her for a tissue from the bedside table.

'I've got snot on your chest.' She blew her nose, and a robin that had perched on the windowsill flew off at the sound.

Lenny watched her clean his smooth chest with another tissue, and he smiled. 'Don't mind, don't care, my love.'

Kath allowed herself to sink into the feeling of vulnerability—not a place she was used to but acknowledged to herself it was okay. She felt an overwhelming desire to confess to him now; to tell him her darkest secret. But bed was never the time to do that. It was too much. And she had to focus on work now. The case was moving so fast. It would keep, she decided as she moved out of his reach and pulled on her dressing gown. She could hear Lane moving about downstairs, heard the kettle and smelt the coffee. 'I love you, Lenny,' she said from the doorway. He moved his body into last night's clothes and followed her downstairs.

Lane had set out two other mugs and had moved herself into the back garden, sitting at the patio table and gazing out at the cattle in the field beyond the trees. Lenny and Kath followed her, carrying their drinks, and Kath lit a cigarette. Noone spoke for a moment, afraid to throw a stick into the wheel of peace and tranquillity. Lenny was the first to break the silence.

'What's the plan for today, then?' He sipped his coffee and looked at Kath. She had outlined where they were up to so far last night within a very amiable atmosphere where Lenny had been polite to Lane and she had not said or done anything to rile him. Instead, she'd filled him in on their progress, extolling the virtues of Byron and his eagerness and talent, expressing gratitude yet again for such an amazing gift and the help he had brought to the team. Lenny had secretly had some reservations about using a psychic and a computer wizard that could hack into all manner of delicate records but he had to admit that it was all working perfectly, hopefully within the confines of the law. He knew Kath had a propensity for skirting the rules and had been forced to back her decisions on several occasions in the past where her judgement had been questionable. But he had had her back then, as he always would, personally and professionally.

'Well'—Kath blew her smoke away from his face—'first, we'll see if Byron has pulled anything from the photograph. I'll need to check on Todd and Miranda, see what's happening with them. The Costains are coming in to make a formal statement but I don't think there's anything else they can provide. It's all about finding Danny now; there may be more clues on his laptop but that's for Byron again. It may just be that there's nothing else there to help us. After all, he did leave it behind. There can't be anything on it he needed, otherwise it would have gone with him to Worcestershire.'

Lane stood. 'I don't know where you plan for me to be but I thought I would just come in with you and take it from there, if that's okay?' She moved past Lenny and laid a hand on his shoulder. She stopped and looked at him and he felt something shift inside. He had politely questioned her about her abilities last night, as gently as he could without sounding like a complete know-it-all, arrogant arse, and she had, in turn, described what she tried to do within each case. He still didn't get the 'feelings' she got but, in deference to Kath, he was prepared to accept it.

'Handkerchiefs,' Lane said. Lenny just stared at her. 'I feel handkerchiefs were important to you growing up.'

Lenny set his lips in a thin line and felt a fluttering in his chest. 'What do you mean?' His mouth was dry now.

She stared at him, the intensity of her brown eyes burrowing into his skull. 'I feel a heat—your mother was very grateful to you.' She removed her hand. She shot a look at Kath and moved into the kitchen.

Lenny looked at Kath, astonishment on his face as he realised Lane was referring to the fact his mother, preparing her son for the world, had taught him how to bake and cook and do the washing and ironing from an early age. His favourite thing, and the first thing his mother had shown him, had been ironing his dad's handkerchiefs. They were just enough to start off with and Lenny had enjoyed the feeling of taking a small piece of creased material and pressing down the heat of the iron, watched over by his mother, and making it into something that resembled a mini ice rink, smooth and white. He could still smell the aroma of the ironed squares.

'How the hell...'

Kath shrugged, grinning inside and blowing smoke, trying not to collapse into a fit of giggles. And suddenly it dawned on Lenny.

'You.' He shook a finger at her and moved quickly into the kitchen where Lane was attempting to make scrambled eggs without bursting into laughter.

'She told you, didn't she?' Lenny said in an accusatory tone. 'She let slip that little nugget from my childhood that only a handful of people know about and you used it on me.'

Lane laughed and held up her hands briefly, then returned to tumbling the eggs in the pan. 'Just a wee joke to start the morning off, Lenny.'

Kath entered the kitchen, put down her empty mug and slid her arms around his waist, giggling into his back. He gave in and let the two women have their moment.

Lane pushed the finished eggs onto plates and set bread into the toaster. 'I told you not to piss off the psychic.'

He smiled as he laughed with them. They ate eggs together, this moment not of dead children and disturbed teenagers but of joy and happiness and contentment. And they revelled in it, as they knew these moments were too rare and should be acknowledged and cherished.

Lane followed in her car behind Kath to the station. It was still early but Kath was eager to get going and guide the team into their next assignments. Traffic crawled behind a tractor and so Lane was able to reflect on the case so far. She wasn't sure how much longer Kath would need her; most of her work had been completed, the main players and locations had been touched by her in the psychic sense. The only person remaining was Danny himself and she wasn't sure she wanted that much close contact with the man he had become. In truth, she was scared she was feeling an overwhelming sense of care for this boy that had felt so conflicted he'd felt his only choice was to resort to murder to clean his own soul. She had no feeling yet from his letters to Miranda. Sitting on his bed had produced the sense of conflict, and she had no handle on how this would pan out when they eventually caught up with him. Kath would let her know what she wanted. She was methodical and had a sense of organisation that looked like chaos but was actually structured.

As the momentum of traffic picked up, so did her thoughts. A few weeks ago, she'd been in New York, helping out on a murder case with the NYPD, and the start of the year had seen her languishing in the cold north winds of County Tyrone with her cousins and uncle and aunt. Whenever she was called upon to assist, the family always joked about how she must have seen it coming. The joke was replayed but never seemed old and they all always laughed. But she never did know where she was going to be next. And she liked her life that way.

The two cars carrying the detective and the psychic finally pulled into the station car park to be met by Shirl who was finishing her fourth cigarette since getting there half an hour before.

'I was gonna text you if you hadn't turned up in ten minutes.' She propelled Lane and Kath through the doors and herded them up the stairs to the office where Ruth and Marvin were standing next to Byron's desk. Kath threw her bag under the table and moved in front of his desk, peering over the monitors. She felt the shift, the knowing, the indescribable sense that something huge was about to erupt.

'Speak.'

Byron took a breath and swept his hair back over his hunched shoulders. 'So, I set the facial recognition software to run overnight with the photograph Lane supplied of Danny. I arranged the schematic to capture and enhance—'

'Stop with the shit and get to the good stuff.' Kath almost barked the words. She had had enough now of all the peripheral stuff and the weird explanations of how the bloody stuff worked. Facts—they were what she needed now.

'I found him,' Byron said.

| 27 |

'Fuck me, we caught a break, you little beauty.' Ruth couldn't help herself. She grabbed Byron by the shoulders, turning his face to hers, and planted a kiss in the middle of his forehead.

'I believe that's sexual assault if you want to press charges,' said Shirl.

'He can press charges later. Now, you need to tell me where this guy is.'

'It's a bit strange,' Byron began, 'I found him on CCTV outside what looks like a derelict building, possibly an old shop, down the bottom of somewhere called The Tything in Worcester.'

'Oh, that's just great,' Ruth said, walking away to the coffee machine and flicking the ON switch with more force than was needed. 'You know what that means, don't you?' She looked at Kath who nodded, sliding herself into her own chair and picking at the leather coming off one of the arms.

'Pirate Sal,' Kath said, nodding to herself.

Marvin was the first one out of the gate. 'Who the hell is Pirate Sal?'

'Ruth, please do the honours.' Kath dug into her bag for her smokes as Ruth pulled herself up to her full height as

if requiring extra grit and bravado for what she was about
to impart.

'Pirate Sal runs Worcestershire and Herefordshire and a
little bit of Shropshire, I now believe. No law enforcement
officers venture into the two main counties without
clearing it with her first.'

'Shouldn't that be the other way around?'

'Yes, Marvin, you would think, wouldn't you?' Ruth
continued, making the coffee at the same time as talking,
raising her voice as the machine spat at her for being so
forceful. 'But that's not the case. Our beloved leader over
there has an up close and personal relationship with her,
which is fine. Generally.'

Lane, Byron and Marvin were looking to Kath for
further details now. Kath pulled her shoulders forward,
gave a cat-like stretch and sank back into the leather. 'You
know they say you shouldn't judge a book by its cover?
Well, Sal is one scary-ass chick to look at.' Kath welcomed
the mug Ruth handed her.

'And?'

'Marvin, patience.' Ruth patted the top of his head as she
passed him to sit at her own desk.

'Well,' Kath continued, 'Imagine Rebel Wilson crossed
with Jabba the Hutt.'

Lane shrugged. 'I've never heard of her before,' she said,
looking at Marvin. He was barely keeping his body in
check, like a Springer Spaniel who knew the ball was
sitting just out of sight behind its owner.

'Her family have been operating in Worcester for years.
Sal took over from her mum when she passed eleven years
ago, and she has a loyal team behind her.'

'What does she actually do, though?' Marvin asked.

'It's going to sound a little bit crazy but bear with me. Her family ran a lucrative but fair protection organisation. When Sal took over, the loyalty and respect went straight to her, no questions. She imports firearms occasionally'—Kath shot Marvin a warning look as his mouth opened, about to run off on its own—'and runs semi-legit massage emporiums.'

'That's copper code for brothel.' Ruth threw the comment at Marvin who threw a middle finger gesture right back at her.

'And some other things we do know about and probably a lot more we don't,' Kath finished.

'And no one arrests her because...' Byron left the question hanging, but Ruth was quick to pick it up.

'Because she basically polices the counties better than we could hope to. And most of the time, we do not have the manpower to deal with some of the shit that goes down. She saves us time and money and retains her standing in the community.'

'So, I really need to know—'Marvin started.

'Yep, already know what you're going to ask. She's called Pirate Sal because she only has one leg.'

'What happened to the other?'

'I shot it off,' said Kath, smiling.

'Whoa.' Marvin leaned forward, completely in awe of his boss right now. 'Tell us.'

'Ruth and I started off together all those years ago in the armed response unit and were drafted in some years back as a favour...well, they called me in because Sal asked for to. And is another story for another time. We weren't always polite girls in skirts, you know. It's a long tale but I'll give you the short version. Sal was in a hostage situation with a really nasty Romanian drug lord and his crew. She messed with the wrong Marine, as they say in the movies. We were called up to respond—'

Marvin's excitement overtook him. He was a big film fan and couldn't help himself. 'It's *Speed*, isn't it? The beginning scenes... you shot the bloody hostage.'

Kath nodded, and Byron let out a gasp. 'It was the only way to incapacitate him. He had Sal as a shield. She gave me a look and I knew what she was asking me to do. She's one scary-ass chick, as I said. So, I shot her in the thigh, hoping for a through and through and praying I was still a good enough shot to miss the femoral artery. That is exactly what happened. He dropped Sal and collapsed, we got him. It was all a bit chaotic and I don't remember all of it; lots going on. We tried to save Sal's leg until the paramedics got there. Anyway, hours of surgery later, it was lose the leg or lose her life. Sal told the doctors to "just take the fucking thing off"—her exact words, I believe. So, they did. We have a very special relationship now. I don't have that much contact with her but when I have to, it's really okay. And she is extremely useful. As I am sure she will be this time.'

While the rest of the team buzzed and chatted about what they had just heard—Shirl having heard it before and Ruth having actually been there—Kath felt her gut tighten. Sal was more to her than she had just let on. Sal had been grateful to Kath for saving her life, her reputation and her business interests and had told her whenever she needed the favour repaying, she would be there for her. Kath had that favour tucked away deep inside her for a rainy day, and she knew now that the rainy day was coming, rolling in with storm force. Her life was changing; Lenny was going to be a permanent fixture and Lane already had an insight into what she'd done. Sal was her way out; her redemption. And it felt good to have that safety net.

'Marvin, take that stupid look off your face.' Shirl picked up her cigarettes and made for the door. Kath stood to follow.

'Yeah, but...wow. Real life John McClane in a skirt. Sorry, Boss... but wow...'

'It was hardly *Die Hard*, Marvin.'

'Don't tell him that,' said Ruth. 'At least ham up our glory moment for the crowd.'

Shirl pushed Kath gently through the doorway, eager for nicotine. 'Come on, Calamity Jane. Need me a smoke.'

They exited to the sounds of Marvin pulling out every shoot 'em up film reference he could think of, and Kath grinned to herself. It had been exciting in the ARU. It was where she and Ruth had met, and they had instantly clicked and become a dependable team. Both their shooting skills were excellent but they both knew the career span of an ARU officer could be short-lived and restrictive. Kath wanted more; to move up the detective ranks. And Ruth wanted to go with her although she had stopped at the point where she was and had no plans to move up. Stability was now the key for Ruth. She knew she was one hell of a support crew for Kath and that was where she knew her place to be.

'So, what's next?' Shirl lit their cigarettes and leaned against the tree trunk.

'I think you and Marvin should go and see Todd and our little redhead accomplice. Take her statement. Unless she wishes to make a full confession, we can't proceed. She's been no help locating Danny but we've already got that covered and she may genuinely not know... to be honest, I feel that's the case.'

'You don't think she's hiding anything else?'

Kath shook her head. 'I hate to admit it but I think she is remorseful. Let's face it, she chose to die in his garden having lived with nuns for years... that's a lot of seeking forgiveness. I don't like it but I can't dispute the facts.'

'These are the facts of the case and they are undisputed,' said Shirl.

'You quoting *A Few Good Men* at me, Miss Shirley? Fuck me, Marvin is having a bad effect on you.'

They laughed and smoked and took in the rising momentum of the day ahead. The case had all its wheels now and was moving forward. Unless one of those wheels came off, it was straight on down the road to the courts and the CPS. Do not pass go. Go directly to jail.

'Ruth and I will go to Worcester. Might take Lane with us as well.'

'This could be the day,' Shirl said quietly. 'This could actually be the day you get him and bring his child-killing ass back here.'

'Copy that,' said Kath.

| 28 |

Miranda was filling Samson's bowl as Todd entered the kitchen. The cat was diving nose first into the pellets and Miranda poured the rest over his ears.

'Your cat is impossible.' She replaced the bag in the cupboard.

'But he adores you.' Todd smiled.

'I was going to make some toast and maybe eggs...if you fancy?' She ventured a look at Todd, her hands pushed deep into her green linen trouser pockets, her red crocheted top revealing a skinny midriff. Todd was glad to hear her even mention food. She hadn't eaten properly since her return from the police station. She had cried in his arms for what seemed like hours, and when she was exhausted of all tears and emotion, she had taken herself off to bed with some herbal tea and a heart that should have been lighter from the confession.

'Yeah, that's great. Help yourself to—' He jumped as he heard the front door open. He had forgotten it was Mrs Tinkerson's day and wasn't sure he was ready for either of them to face her. She entered the kitchen with her usual basket and set it down on the table, firmly pushing Samson away from her leg.

'Weather's too warm for much cooking at the moment, so I've prepared a quiche and salad for you. Both.' She cast a glance at Miranda who had shrunk back against the worktop.

'Thanks, Mrs T.' There was an uncomfortable silence as Mrs T took off her cardigan and went to the utility room to get her cleaning caddy. Todd shrugged at Miranda, smiled and handed her the eggs from the fridge. Mrs T marched through the kitchen and went straight up the stairs.

'She always makes me feel like I've done something naughty,' Todd said, lowering his voice and grabbing his cigarettes off the table. Miranda handed him coffee she had made earlier while pacing the kitchen and waiting for him to come downstairs. He had such a calming effect on her now. Every time she was parted from him, there was a danger in her; a feeling that could turn to dread if she didn't keep a handle on it. And the way to do that was to stay within his reach.

They moved outside with drinks and smokes and walked like old friends through the grass, Miranda pointing at plants, pretending to know what they were; Todd nodding and smiling, pretending to be the slightest bit interested. The cuffs of his jeans soaked up the moisture from the sudden overnight storm while dark stains spread up Miranda's trouser legs. But neither of them paid a mind to the damp and the mini cobwebs that brushed the fabrics and clung to their hair as they passed under the overhanging small trees and shrubs bearing coloured jewels of blooms, large and small. They both understood time together may be short now; the police would be back. Miranda had yet to make a formal statement and there was more to reveal and examine. But they could both play make-believe until then and enjoy the soft snorting of cows that floated to their ears from the meadow at the bottom of the garden.

They both turned to face the house as they heard tyres crunching across the gravel on the front driveway. Andrew appeared from the side of the house and stopped as he saw Miranda and Todd standing in the middle of the grass. Even from a distance, Todd could sense the tension in Andrew's body as they walked towards him.

'Just came to check on you to see you're okay,' said Andrew, making a point of ignoring Miranda who moved ahead of the two men into the sanctuary of the house.

'I'm okay, mate. Really.'

'What's happening with her?' Andrew slipped an arm across Todd's shoulders, stopping him from following Miranda.

'I think the police are coming by, probably today, to... I don't really know... maybe take her back to the station.'

'She should be locked up,' Andrew said.

'Come inside, mate.' Todd manoeuvred him gently through the door into the kitchen. Miranda was in the utility room, busying herself with doing not very much but wanting to keep out of Andrew's way. The two men walked in silence to the lounge. Miranda flitted from kitchen to utility room and back again. Mrs T was still upstairs, and she wanted a place to hide away from people that would judge her; that wouldn't understand.

'I don't understand you, Todd.' Andrew sank into the armchair. 'Why is she still here?'

Todd perched on the edge of the sofa. 'I can explain.' He leaned forward, arms resting on his knees, hands talking as much as his mouth as he told Andrew about his heart to heart with Miranda, her confession and his willingness to forgive her. Andrew listened quietly, trying to understand his friend and his motives. He wished he could get it but his anger got in the way every time. When he felt Todd had finished, he leaned forward to the coffee table between them. Dozens of photographs were spread across the surface—random shots of Todd when he was younger including school photos of their friends. He plucked at a corner of one hidden beneath a pile and stared at it, grinning.

'Christ. I'd forgotten about this.' He turned it to show Todd.

'Yeah, I got them out to show Miranda.' Todd smiled. 'We got talking about when we were young. She hasn't got many photos herself, just the odd one of her mum—they reconnected about eighteen months ago. I told you she was fostered, right?' Andrew nodded and Todd continued, not wanting to break the thread. 'Well, her real mum sent a letter to the fostering people and asked for it to be sent on to Miranda. They obliged and Miranda agreed to meet up with her. Her mum dropped dead from a brain aneurysm six months later.' Andrew felt a stirring of emotion for the girl, abandoned then getting to face the woman who had done it before losing her all over again.

Todd went on, 'She was asked if she wanted anything from her mum's house. She took a few bits of jewellery, her birth certificate, a few photos and that was about it.' His face clouded as he thought back to the previous evening and her reliving the experience of reuniting with her birth mother.

Andrew passed him the photograph. It showed Todd and Andrew as fifteen-year-old boys about town, snowy mountains in the background, other people visible beyond the smiling faces outside the ski resort cafe.

'Yeah... the school skiing trip to Austria. God, we look so young.'

'Handsome and carefree,' said Andrew. 'Billy Big Nose took that one. He ate more snow than anyone.' They laughed, and the tension eased. Andrew moved to sit next to Todd, pushing his fingers through the other photos. He glanced back at the photo in Todd's hands and pointed to a couple of girls in the background.

'A memorable trip with those two.' He pointed to a blonde and a redhead. A spark of remembrance fired in Todd's brain as he recalled the other schoolkids at the same resort from a girls' school across the county.

'Lots of flirting, lots of hormones. Our first times.'

Andrew snorted. 'Your first time, mate. I had experience under my belt and the blonde knew it. Can't remember her name, though.'

'Shame on you,' said Todd. 'I think she was Sally, and the redhead was...' He fought to recall the name and grimaced. 'I'm ashamed to say I can't remember my conquest. I hope they don't look back at that trip now and think we were dicks.' Scenes came back to him; him and Andrew on the slopes, both taking quickly to the sport and showing the other boys just how it should be done, taking the piss for days out of Billy Big Nose who failed to do a run without tumbling into white powdered snow. Then the evenings and sneaking into the room the two girls shared and getting to grips with the acts they had only seen in magazines and heard others talk about.

'Good times, mate.' Andrew grasped Todd's hand and they enjoyed the moment. Andrew knew their friendship would survive this stage of Todd's life, however difficult it would be for the both of them.

They heard Miranda approaching the doorway and released their hold. She was holding a wooden tray with two mugs of coffee and a plate of biscuits on it. She had heard the laughter from the kitchen and decided to try and make some sort of peace with Andrew. He was such an important part of Todd's life.

Todd held up the photo for her to see as she stood next to them. 'What a couple of dudes, eh?'

For a few seconds, the tray seemed to hang in the air, *Matrix*-like, coffee spilling from the china mugs, cookies tossed in the air like juggling balls. The tray bounced off the edge of the table as the brown liquid seeped into the cream carpet. The two men stared down at the chaos.

'I have a question,' Miranda said in a hushed voice. 'What are you doing with a photograph of my mother?'

| 29 |

'By the way, how did the date go?' Kath asked as she sat back at her desk. Marvin shuffled papers and pretended to look busy.

'Um...yeah...great, thanks. Might do it again.' He got up and went into the toilet. The women all cast glances around the room and then focused their attention on Byron.

'Spill the beans or we'll have to employ our arsenal of interrogation tactics.' Ruth jokingly glowered at him. Byron was still slightly intimidated but determined to stand his ground.

'He just said he had a nice drink and then took her home.' Byron put his head down, his hair providing perfect cover, and let his fingers fly across his keyboard. Marvin had asked him not to tell the rest of the team his date had been with Kerry Harris, his former colleague. He had had a bit of a thing for her, the first woman he had even looked at seriously since his breakup with his wife. He didn't want it to be just a casual thing; he was winding himself up to being serious about her, if her dad would let him.

The women made humming and tutting noises in an attempt to unnerve Byron, but he remained resolute and silent. Marvin returned and Ruth slapped him lightly on the back.

'It's okay, we're just looking after your best interests, you know that.'

Marvin nodded. 'I know, it's just that I really like her. I don't want to jinx anything, you know?'

'So...' Kath stood to address the room, her brain now switched to attack mode regarding the case. 'Ruth, did you get anywhere with the foster records for Miranda and Danny?'

Ruth went to her desk and tapped a few keys. The monitor sprang to life. 'Miranda Allendale has nothing, same with Danny Halstead, Daniel Halstead... tried all sorts. I passed it to Byron to do one of his algo... well, you know. If we can't find out by conventional means—I even telephoned the main office, but they won't do anything without a warrant—I thought we could apply for the warrant, but Byron might get something a bit quicker.'

Kath nodded. 'Okay. It might not matter that much now. We have her and we'll have her statement, maybe even a confession. And tonight, I believe we'll have Danny.' She turned to Lane. 'Do you want to come to Worcester with us? If we catch Danny, you may be able to get something from him we can't if he doesn't decide to play ball.'

'Sure thing. As long as I can meet Sal, too.' There was a twinkle in Lane's eyes.

Kath grinned. 'Be careful what you wish for, my lovely. Ruth, you're with me and Lane. I may let you drive.' Ruth moved the muscles of her face into a sarcastic smile. She was the better driver and Kath knew it.

'Marvin and Shirl, go to Todd's, get a feel of what's transpiring between the two of them. Take a statement

from her. You don't need to separate her from Todd if
she's happier with him around. It's weird how she can't
seem to function without him. This connection they have
is... I can't explain it.'

'I think I can,' said Byron, standing, his chair hitting
the wall hard behind him. 'The DNA results came back
from the swab we took from Miranda. It revealed a familial
match with Todd.'

There was a hush across the room.

'Ladies and gentlemen, Miranda is Todd Prospero's
daughter.'

'You're what?' Andrew was the first to speak. Todd simply
stared at Miranda, unable to process what he was hearing.

Miranda's world was in sharp focus now. She felt the
warm coffee turning cooler on her ankle, wondered what
Mrs Tinkerson was going to say at the mess on the carpet
as the coffee spread like bloodstains, saw the stray curl
on Todd's forehead he regularly pushed away just for it
to always return to the same place, Andrew's hands with
tapered fingers. *I bet he plays the piano.* Was that someone
knocking on the front door?

Mrs Tinkerson was now standing behind Miranda,
having heard the crash. She took in the scene, the three
adults staring from one to the other, the crumbs and liquid
on the floor, the wooden tray at an absurd angle leaning
on one corner propped against the coffee table strewn with
photographs now spattered with coffee.

'I'll get the door,' she said.

Todd stood, the photograph still in his hand. He looked
at it now, then back at Miranda. He held it out to her,

and she moved forward to take it from him. Andrew also stood, sinews taut; he wanted to fight but couldn't explain why.

'A school trip to Wildkogel, Austria. This is her and her best friend, Sally. I have a similar photo I took from her house when she died. This is you?'

Before he could reply, a short woman bustled into the room, Mrs Tinkerson following and protesting.

'Miranda?' The woman stopped. She knew there were others in the room but could only focus on the red curls of the person facing away from her. Miranda turned at the familiar voice, and a sob escaped her throat.

'Ida?'

The two women embraced, Ida's head resting against Miranda's collarbone.

'Who the hell is this?' Andrew found his voice, harsh to his own ears but not caring anymore.

Ida released her hold and looked at Andrew. 'I'm Miranda's foster mother.' She looked up at Miranda's face, tiny tears nestling against one cheek. 'The police came to see me. They told me you'd turned up here, and I just wanted to see you, to say I—'

'Don't.' Miranda pressed her finger to Ida's lips. 'Not now.'

She still had the photo in her hand, and she turned back to Todd who had moved closer. Ida stepped back, unsure what to do now she was here. She hadn't really thought through any of this. She had been wrestling all night with the need to see her and had even driven to the house past midnight because of a strange desire to be closer to her foster daughter. The house had been dark, and she had sat there for a while, looking up at the windows, wondering where Miranda was, which room she was in, if indeed she was still there. What if she had run? Reason had finally overtaken her, and she returned to her bed, unable to sleep but running through all the possible scenarios in her head. This scene had not been one of them, and she felt displaced and awkward.

'Tell me,' said Miranda. 'Just tell me you knew her.'

Todd took her hand containing the photo. His heart was beating loud and fast, skipping and tumbling as his brain tried to regulate the rhythm. Andrew stepped forward and put a hand on Todd's shoulder, staring at Miranda through narrowed eyes as his mind turned over the information.

'What is your last name?' he asked.

'Allen-Dale,' she replied. 'It's hyphenated. My mum wasn't actually sure who my father was, so she made a surname for me from the two possible guys.'

The six-foot-two rock star who had commanded stages and arenas around the world, made girls and women and grandmothers faint from pure joy buckled against Andrew who gathered him into his arms and positioned him on the sofa, Todd's face now white, his brown curls sticking to his skin with a sheen of sweat Andrew recognised.

Miranda cried out and threw herself next to Todd, eyes wide, looking at Andrew for answers. Andrew pulled his phone from his pocket, gave his details to the dispatcher and ordered a paramedic team.

'I don't understand,' Miranda muttered as Andrew made Todd more comfortable.

'Todd, look at me. Focus, mate, come on. Regulate your breathing. Remember what I taught you. Breathe with me.' Todd's eyes were glassy. He tried to make his eyes focus on Andrew but wanted to look at Miranda. Blood pushed through his ears like listening through a big seashell at the beach where they told you if you listened hard you could hear the sound of the sea. It was so loud, he could barely make out the words from the lips of his friend.

Miranda went to stroke Todd's face. To move back that annoying curl. Andrew grabbed her wrist and halted the movement. She tried to shake him free but his grip was firm.

'Prospero is Todd's stage name. His real name is Todd Dale.' Andrew took a deep breath.

'I really don't want to say this but… your father is having a heart attack.'

| 30 |

Kath pulled up behind the ambulance. 'What the hell?'

Ruth was out of the car almost before it had stopped and made her way inside, followed by Kath. The room was busy with people. Two paramedics were attending to Todd who lay on the sofa, Andrew was talking to them and Miranda was standing next to the sofa, crying. Ida Costain was in the hallway, hands fluttering in front of her, not knowing whether to go or stay. Mrs Tinkerson was standing in the kitchen doorway with a cloth and dustpan and brush in her hands, her lips in a straight line, taking in the chaos.

'Is he going to be okay?' It was the only question Kath could think to ask given the way Todd looked and the paraphernalia surrounding him from the paramedics.

Andrew stood to give the medics room to manoeuvre Todd to the ambulance. 'He's had a small heart attack, I believe. I'm going with him to the hospital; get him checked out and stabilised. He's had'—he looked over at Miranda who was hovering, wanting to rush to the ambulance—'a big shock. We all have.'

'We have some shocking news of our own to impart, but given his already compromised state, I think it can wait.' Kath was about to reveal their news but Andrew stopped her.

'Would it be anything to do with Todd and Miranda being father and daughter by any chance?'

Ruth's mouth dropped. 'Yes. How the hell did you know?'

'She'll tell you,' Andrew said over his shoulder, nodding his head toward Miranda.

'I want to go with—'

Andrew spun around so fast he knocked against Kath who tumbled into Ruth. She steadied herself, ready to intervene if necessary, as Andrew had the look of unlawful acts in his eyes. Andrew's face was inches from Miranda's, and his spit flew against her cheeks.

'You have done enough fucking damage for one day, don't you think? Stay here. Stay away from him.' He moved outside, and the ambulance set the sirens on and pulled away.

Kath and Ruth looked at each other. This was not how it was supposed to have gone. Mrs Tinkerson pushed past everyone and began clearing the mess from the carpet. Kath was still trying to process what had just occurred and so let the woman continue her cleaning. Ida moved into the doorway, and Kath's hackles rose ever so slightly. Another bloody complication she was not equipped to deal with right now.

'I'll drive you to the hospital if you want,' Ida offered, holding her hand out to Miranda. She glanced at Kath, aware the police officer may try and stop her.

Kath sighed. 'For fuck's sake,' she said under her breath. 'Yes,' she said out loud. 'Go; do whatever you need to do. This will keep, I guess.'

As Miranda and Ida left the house, Ruth shook her head as she watched the housekeeper expertly removing china shards from the shag pile. 'Guess she won't be skipping town any time soon. At least that's in our favour.'

Mrs Tinkerson stood and addressed the two officers. 'That girl has been nothing but trouble since the day she set foot in this house.'

Ruth took a gamble. 'What is your understanding of how she came to be here?'

'Mr Prospero said she was a family friend staying for a few days.'

Ruth raised an eyebrow. This would be interesting. 'But you weren't convinced?'

'The girl had no clothes with her, nothing except a straw bag. 'I cleaned the room, happened to look in the wardrobe in case anything needed dry cleaning... or something.'

Ruth was not going to challenge the nosiness of the housekeeper. She said nothing, hoping she would continue. An old trick of police officers. Generally, they made people wary. People either wouldn't shut up and spilled their entire life story or, if you just shut up and didn't respond, they would fill an awkward silence for you.

'Then, a few days later, the wardrobe and chest of drawers were full of clothes. There was a bag in the bin from Tianna—an exclusive little women's shop in Bridgnorth.'

'You'd make a good detective, Mrs...'

'Tinkerson. Mary Tinkerson. I live in Ironbridge and come here twice a week to keep house.'

'And you've been here how long?' Kath asked.

'Ten years in October. The first eighteen months, I had to work around Mr Prospero. He was severely depressed after the tragic events concerning his child and then his wife. He put a postcard in the village shop—I believe it was Dr Taylor that prompted him to do it—and my friend who lives nearby told me about the job. I had a rather strange interview, I suppose you would call it, and we agreed on terms. I looked after him. I still do. And I can just tell that girl is no good.'

'Thank you,' Kath said, pulling out her phone. 'We will be in touch if there's anything else we need from you.'

Mrs Tinkerson picked up the dustpan and brush and went to the kitchen.

'She's a little bit on the scary side but good for information,' said Kath, getting into the car and putting her phone in the slot under the satnav. 'Will you phone Lane and tell her to meet us outside the station? We need to get going to Worcester. Then call Shirl. Tell her what's just happened and to keep in touch with the hospital. I want to know he's going to be okay.'

Ruth made her calls as Kath sped towards the station. *What a fucking day this is turning into*, she thought, narrowly missing a hedgehog. All this and a meeting with Pirate Sal on the agenda.

'There's not enough nicotine and caffeine in the world for all this shit,' she muttered.

Lane was waiting outside the station with Marvin who was moving from one foot to another. The weather had finally broken after the small storm in the early hours bringing minutes of torrential rain with moments of calm and silence and then another shower. Lane had donned a lightweight jacket, her overnight bag beside her on the grass. It was a given for her that she always had an overnight bag in the boot of her car with a change of clothes, a T-shirt to sleep in and duplicate make-up and the stuff required to get it off again at the end of the day. Ruth buzzed her window down to speak to Marvin as Lane got into the back seat.

'Shirl told me. How is he? Do we know what happened? Can I—'

'Yes, Marvin.' Kath leaned across. 'You can liaise with the hospital. I think he will be okay. He's just had a massive shock. Seems to be the order of the bloody day.'

Marvin nodded. 'Thanks. I'll keep you posted. Anything else you want me to do?'

Kath slammed the car into reverse and Ruth winced at the sound of the gearbox complaining. 'Nothing comes to mind. Stay by the phone.' Kath put her foot hard on the accelerator and drove away.

Marvin took a moment to breathe and look up at the trees. 'Let him be okay. Just take care of him. For me. For all of us.'

'So, are you going to give me a little more of a heads up on Pirate Sal?' Lane leaned forward, head poking through the gap in the two front seats like a tortoise eager to grab a lettuce leaf.

'Okay,' said Kath. 'Quick life history. She was born Salaberga Hoffman. Dad was German, Mother... not actually sure. Anyway, she went to an exclusive girls' school in Worcestershire where she began... cultivating friends and trying out her family history prowess on the underlings. Even as a kid, as a teenager, she was not a chick to be messed with.'

'So, German name. Bit of a mouthful. I can see why she shortened it.'

'It's a very appropriate name. It means "she who defends the sacrifice"'

There were a few seconds of silence as they all took in the significance of the name.

'Anyhow,' Kath continued, 'she had always known about the family business, and it seemed there were no more children on the horizon, no siblings and no male to carry things on, so her devoted parents nurtured her and brought her up to be the figurehead. Retirement isn't really an option in the criminal underworld—someone's either gonna take you out or you die in a hail of bullets trying to get the other guy, kind of thing.'

'All sounds a little dramatic for a teenager.' Lane was trying to figure Sal out; evaluate her psyche before she met her. It wasn't working well in her brain.

Ruth came into the conversation. 'Dramatic doesn't even come close. The kid had seen more death—murder actually—before her twelfth birthday than I've witnessed in my career. I hear tell, and I don't know whether it's an urban myth, her father passed her the gun to kill a particular guy. She did indeed kill him and Daddy smeared the guy's blood on her forehead like they do at the hunt when the kid is present at the first kill.'

'Shit.'

'Like I said, there are some weird and wonderful stories floating around out there. The other part of that story is Dad apparently cut off the guy's thumb and had it framed for Sal. It now hangs on her bedroom wall.'

'Cute story,' said Lane, sitting back and looking out the window. 'Can't wait to meet her.'

| 31 |

The house wasn't as tacky as Kath remembered. The mock Georgian mansion had now been tastefully adorned with climbing plants across the facade, the front gardens landscaped as per Capability Brown's instruction manual and there was the sound of water as the women exited the car. Kath spotted a koi carp pool with a running water supply giving a calm air to the home of the underworld killer.

The man at the front door was sharply dressed, his tailored suit barely encasing his upper arm muscles. He had a tight curl afro and brown eyes that flitted across Lane's face and body with barely concealed admiration.

'Come this way, ladies. Sal is in the drawing room.' He opened the heavy front door and led the way inside.

'My my,' Lane whispered. 'Oh, my day just got a whole lot better.'

Kath smiled and shushed her, eyes taking in the black and white chequered hallway floor and occasional tables with huge bouquets of flowers on them.

'If you didn't know better, you'd think it was a *Poirot* episode or a murder mystery weekend,' Ruth muttered, slightly envious of the space. She loved her three-bed new-build on the outskirts of Shrewsbury but was in a constant state of decluttering to keep the energy flowing and the spaces free from negative vibes. The man stopped at a pair of double doors and gestured for them to go in. Lane smiled at him as he passed them to go back to his post.

Kath nudged Lane with her elbow. 'You're here to work, remember?'

Lane shrugged and grinned.

Kath pushed open the doors, and the two detectives and lusty psychic were greeted with the picture of a black-haired woman kneeling between the open leg and stump of Pirate Sal. The three visitors stood open-mouthed as Sal gasped and grabbed the arms of her wheelchair as an orgasm ripped through her. She let out a sigh like air out of a tyre, and the kneeling woman stood, wiped her mouth with the back of her hand and leaned over and kissed Sal. She moved towards the doorway, and the three women parted to let her through, leaving plenty of space to let the bulky frame pass. She glanced at the women, a sly smile playing at the corners of her lips, and pushed a hand through her black hair, shaved at the sides but with an Elvis quiff that L'Oréal products would never touch.

Sal pushed her dress down and held out her arms. 'Hey, Cagney and Lacey. Nice to see you. And you've brought me a little gift, I see.' Sal eyed up Lane like a Texan picking out a steak. 'Come, sit with me.'

'Gardens are looking good, Sal,' said Kath, sitting at the end of the sofa nearest to Sal in her wheelchair. Ruth and Lane sat next to Kath; they looked like the three wise monkeys sitting on the branch.

'That's Zelda's handiwork. You've just been briefly acquainted. Been with me three years now.'

'She's no Rachel de Thame, is she?' said Ruth under her breath.

Sal smiled. 'Zelda might not be pretty but she has a passion for gardening, and she's adapted some of the space outside so I can use the wheelchair safely and admire her handiwork. She also has a fucking amazing tongue.'

Heat rose in the cheeks of the three women on the sofa.

Kath cleared her throat. 'Anyway, shall we talk about why we're really here?'

Sal made a sweeping gesture with her arm. 'Please, continue.' Her arm fat wobbled with the movement, and she set her hand back in her lap, smoothing the creases from her long blue dress.

'We'd like to go to your club tonight. This is the guy we're after.' Kath passed her the photograph of Danny and Miranda from Ida's house. Sal studied it for a moment.

'Yes, I know him. And he's the one who killed Daisy Prospero?'

'There's little doubt now.'

'Take the sick fuck down with my blessing. All I ask is you minimise the fuss and disruption, if possible. The clientele at the club pay me a lot of money—and I mean a lot of money—to have the safety of anonymity so they can indulge in their particular likes.'

'All tastes catered for, eh, Sal?' said Ruth.

Sal leaned forward as far as her torso fat would allow. 'You have no idea, lovely.' She smiled at Lane. 'You could make some serious cash if you fancied a career change. I see you in leather and chains.'

Lane faked shock but she was secretly flattered. There was something quite mesmerising about Sal. 'I'll give that thought due attention. Thank you,' Lane said graciously.

Sal grinned back at her. 'I guess you can be a psychic forever though, no retirement, no expiration date. Quite a good long-term investment really.'

They all laughed.

Sal rubbed her thumb across Danny's face, feeling the silky sheen of the photo paper. 'He'll be on stage tonight. Usually, he's second on. Check with Erasmus when you get there.'

'He's still around then?' asked Ruth.

'Can't get rid of him; he knows too much... unless I *get* rid of him, if you catch my drift.'

'We always catch your drift, Sal,' Kath said.

'Well'—Sal started to manoeuvre her wheelchair forward—'I've had lunch prepared on the terrace if you'd like to join me.' She moved towards the door. Kath looked at Ruth and Lane. She knew they were both itching to spend more time with Sal and look around the house. They had plenty of time to kill before the show that evening and they hadn't stopped for food for quite a while.

'That would be lovely, Sal. Thank you.' They stood and followed her through into another large lounge area with huge French doors that opened out onto the terrace as Sal had described. Although the day was overcast, the air was close and it was still warm enough to enjoy the outdoor space.

'May I use your bathroom?' Lane asked.

Sal smiled and pressed a button in the arm of her wheelchair. 'Sure thing.' The attractive doorman appeared as if he'd been hiding behind the curtain, waiting for instructions. 'Marcus will show you where to go. The lunch is all cold cuts and salad, so nothing will spoil if you feel the need to have a little guided tour with him on the way back.'

'My day keeps getting better,' Lane said, walking into the lounge closely followed by Marcus.

'You're a naughty girl, Sal,' said Kath, sitting at the glass-topped table, admiring the plates of meat and fish, aubergine slices, avocado and smoked salmon nestling on a bed of frothy dill, and bowls of multicoloured salad items.

'My middle name,' replied Sal, passing some tongs to Kath. 'By the way, before the lovely Lane comes back, I know who she is and what she does, and I want to say I hope you didn't bring her here to get stuff out of me or give me a psychic therapy session.'

Ruth grabbed a bowl of peppers, endive and fennel and spooned some onto her plate. 'No, you're okay. She's been extremely helpful on this case and won't be dipping her toe into your emotional pool.'

'So, how's this new job working out for you, Kath?'

Kath had filled her plate and was slowly working her way through the delicious assortment. 'It's really good. I wasn't sure at first—it's a big transition for me—but I have a good team around me and it feels right. We are on the way to getting our first result and that's satisfying.'

'If you need my assistance with this guy, just ask. But I feel you really want this one all to yourself,' said Sal. She put down her fork and laid a hand over Kath's. 'And you know you still have that favour in the bank, don't you?' She squeezed gently, and Kath's heart rate increased to a roar in her ears.

Ruth busied herself with filling an already overflowing plate, pretending not to listen.

Kath looked at Sal. 'That day might be very soon.' She squeezed back. They released hands quickly as Lane appeared in the doorway.

'Worked up an appetite, then?' Sal asked, gesturing for Lane to take her seat.

'Your bathroom is lovely; very welcoming,' said Lane non-committally, sitting down and tossing her curls over her shoulder. 'I particularly like the frame above the toilet with what appears to be a human thumb in it. Care to tell the story?'

'Happy to share,' said Sal, passing her a small bowl of mayonnaise. 'But you may want to wait until after you've eaten.'

Lane laughed and then turned to the sound coming from the large shed at the far end of the garden area.

'Don't worry,' said Sal with a mouthful of food, 'that's just Zelda in her workshop. She's been creating some metal sculptures for the garden. Very handy with an oxy-acetylene torch. As several people have lived to testify.'

Ruth swallowed, not sure if she could get the next sentence out without choking. 'So... Zelda the welder? Nice.'

'Everyone needs a nickname,' said Sal, smiling. 'I like that, actually. Sounds like the title of a kid's book.' She turned to Lane and started talking as Ruth leaned into Kath and whispered in her ear.

'Not a book I'd read to any kids I know.'

| 32 |

The weather had properly broken now—not unusual for August. The sky was fat with dark grey clouds and thunder rumbled in the distance. The humidity had increased, making bodies sweat just standing still. The air con in Kath's car was keeping the three women almost icy to the touch but they knew a wall of heat would greet them as they stepped out. The road was fairly quiet. It housed a smattering of restaurants, takeaways and pubs dotted with a few small bespoke shops, some of which had fallen foul of the economy and been left to broken and boarded-up windows and layers of grime on the paintwork. Kath found a spot to park as close to the club as she could get. If they were going to successfully pick up Danny tonight, she didn't want to have to walk too far to the car with him. Sal had phoned ahead to the muscle on the door so that entry would be a smooth transaction. The Butterfly Burlesque Club had been started by her three years ago. The frontage was another one of those boarded-up former shopfronts, plywood covering the picture window adorned with graffiti and a patch of a brown substance Kath didn't want to think about naming. Two CCTV cameras were situated above the door. There was no indication from the outside to say what lay inside the building. Sal had confirmed that Danny performed there several nights a week—her star turn, she had called him, and now that star for her was tainted by his actions. She had said the club catered to a very eclectic clientele but would say no more. Admittance was by invitation only and the vetting process for membership was extremely thorough.

Kath knocked on the solid wood door and looked up at one of the cameras.

Ruth pulled down her blue polo shirt. 'I actually feel a little underdressed for this,' she whispered to Kath.

'From what Sal told me earlier, I don't think anyone's going to pay us much attention,' Kath replied. The door opened and a tall, thin Asian man dressed in a black suit and black shirt stood back so the three women could enter. The small lobby area was dimly lit, the last bit of daylight disappearing as the man closed the door behind them. They waited, not knowing where to go next. The man walked to an interior door ahead of them and opened it, a smoky haze filtering up the dark stairway below them.

'Down the stairs, ladies. At the bottom, turn right and follow the music.'

Ruth looked at Kath and made the move to go first. Lane followed next with Kath bringing up the rear. The stairway was darker than the lobby, neon exit signs giving the only illumination. Kath heard the door close quietly behind them and turned back. Years of being a police officer had taught her to always know where the exits were and how she could get out of a situation should she need to. Now, she fought down a desire to run back up the stairs and hammer on the door to be let out. A bass rhythm reverberated through their bodies, the claustrophobic atmosphere adding to the already humid evening. They all turned right at the bottom of the stairs as directed and the stairwell opened out into a large room.

'Wow,' said Lane under her breath.

Individual tables and chairs were dotted around the room. Along one wall was a stage which held a woman with a huge Mohican and chains strapped across her thin, naked body. She stood next to a small mixing deck and turntable—the source of the pulsating sound. Most of the tables were full, groups of twos and threes sipping drinks and chatting. The lighting was still subtle; tall floor lamps with heavy shades stood around the perimeter competing against muted footlights at the base of the stage.

Ruth coughed, her hand covering her mouth as she tried not to draw attention to her and her companions.

'Guess they didn't get the Government memo about the indoor smoking ban,' Kath said in Ruth's ear.

'I hope we don't have to be here too long,' she replied.

A bar area was positioned to their right, running down one wall with a variety of padded stools on the customer side and two young men behind the polished wood, attending to optics and glasses.

'Let's get drinks. Try and look as if we should actually be here.' Kath moved to one of the stools, realised it was too high for her to climb onto with any kind of grace and decided to slouch as nonchalantly as she could against the bar. Lane and Ruth climbed onto stools, and one of the bartenders approached them with a tray holding three old-fashioned champagne glasses, reminding Kath of her early drinking days of ordering Babycham in the vain hope of looking sophisticated. The boy had a shock of dark hair and a beautiful face that was expertly made-up, complete with very long false eyelashes and a Cupid's bow that made Kath envious.

'It's a sad day when men look better in make-up than I do,' Kath said, smiling at the boy as he placed the three glasses in front of them.

'Vintage champagne for Sal's guests,' he said.

The women eyed each other; Kath knew what they were all thinking but she pushed the thought down. 'Thank you. That's very kind.'

Ruth looked at her watch. 'Sal said Danny was on after the first act—Althea, Queen of the Night.'

'That's correct.'

Ruth nearly fell off her stool at the words uttered by the six-foot-seven man who had quietly appeared at her side. 'Shit... Erasmus, don't do that.'

Kath turned to Lane. 'Let me introduce Erasmus Bookbinder, one of Sal's long-time...associates.' She was going to say friend but the description seemed out of place.

'Nice to see you again, DCI Fortune, DS Goodwin. And I am very pleased to meet you, Ms Petreus.' He held out his hand to Lane who took it as she looked at Kath.

'You know some interesting people.'

'Your reputation precedes you, Ms Petreus.' His voice was clipped, hiding the Black Country accent he had fought hard to diminish.

'Nice outfit,' Lane commented.

'This old thing?' He gestured up and down his body, brushing the black leather trousers and silky white shirt which was adorned with what looked like hat pins and small daggers. 'If you need anything, just ask one of our sweethearts behind the bar. I'll be down in the Basement of Base Delights, overseeing the Punishment Princes.' His one eye twinkled, the other covered with an eye patch. The ugly scar at the corner of his mouth crinkled as he smiled.

'Of course you will,' Ruth muttered.

Erasmus moved away in a gliding motion towards the door next to the bar. Lane was laughing quietly to herself, brushing imaginary lint from her linen trousers. 'I know why we're here is really serious, don't think I haven't forgotten that, but I have to say I'm really enjoying myself.'

'I'm sure Marcus the muscle man is saying exactly the same thing to his mum as she serves up his tea,' said Ruth.

Lane feigned an outraged expression but couldn't hold it and giggled like a teenager caught behind the bike sheds. 'Anyway, as I was saying, Erasmus seems like an interesting character.'

Kath downed the rest of her champagne and put down the glass. 'Don't be fooled by his appearance. His real name is Mark Thomas. The eye patch is just for show—he feels it adds gravitas to his personality.'

'Works for me,' said Lane. 'I am wondering what goes on downstairs, though.'

'Take up Sal's offer of a job and you won't need to wonder anymore,' replied Ruth.

'Come on...spill the beans.' Lane nudged her in the ribs and Ruth pointed at Kath. 'She'll tell you.'

Whilst Lane had been enjoying the tour of the bathroom at Sal's house, Sal had explained to Ruth and Kath just what sort of club the Butterfly Burlesque was and what went on there. Before Kath could speak, a woman appeared on stage and announced the show would be starting in ten minutes. Her smile was as bright as her neon green dress, and she manoeuvred the motorised wheelchair with obvious experience.

'It's a cliché but losing her leg has really changed Sal. She was always broad-minded and open and accepting of people's differences but she soon came to realise, even in today's mixed-up world, the disabled and the 'different' people are still marginalised and segregated and not in a good way.'

'I see that.' Lane nodded.

'This club is for people to be able to express themselves; be who they want to be without judgment from the everyday world. We're still hung up on men and women, stating the two specific genders most of us have only ever known. This place allows people to experiment and let out sides of their personalities they feel they have to keep hidden.'

Ruth grimaced. 'I know I'm old-school but it's fucking difficult nowadays not to upset anyone. I'm not afraid to say I'm at a loss sometimes how to address people in case I offend them, and they take me to bloody court for calling them something I shouldn't. They just don't like it. They get upset because I state the bloody obvious, but how am I to know if they want to be known as this, or that? Christ, sorry, I'm ranting.'

Kath continued, 'Yeah, you're right. Our likes and dislikes are still judged. So, downstairs is a collection of rooms that cater for those likes others would say were deviant or misguided. Sal said there are women and men who dish out pain and humiliation for those who want it, performing acts we as police officers would see as arrestable offences.'

The bar boys had snuck up and set fresh glasses of champagne behind them. The women all reached for their glasses at the same time.

'There's even a room where men get dressed up in romper suits and nappies and play tiny children being looked after by 'Nanny'. They get baths and covered in nappy cream and talcum powder and suck from baby bottles and... breasts.'

Lane's eyebrows shot up as she sipped her drink.

Kath went on, 'Apparently, there are high-ranking police officers, judges, council officials who lead such stressful lives that this is their way of relaxing and letting go for an hour or so.'

'No judgement here,' she said, setting down another empty glass. 'I'm just weirdly fascinated, but...' She stopped and put her hands to her solar plexus, her breathing becoming laboured.

'What is it? Lane, are you okay?' Kath grabbed her arm as Lane swayed on the stool. She took a breath and let it out slowly between her lips as her body centred itself. 'I can't explain it to you but I felt something shift. I think it's to do with Danny.'

The jovial mood was now lost to the three women as Lane collected herself. Ruth, too, felt a different energy. She had never claimed to be able to do what Lane did but she did have moments of unexplained clarity, visions, energy shifts and spikes. She generally kept it to herself, but something was welling up in her now, the joking and the banter lost to the feelings.

When Lane spoke, it was more deliberate. 'Tell me, Kath, why didn't we just pick up Danny when we arrived? We could easily get backstage, after all—we have Sal's blessing. So, why wait and watch his act?'

'That's a good question,' Kath said, turning her hands out and shrugging her tension-filled shoulders. 'I just have the feeling we need to see him perform. Maybe, I don't know, it'll give us more insight.'

Ruth interrupted, her senses on high alert now. She was feeling nauseous, and an unpleasant heaviness sat in the middle of her chest. 'Surely we should have just grabbed and gone. We have enough evidence.'

Before Kath could offer any further explanation, the woman in the wheelchair appeared on the stage and the audience applauded. She held up her hand to silence them.

'Ladies and gentlemen, I have an announcement. Unfortunately, due to illness, Althea will not be performing this evening.' A collective groan went up. 'But...' the woman continued, 'I am pleased to say our following act is ready to go and is eager to perform for you. People'—she reversed her chair and made to go off into the wings—'I give you Marguerite.' She exited, and the audience applauded, a few whistles ringing out around the room.

'I thought Danny was on after Althea... I don't under...' The words froze on Ruth's lips as a large wardrobe-type cupboard was pushed onto the stage. A white light lit the item from above, and now it was clear exactly what it was. A clown cupboard. Jointed arms hung from the sides with big fat hands dangling from the end of each arm. The head on top of the cupboard was huge and grotesque; a white face with red, black and yellow circles around the eyes. Huge black eyebrows raised themselves in surprise. The mouth was set in a grin, a red interior with off-white teeth that were out of proportion to the rest of the face. The hat sat on top of the cupboard, a vibrant yellow with swirls of green plaster poking from beneath as hair.

'Dear fucking God...what fresh hell is this?' Ruth muttered.

The music was a seductive rhythm, a sound to sway to, a sound that beckoned with its finger to come and join in. After a few bars, the music built to a crescendo, and suddenly the arms flew upwards and positioned themselves in a crucifix pose. There were a couple of startled gasps from the audience, and Ruth felt her champagne bubbling up into her throat. The cupboard doors were flung wide as the music slowed back to its seductive pace, and from the interior emerged the performer. He held two large, feathered fans in front of him, shielding his body. But his face was exposed, and Lane sucked in her breath at the beauty of him. The blonde man smiled, perfect white teeth gleaming behind red lipstick. Long eyelashes fluttered as he glanced at audience members and flirted with them. The make-up had been done with an experienced hand and his natural hair seemed to float like a halo around him. He fluttered the fans, releasing one out to the side, then quickly swapping them so that the audience could not see the treasure that was underneath. He turned his back and performed the same manoeuvre, allowing glimpses of stocking tops. He wore the highest stiletto heels Kath had ever seen, and she was mesmerised by his ability to move in them. He turned back to the audience, and the music built up again. Lane pushed her hands to her chest, and Kath saw distress in her eyes but turned quickly back to the stage.

The music was a couple of beats to the end as the man on stage with his beautiful face and beatific smile held the fans out to the side to reveal his body. As the audience clapped and whooped with appreciation, Kath swallowed down a mouthful of bile that had risen from her belly. Across his chest, the man had a pair of enormous rubber breasts strapped on, the type that reminded Kath of naughty cartoon postcards from the 1950s. The nipples and areolas were highlighted even further with the same shade of red lipstick that adorned his mouth. The sight was shocking enough but the real surprise was the tattoo of a uterus that spread across his lower torso, artwork so expert it looked as if his body had been slashed open by Jack the Ripper to reveal the beauty inside. The tattoo ran down to his pubis, his penis and testicles tucked back between his legs and held by delicate lace panties in a shocking pink hue. The spotlight from the stage illuminated the image of a tiny foetus, and Kath reached behind her with one hand, unable to look away from the horror, grabbed an empty champagne glass and filled it with stomach acid and vomit.

The man on stage waved and bowed and flicked his fans in a flirtatious manner. He then made his ways to the wings, stopping to give a wink and a final wave before disappearing behind the velvet curtains.

'We need to go. Now.' Kath pulled Lane off her stool. Ruth followed but pulled Kath's arm to halt her motion.

'Wait... what are we doing?'

Kath faced her. 'We are going to arrest that sick bastard, that's where we're going.'

'Him?' Ruth looked at the stage and then back at Kath.

'Yeah, him,' she replied. 'Marguerite is Spanish for Daisy.'

| 33 |

Marvin liked hospitals. He was the antidote to the cliché clung to by so many. He liked the smells, the business, the sense of bad stuff being made right. It was like the atmosphere echoed his own life path. Medical professionals sutured wounds—he and his colleagues sutured emotional wounds, mending whole families, whole communities. He'd dated a nurse and a health care assistant by the time he was twenty. He would linger around the hospital corridors, waiting to pick them up from a shift, soaking up the goodness of the building. This visit was different. He was focused on his destination, and the atmosphere was lost on him as he hurried down the main corridor of the Princess Royal Hospital to the AMU where Todd was still being attended to after his admission earlier. Marvin had telephoned the unit about an hour after Kath had told him what had happened. He'd paced the office, and eventually Byron and Shirl had yelled at him to make the bloody call and get his arse over to PRH to check on his beloved rock star.

He held up his credentials for the sister to see and craned his neck whilst talking to her, explaining he had come to check on Todd.

'You're not going to lock him up, are you?' The sister took him into the unit, to the end bay. The curtains were closed but Marvin spied Todd through the gap, lying back on the pillows, looking tired and worn.

'No, I'm not. Thank you.' He waited for her to leave, which she did, reluctantly, looking back once to see what was transpiring. She knew who Todd was. Hell, the whole bloody world knew who Todd was unless they'd been living in a cave. But the staff had pushed aside their excitement at seeing the star and attended to the man who was having trouble catching his breath and wearing a waxy glow.

Marvin pushed aside the curtain. 'Knock knock.'

Todd turned to him and smiled. 'Who's there?'

Marvin replaced the curtain and sat on the bed. 'Just a guy coming to see how you're doing.' Marvin suddenly caught himself and was about to stand. What the hell did he think he was doing sitting on Todd Prospero's bed? But he rethought and gathered himself, his confidence growing. This was a regular guy who was involved in a police investigation, a regular human with the same blood and sinews and bones as the next man.

Todd held on to Marvin's arm. 'Thanks. It's nice to see a friendly face. It's been a bit of a morning...' He let the words trail off.

'I know what happened,' said Marvin. 'Are they keeping you in? If not, I'm your lift home if you fancy getting out of here.'

Todd managed a grin and pushed himself to a more upright position. He was still clothed and on the top of the bed. 'Andrew's gone to talk to the doctor. I'm feeling better. I don't really want to be here, and I told Andrew to get me released or I'll self-discharge.'

'Stubborn arsehole.' The curtain pulled back and Andrew looked at them both. Marvin stood. 'DC Marvin Henshall.' He held out his hand and Andrew shook it.

'Dr Andrew Taylor.' He turned to Todd. 'I've spoken to the consultant. He's happy to release you into my care if I can't persuade you to stay for the night.'

'Please, Andrew, I'm feeling much better. I just want to go home. Please.'

Andrew nodded. 'Okay, I thought you may say that. I've phoned the surgery and I'm taking the rest of the day off plus tomorrow. I'll stay with you at your place, just to be on the safe side. Mr Khan will give you a final check over and then he has agreed to let you go home, as I'll be with you.'

Todd sighed his gratitude and leaned back against the pillows. 'Marvin has said he'll take us back.' He paused. 'Where's Miranda?'

At the mention of her name, Andrew's face darkened, but he pushed down his annoyance. 'She's with that woman who came with her. They're in the cafe, I think. I... it was suggested they keep a distance while you get checked over and stabilised.'

Todd shook his head. 'I still can't believe what's happened.' He looked at Marvin. 'Do you know?'

Marvin nodded. Kath had filled them all in and he was as gobsmacked as everyone else at the revelation that Miranda was Todd's biological daughter. The repercussions were going to come thick and fast but Marvin's job and first priority was to get Todd home safely and take it from there.

Andrew moved away and stepped past the curtain. 'I'll chase down the consultant and get you out of here. Thank you, Marvin, for the lift home. Much appreciated.'

He left to find the doctor, and Marvin placed himself back on the bed. He was unsure of what to tell Todd now they were on the verge of finding Danny. And he knew the fact of Miranda and Todd being related in the way they were would change the dynamic and possibly the final outcome of the case. He made an executive decision and decided to keep quiet unless specifically asked. Then he would not lie to Todd. He heard Andrew's voice with another voice accompanying him, moving towards the bay. He stood again.

'I'm going to wait in the main entrance for you and then I'll drive you and Dr Taylor back to yours.'

'Cheers, Marvin. Or should I call you DC Henshall?' He smiled. Marvin smiled back.

'Marvin is just fine.'

The café at the hospital was always a hub of chatter and bustle and bodies sliding past tables and clattering crockery as people placed trays on the dirty tray rack at the entrance to the eating area. Miranda and Ida sat in the conservatory-type structure away from the main thoroughfare with coffees gone cold and ripples of shock still running through both their bodies. Miranda had told Ida everything that had happened since she'd arrived in Todd's garden. Ida sat with a shredded serviette in front of her and had started on another.

'I didn't know,' she said again, having already mentioned it countless times since the car journey to the hospital. 'I wish you'd come to me.'

'I couldn't,' said Miranda. She bowed her head. 'I was so ashamed of what we'd done.'

'I thought I'd raised two happy, healthy children.' Ida's fingers worked on the flimsy, white paper. 'Teenagers always change... it's the hormones. I knew that. I just didn't realise…'

Miranda put her hands over Ida's to halt the motion. 'You couldn't have known. I didn't want to be a part of this nightmare but Danny was so... he felt so helpless. I just wanted to help him, but I knew... Oh God, it was so wrong. And now I know she was my sister.'

Ida was sitting with her back to the view of the car park but Miranda saw Todd and Andrew with the young detective constable moving towards a car. She stood, her chair legs screeching across the linoleum floor.

'There he is. I need to see him.' Before Ida could grab her, Miranda had turned and pushed through patients and visitors and was making her way down the corridor to the main entrance. Ida followed, leaving a trail of white confetti behind her.

Marvin opened the back door of his car and settled Todd into the seat. Andrew got into the passenger side but jumped out at an awkward angle as he saw Miranda running towards the vehicle.

'Todd,' Miranda shouted, trying to move past Andrew to the back of the car. Marvin stepped in front of Andrew and firmly held Miranda's arms as she struggled in his grip to get a glimpse of Todd.

'I think it's best if you let us leave. He's still recovering from his heart attack.'

'This is all my fault,' she mumbled.

'Too fucking right it's your fault. Stay away,' Andrew barked. He stood behind Marvin, his hands itching to grab Miranda and throw her to one side. He was generally a mild-mannered, good-humoured GP who his patients adored and his friends admired. But when he was riled, he was a force to be reckoned with and had come close in previous years to losing his composure and doing something he knew he would regret. Luckily, he wasn't one to act purely on impulse.

Marvin continued to stare at Miranda, still in his grip. 'Dr Taylor, please get into the car.' His voice held the authority of his office, and Andrew swallowed his grievance and got in as instructed. Todd gazed at Miranda through the window and put his hand on the glass. She let out a sob and relaxed.

Marvin released his hold and she stood staring at Todd. 'Perhaps it would be best if you stayed away for tonight.' As Marvin spoke, Ida appeared behind Miranda, putting a hand on her arm.

'She can stay with me tonight,' she said to Marvin who nodded and moved around the car to the driver's side.

'Come on, love. Let's go to my house.' She gently pushed Miranda aside as the car purred into life and moved slowly away.

Miranda gave a wave to Todd as he watched her as far as he could through the car window until his head could not turn any further.

'See you soon... Dad,' Miranda whispered.

| 34 |

The applause died in the ears of the three women as they turned to look at each other.

'We're walking into a whole new world of pain.' Ruth turned to Kath. 'Plan?'

Kath pulled out her phone. 'I'm on it. You get Erasmus.' She dialled a number and moved away further down the bar. Ruth beckoned to one of the bar boys. 'Erasmus. Now.'

'Yes, Ma'am.' He quickly moved from behind the bar and went through the door Erasmus had disappeared behind earlier. Kath nodded to herself and looked at Ruth as she ended the call. Before they had made their way to the club, Kath had called Detective Chief Inspector Mary Amos. They had done some of their early training together and had stayed in touch, albeit sporadically, for many years. Kath had asked for a backup car at the club after explaining the situation and briefly filling her in on what was about to go down. Mary had agreed to send an unmarked car, complete with three officers, so that Danny would not have to be in the vehicle with Kath, Ruth and Lane.

Erasmus appeared at a pace and headed towards Kath.

'Take us backstage, Erasmus.'

'Okay. Do you need any further assistance?'

'It's waiting outside. It's an unmarked car, so don't panic,' Kath replied as Ruth and Lane followed her. Lane held her hands to her chest.

'You alright?' Ruth asked her as they followed Kath and Erasmus through a curtained doorway, into another corridor.

Lane simply nodded. She had met many perpetrators in her career as police liaison, advisor, whatever label they wanted to put on her. But she was feeling a real anxiety rush at the thought of coming face to face with the man that had appeared on stage.

Erasmus stopped at one of the closed doors down the corridor and gestured. 'I think you'll find what you're looking for in there.' He leaned forward to whisper in Kath's ear. 'I can take care of him for you if you'd like. Ten minutes with me and he will tell you everything you want to know.'

Kath raised an eyebrow. 'I appreciate the offer but this has to go by the book. And by that, I mean *our* book.' She felt that sudden pang deep in her gut. The hypocrisy of extolling the virtues of the criminal justice system versus personal retribution. The memory was so far in the past but every now and again, it was so present with her it seemed like only hours had elapsed since it'd happened. Erasmus took a step back. He pulled a pack of smokes from his shirt pocket and lit one, causing Ruth to want to cough but suppressing the reflex so as not to advertise their presence outside the door.

Kath turned the round, old-fashioned doorknob and pushed hard, the door swinging open more easily than she'd anticipated. It crashed back on its hinges, and Danny, sitting at a triple-mirror dressing table, saw Kath standing in the doorway and turned slowly on his padded stool.

'Ooh, fans... do you want a signed photo? An autograph?' Danny stood. He had put on jeans but the rest of him was naked, the tattoo peeking above the low waistband.

Kath flourished her warrant card. 'We are here to take you into custody regarding the murder of Daisy Prospero.'

Danny stared at Kath. 'Murder?' He spread his arms wide, the muscles in his torso and arms straining. 'Daisy is not dead, dear ones. She is here. Behold her beauty.' His smile revealed perfect white teeth and his blue eyes sparkled with his words. Kath was so fixed on staring at his face she did not realise Lane had passed her and was now stood in front of Danny. She put her hands on his chest, and he let her feel his hairless skin.

'You feel her, don't you?' he whispered. 'In me, with me, belonging inside me.'

Lane couldn't speak. The energy flowing from Danny's hairless chest disrupted the neurons in her brain, and she had to fight to keep aware and focused.

'You need to come with us. We need to understand. Tell the story.'

He gently took Lane's hands and pulled them away from him. 'Why, of course. That's only natural that you should want to see the wonder of me.'

The atmosphere in the room was like something from a Derren Brown show. Ruth suddenly snapped back from the trance-like state she had also found herself in and grabbed a shirt from the chair next to her. She threw it at him, missing Lane by centimetres, and he caught the material in the soft hands that had squeezed the life from a child.

'Get dressed,' Ruth barked. 'And say your goodbyes to this place.'

The journey back to Telford was a sober affair. Lane sat in the back of the car, Ruth and Kath in the front, making occasional comments about what was going to happen when they got back. Ruth had texted Shirley, Marvin and Byron to update them. The car following them with Danny onboard was almost nose to tail as Kath put her foot down hard on the accelerator. Danny had come quietly with an almost serene look on his beautiful face. He was still fully made-up, and the three detectives from Worcester CID had made a good show of not revealing any emotions as they'd opened the door to let Danny into their car. Lane had felt strongly that there would be no trouble from Danny. He was revelling in the attention but not talkative, just staring at the night sky almost as if seeing the stars for the first time. Kath was grateful for the backup. It did not seem right that they escort him in her vehicle. Truth be told, she did not want him in her car, that close to her, breathing in the same air. They were all feeling the weight of the day as the signs for their destination brought them closer to home, and she was relieved to pull into Malinsgate. She had phoned ahead to tell them she wanted Danny booked into custody. There was a palpable tension as she and the officers from Worcester surrounded Danny and propelled him towards the rear reception and into the custody suite.

Kath shook the hands of the three other officers and thanked them for their help. There was no banter, no camaraderie. It was not an occasion for light-hearted police chat. As they left the building, the duty sergeant leaned forward. He was an old-school officer who had been around at the time of the Prospero case. Kath could see his bearded chin clicking from side to side in irritation.

'Can we speak candidly?' he asked. Danny was looking around the walls, the floor, raising himself up on the tips of his toes and down again.

'Of course, Bob.'

'That's the fucking freak who murdered little Daisy?'

Kath knew he was only echoing what a lot of people would be feeling and thinking but she had to tread the fine line. 'Bob, this is going to be hard for many of us. But this is the last leg now. He will be processed according to the law and we will get justice.'

Bob Craddock looked over at Danny, his hands curling into fists under the desk. 'If I was ten years younger...'

Kath managed a smile. 'If you were ten years younger, you'd still be too old to do what you're thinking about doing.'

Bob returned a weak smile and moved the computer mouse to bring the monitor back to life. 'Do you want suicide watch?'

Kath thought for a moment. 'Better be belt and braces on this, so yes. Can you also book him in for a psych evaluation for in the morning?'

'Oh Christ,' Bob muttered. 'We're not going for "the crazies made me do it", are we? Please don't say that.'

Kath fished in her jacket pocket for her cigarettes and pulled them out with her lighter. 'Like I said, we need to do this by the book. Get in touch with the duty solicitor first thing as well. But keep an eye out tonight, okay?'

Bob mumbled his displeasure while typing.

'I said okay, Sergeant Craddock?' She gave him a look halfway between pleading and don't fuck with me.

'You can rely on me, Detective Chief Inspector Fortune.' He beckoned to the two uniformed officers either side of Danny.

'Thank you.'

Kath pulled a cigarette from the packet, eager to smoke it as soon as the building was behind her.

'Don't go.' Danny's voice bounced off the walls, and Kath stopped but did not turn. 'I have so much to tell you; so much to share. A story of exquisite symmetry. A story of blooming and becoming.'

Kath marched towards the double doors and hit them hard, crushing her cigarette and a little bit of her spirit.

| 35 |

Lenny looked at his empty wine glass, grabbed the bottle from the fridge, returned it and flicked on the kettle. He had already spent two hours and two large glasses of a fruity little white mooching around Kath's cottage, anxious for her return. She had texted him to let him know what was happening and asked if he could be at her place for when she got back. The hands on the kitchen clock had both passed the beak, signifying the move into a new day, and he knew he wouldn't settle until she was in the house and in his arms. He went upstairs to the bathroom to recycle the wine. As he dried his hands, he thought he would show his absolute potential in his homemaking skills and put a new toilet roll on the holder. He opted for the small cupboard under the basin and found the stash of plain white tissue.

'That's my girl,' he muttered. 'No frills. Plain and unfussy all the way.' As he pulled a roll towards him, he heard a faint noise like something had fallen over. Slightly mortified at what he might find but not wishing to leave any kind of mess, he knelt further to see what it was. He picked up a lipstick and sat back on his haunches. The gold tube looked like the lipstick his mother used to have in the '50s. Kath had never been one for wearing a lot of make-up; running around with the armed response unit and on various crime scenes in all weathers, sweating, wiping cobwebs and assorted muck from her skin had made her realise it was just not possible to maintain the kind of look Maybelline were insistent on ladies having, so she'd tailored her look to a little mascara and the odd swipe of lip gloss. Lenny removed the outer tube and twisted the bottom to reveal the colour inside. The texture of the bright orange pigment seemed old and worn, flattened down to the base of the inner tube, remnants peeking just above the rim. He'd never seen her wear this vibrant colour and was confused as to why it was apparently hidden behind the toilet rolls. He put the two tubes back together and replaced the lipstick where he had found it. He might ask her about it later but now it was time for a cup of tea and late-night US crime shows.

Kath dropped Ruth back at Madeley station to get her car. As Ruth moved to get out of Kath's car, she turned to Kath. 'If he's seven kinds of crazy, where do we go with this?' That had been the only thought running through Kath's brain as they had driven back from Worcester, and she was reluctant to voice what they were all thinking.

'Don't think about it anymore tonight.' She looked at the dashboard clock. 'I mean, this morning. Get some sleep. Regroup tomorrow.' Ruth patted her arm and said goodbye to Lane who moved into the passenger seat as Ruth walked through the rain that had just begun. As Kath nosed the car towards Bridgnorth, the drops became bigger and soon the wipers were working hard to disperse the downpour.

'Reflects my mood exactly.' Kath peered through the sheets of water running off the windscreen. 'What are your plans, now?'

Lane wrapped her arms around herself. 'I'll say goodbye to the team in the morning and then head off if that's okay. I can't see you really needing me for anything else.' Kath took a moment. Lane had done what she'd wanted her to do; there didn't seem any reason for her to stay.

'No, I think you're right. I can't thank you enough for what you've done.' She pulled into her driveway and killed the engine.

Lane turned to her, the rain thrumming on the roof of the car. It was now impossible to see outside or in. 'I told myself I wouldn't say anything but I have to ask—'

Kath stopped her with a hand on her thigh. 'I have a plan. I've always had a plan, and I think it may be time now to execute it.'

Lane nodded. 'Okay. With Sal's help, by any chance?'

Kath smiled in the dim haze of the porch light trying to break through the rain barrier. 'Yes. With Sal's help. I can't tell you—' Before she could continue, the front door opened and she could see the fuzzy outline of Lenny in the doorway, probably wondering why they were sitting in the car having pulled up minutes before.

'Let's go in,' she said, and they dashed the few feet from the car to the warm interior of the cottage.

Andrew woke with a start at the noise from upstairs. He pushed the duvet off him and moved quickly up the stairs, taking them two at a time, scared he might find Todd collapsed on the bedroom floor. He pushed open the door to Todd's bedroom to find his friend setting a small table upright and repositioning the lit table lamp that now had a dented shade.

'It's alright, mate. I just knocked into it.'

Andrew sighed and put his hands on his hips. 'How are you feeling?'

Todd yawned and stretched. 'Bit woozy, I guess. But I'm fine, really. Coffee?'

'Maybe herbal tea,' Andrew suggested as they moved downstairs, into the kitchen. Todd made disparaging noises as he flicked the kettle into life. He reached up into the cupboard to look at the assortment of teas Miranda had purchased from the health shop in Bridgnorth on their day out. Samson appeared through the cat flap at the sound of humans in his favourite room and rubbed himself around Andrew's legs. Andrew scooped up the ginger ball of fluff and nuzzled into his fur before realising the water from his coat was seeping into his shirt.

Todd raised an eyebrow. 'I swear that damn animal loves everybody more than me.' He picked out two sachets of camomile and tore them open, placing the bags in two china mugs.

Andrew laughed and put Samson down. 'You're a disgusting boy, Samson, mousing in this weather.' He tried to brush the raindrops from his chest but the warmth of the cat had already pushed them through the fabric and Andrew was left with a damp stain coupled with a couple of leaves and a muddy paw print.

'Hey, I want coffee, not that green crap.' Andrew shook his finger at the camomile tea bag.

'Oh, great,' Todd muttered, 'the health professional wants to poison his body with caffeine while I have to drink this bag of lawnmower cuttings.'

'This health professional has not just had a mild ischaemic attack,' Andrew replied. Todd had no real comeback to that. The episode had scared him, he had to admit. He had always looked after himself, not excessively or with any kind of moral superiority, but he ate modestly and well, drank little and had cut down his cigarettes to a handful a day. He wanted desperately to talk about Miranda, about what had transpired, but he was afraid Andrew didn't want that and he needed some support now, not a lecture. He spooned instant coffee into another mug and added water to both their beverages. They sat at the table, Todd craving a cigarette, Andrew sipping his coffee. He swallowed his feelings with his liquid.

'Okay, talk. I'm here to listen, not to judge. No wisecracks unless I can't help myself.'

Todd held the teabag by its paper label and dunked it up and down in the hot water, blinking through the steam, hoping to find some sense in the mess that had thundered into his life. 'I have another daughter, Andrew.' His friend nodded but said nothing. 'I knew I had a connection with her, just felt something so strange I couldn't make any proper sense of it, and now... from all the pain comes something good and I can't imagine my life without her.'

Andrew was struggling but pressed his lips together and breathed steadily through his nose. 'You might have to... the police haven't finished yet...'

Todd halted the teabag motion and stared at his friend. 'But she didn't do anything. I told you what she said. She didn't do anything, she was just...there.' His words were becoming more urgent now.

'Drink your tea. You need more sleep. We'll pick this up later when the sun's up.' He pushed his chair back, feeling anger growing inside and fighting to get out. He threw the rest of his coffee into the sink and turned the tap on so hard the water splashed onto his shirt, making the damp stain from the cat even wetter. He grunted and stepped back, grabbing a tea towel off the back of Todd's chair.

Todd spun round and grabbed the towel. They both held it, their eyes holding a stare filled with anxiety and fear from Todd and rage and disgust from Andrew. He pulled hard but Todd hung on.

'I'm not ready to do this yet,' Andrew said, letting the cloth go and stepping back.

Todd stood, still holding the towel in his hand that had now become a fist. 'But I am, Andrew. I need to talk about this. You're the only person I can do this with—'

Andrew pointed. 'You might be ready but I can't do this, mate. I want to say so much but I'm biting my tongue so fucking hard I'm tasting blood.'

Todd threw the towel onto the table and moved into Andrew's space. 'So, don't hold back. Don't flatter yourself that you're gonna give me another heart attack by expressing your opinion.'

Andrew blinked as Todd's breath stung his eyeballs. That was exactly what he was afraid of; he didn't want to raise Todd's blood pressure and see him admitted to hospital again. The consequences might not be so mild next time around and, on a completely selfish level, Andrew did not want that on his conscience.

'I can't pretend.' Andrew steadied his voice and stepped back, his body resting against the sink. 'From the moment I saw her lying on the couch with vomit around her mouth, I knew she was trouble. And I was right.' His chin trembled like a Hollywood starlet as he tried to keep his emotions in check, but he could feel the energy pushing, desperate to be out of his mouth and he knew once the words were out, they could not be unspoken.

'I hated Carmel.'

'What?' Todd's words stunned him. 'Where the hell did that come from? And what has that got to do with anything. And why? What do you mean...?'

Todd spread his hands. 'Just saying I didn't trust her from the moment you introduced us.' Andrew was about to protest but Todd silenced him. 'No, my turn now. When you announced, no... wait...*she* announced your engagement, I smiled and wished you well. I kissed her on the cheek. I got you that fucking horrible gravy boat thing she wanted for a wedding present and I sat through endless dinners and parties and watched you beam with happiness while I just wanted to hit her with a large rock.'

Andrew was fighting feeling deflated by the news coupled with a fierce disappointment at Todd's revelation.

'And when she left you—and I always knew she would—I supported you and was there for you. I never said, "I told you so". I never said, "good riddance" I was a friend. Your best friend. And I gave you what you needed.'

'Maybe what I needed was a little honesty from my best friend.'

'Maybe you wouldn't have listened to what I had to say. It can get awful cold up there on the moral high ground.'

Andrew's shoulders sagged a little, knowing Todd was right. He had been obsessed with his first wife. They had been young, and he knew he was punching above his weight and he had always felt, deep down, that he would lose her. He just didn't think it would only be two years and couple of months into the marriage.

'Okay. I don't really know what to say except maybe thank you for not telling me you hated the love of my life.'

Todd moved to the back door and opened it, letting the sound of the heavy rain into the room. He grabbed his cigarettes from the counter and pulled one out, not even bothering to look at Andrew as he lit it and inhaled deeply before blowing the smoke into the darkness. Andrew wanted to take it from him and crush it into the white porcelain of the sink but he didn't want to escalate the situation.

'I'm gonna go back to the couch and try and get some more sleep.'

Todd watched his back, then turned to the safety of the rain and the dark night. His heart was beating fast but it felt normal, regular, what you'd expect from a heated exchange. Samson sat next to him, looking at the rain that was now coming down heavier and deciding that inside watching it was better than being outside in it.

'You love her, don't you, boy?' Todd bent to tickle the top of the cat's head, and he mewed softly in response. 'As long as we both love her, that's all that matters.'

| 36 |

The morning was decidedly cool for late August. Lenny had surprised Lane and Kath with a full breakfast of fried goods and left them to it. Kath had messaged her team and told them to meet her at the station for a formal goodbye for Lane. The office temperature was bearable now the weather had broken and Ruth was back in tidy mode. Marvin sorted drinks for everyone and they all grabbed chairs and sat in as much of a circle as the office layout would allow. Byron was still tapping away at his keyboard, and Kath nodded at him but left him doing whatever it was he was doing.

'So, this is where we're at.' Kath quieted the chatter and they all looked at her. 'Todd is fine, albeit very shaken by his hospital admittance. Dr Taylor has taken it upon himself to keep an eye on him. He's coming to terms, in his own way, with the fact Miranda is his daughter.'

'I don't think any of us saw that one coming,' said Ruth, flattening and refolding the yellow duster balanced on her knee.

'I know.' Kath shook her head. 'But the fact is, we actually only have Miranda's confession to Todd that Danny killed Daisy.'

'So, Danny is denying all knowledge?' Marvin frowned, struggling to understand how the case was going to pan out.

'Not denying exactly,' Kath tried to explain. 'He goes by the name Marguerite now. He says Daisy is not dead but lives inside him.'

'If we can't get a confession, surely there's no case for the CPS to move forward with...' Shirl curled her hands around her warm coffee mug. 'Does this mean we can't get him for what he's done?'

'In his eyes, he hasn't done anything,' Lane cut in. 'Daisy's spirit, essence, whatever he wants to call it, has just moved from one body to another.'

'Are you defending him?' Marvin's voice had an uncharacteristic snarl to it, and Lane was taken aback by the force of his words.

'Not defending, Marvin, I'm just being objective—telling you what he feels and thinks. Just because it doesn't fit the scenario we want it to doesn't make it wrong.'

Kath held her hands up as everyone started to talk over each other, working out how the system could prosecute the killer they had caught but had no substance for a case. 'I am going to sit in, or rather watch from the mirror, the interview with Danny—Marguerite—with the psychiatrist. We'll tape the session, and the judge can have a look at it and decide if he's fit to stand trial. I haven't actually charged him with anything yet; he is merely helping us with our enquiries.'

'That's the crap we send out to the press. I can't believe he's going to get away with it,' Marvin muttered. 'That poor man needs closure for the death of his little girl. We have to fight for that, don't we?'

'Yes, we do, Marvin. But, as I said, we only have Miranda's statement to Todd. If she decides not to tell us formally about what she witnessed, we can't move ahead. If the perpetrator denies all knowledge of the act because she isn't dead, because she is... him... Christ, it can all get more complicated, but that's the remit of the psych evaluation. So, yeah, there may not be a case to answer to. The judge may well decide he's not fit to stand trial.'

'Then it's all been for nothing,' said Ruth. 'Our first fucking case and all the work and we can't get a conviction or closure for Todd.'

'Maybe Todd would have wanted to press charges. We could have gone down that road. But, in light of what has happened with him and Miranda and this bond they have built, I don't really think he's going to want to have his own daughter prosecuted for witnessing something that, in Danny's eyes, didn't happen.'

'Where's Miranda now?' Shirl asked. She thought Marvin had told her but with all the information flooding her brain, she was finding it difficult to recall pertinent items.

Marvin cleared his throat. 'She went to stay the night with her foster mother, Ida. Andrew—Dr Taylor—didn't want her around Todd when he left hospital. I guess she's still there unless she's gone back to Todd's house by now.'

There was silence as they all digested the information, scenarios running inside all the brains in the room, trying to come up with a workable solution. The only sound was coming from Byron's fingers. When he stopped, Kath looked across at him.

'Byron, anything you want to add?'

He lifted his mug to his lips, realised there was nothing in it and put it back down. 'Yeah, I think I do.'

'Spit it out then, lad,' said Ruth. 'There can't be any more surprises in this bloody box of tricks.'

Byron cleared his throat. 'Did you say Mary Tinkerson is Todd's housekeeper?'

'Oh God,' said Kath. 'What's she got to do with this unholy mess?'

'Nothing much,' said Byron, 'except for the fact she's Danny's maternal grandmother.'

| 37 |

'What the fuck...' Shirl spun round in her chair to face Byron. 'You have got to be kidding.'

Byron shook his head, stood and stretched.

'How the hell did you come across that?' Ruth asked.

They were all looking at him now for an explanation, fighting to fit this particular weird shaped puzzle piece into the overall picture.

'Sometimes it's the simplest way that's the best.' He moved from behind his desk, hunching his shoulders quickly up and down to remove the stiffness. He had got in early yet again and been hard at work for an hour and a half before the rest of the team had arrived.

'I was looking for Danny's parents, seeing as how the foster records had been sealed, and I was going to do a bit more'—he hesitated to use the word 'hacking', instead finding a more suitable alternative—'investigating when I realised I could just go onto one of the genealogy sites and try my luck there.'

'That'll make a great TV advert. Are you related to a child murderer? Try our new site for a free two-week trial run and find out more about your family.' Ruth threw the duster across the room and then stood to retrieve it. It was too messy to leave the yellow fabric haphazardly lying on the floor.

Shirl gave a faint smile and picked up her cigarettes. 'Not enough fags in the packet for this little nugget.' She marched out the door, glancing at Kath who nodded. She would follow when she'd heard more about this latest revelation.

'Let's have it, Byron,' Kath said, leaning back in her chair. He remained standing.

'Well, Mary Tinkerson had a daughter—Harriet—who got a taste for heroin. Not a nice story but not unusual. Bit clichéd but she threw the girl out, left her to her own devices. She went on to have Danny and actually registered his birth under the father's name: Halstead. Which is where I found him. Simple enough.'

'Father and Mother... where, exactly?' Kath asked.

Byron flicked his fingernails against his fingers—a habit that had always driven his mother crazy but was his stress relief. Noone in the office had mentioned it, realising the motion for what it was. 'Harriet died soon after giving birth. Not surprisingly, a drug overdose. Dad, Ricky, went the same way. Don't think they were actually together as a couple, so to speak, maybe just drug buddies. I don't really know. Baby Danny was found in the flat where Harriet was squatting. The other members of the household had no apparent interest in anything but opiates, so the baby was in a pretty poor state when someone finally called the police about the smell coming from the squat—Harriet's dead body.'

'Jesus.' Marvin felt immediate sympathy for the child but then remembered who he had grown up to be and hardened his heart.

'Harriet, amazingly, was not in the system, so police couldn't identify her, so Mary Tinkerson had no idea about her daughter or that she had a grandchild. Still hasn't, I guess. She never filed any missing person reports. Just maybe wanted to forget she had a daughter. So...' He shrugged to signify he had finished divulging the information, and Kath grabbed her smokes.

'Let me think,' She moved towards the door but turned back to Lane who had mostly been keeping quiet and wondering whether she was still required. 'Sorry, Lane, I've been a bloody awful host. Do you want to stay? I don't know that there's anything you can do...'

'No, I think I'm all done. I don't really think you need me anymore. Happy to be on my way if that's okay.'

'Yep, that's fine. Say your goodbyes and I'll see you off downstairs at the car.'

Lane moved forward first to Marvin who was about to hug her but stepped back. 'You're not going to give me a message from my dead grandfather or anything, are you?'

Lane laughed. 'I'm not like that TV show where the woman touches someone and gets visions and messages from the dead all over the place. Come here, sweet wee boy.' She pulled him into her and they hugged, then he leaned back, still holding onto her arms.

'It's been a real pleasure working with you, Lane.'

'You too, honey.' She brushed his cheek with her hand which reddened, then she moved onto Ruth. They embraced and laughed about something Lane muttered. Byron stood in the corner near his desk, not really sure whether he also wanted to be as close as a hug would involve.

'Byron, you've a real gift.' Lane approached him and he decided a hug would not be the worst thing that had transpired that morning. Lane frowned as she released him, feeling his energy become unsettled like the nap on velvet when you brush it the wrong way. 'Maybe we'll meet up in the future.' She stared at him, leaving him unsettled.

'Yes. Take care.' He turned quickly back to his desk, and Lane grabbed her bag.

As she started down the stairs, she turned back, hearing footsteps behind her, and smiled at Byron at the top of the stairs.

'Lane...'

'I know, honey. I know. Let it run through you. It'll be fine.'

He sighed and waved a hand, returning to the office. Ruth stood behind him, a puzzled expression on her face.

'Look after him, Ruth.' Lane continued down the stairs and out into the overcast day where Kath and Shirl were smoking by their favourite tree. Kath moved to join her. Shirl threw her cigarette butt to the dirt and gave Lane a hug.

'Nice working with you. Do it again, maybe?'

'Maybe.' Lane nodded and moved towards her car where Kath was waiting.

'Words seem a bit redundant... the old thanks and all that, but you've been a real asset and I am really grateful.' *Not grateful you picked up on my secret but beggars can't be choosers, can they?* Kath brushed the thought away as Lane threw her bag onto the passenger seat.

'Anytime, Kath. I just hope you can move forward with a suitable conclusion.'

Kath knew she wasn't just talking about the case and chose to just smile and step back as Lane pulled away with a wave.

A uniformed PC opened the door to the station and peered around the side of the building. Seeing Kath, he beckoned her over.

'Just got a message from Malinsgate. They've been trying to ring you. The duty solicitor has turned up along with the psychiatrist. Apparently, they've been trying your mobile.' Kath nodded and muttered her thanks, pulling her mobile from her pocket and realising she had switched it to silent. She had four missed calls, and she gestured at Shirl to follow her back upstairs.

Kath caught her breath at the top of the stairs and Shirl barrelled into her. 'You need to get to the gym,' she said, moving past her. Kath put her hands on her hips, trying to steady her breathing.

'Me and gym have a very absent relationship.' Kath wheezed and sat, her breathing regulating to a normal rhythm. 'I'm off to Malinsgate in a minute. Ruth, do you and Marvin want to head over to Todd's and see this Mrs Tinkerson... let her know what we've found out?'

Ruth nodded and grabbed her jacket. 'I've got her home address if she isn't at Todd's. I think it's one of her days to be at his house, so we'll head there first. Also gives Marvin a chance to check on his man crush.'

Marvin pulled himself up to his full height of six foot. 'Mock me all you like. I don't care.'

'Anything you want me to do?' Shirl rolled a pen between her fingers and looked at Kath.

'Yeah, give Ida Costain a call, see if Miranda is still with her.' She paused. 'I'm kind of at a loss at the moment, if I'm honest. It's all got even messier than it was before. I think I'll know more when Danny has said his piece to the psychiatrist.'

'It's okay not to have all the answers fall in your lap,' said Shirl as Kath stood to leave.

'I know,' she replied. 'But my lap is completely empty and I don't like it.'

| 38 |

'How many kinds of crazy are we looking at?' Suki Lapido settled herself into the chair of the interview room. The twinkle in her eyes and soft Ghanaian accent lifted Kath's spirits a little in light of what was to come.

'Double figures,' Kath replied. She stood and fiddled with the recording device and then repositioned the video camera.

'Just another day at the office, then?' Suki smiled, revealing perfect white teeth behind a vibrant red lipstick. She pushed her headband further into her mass of grey curls and reached for her pad and pen from her briefcase.

'It's a tough one,' Kath said, putting her hands on the table and leaning forward. 'I have a witness that saw him strangle Daisy Prospero but he has told us she is not dead and lives inside him.'

Suki nodded and scribbled something on her pad. 'Have you charged the witness? Is there a statement?'

Kath looked around the room; anything to avoid Suki's gaze. 'No and no.'

Suki smiled. 'I've never known a case you were involved with that wasn't complicated, so I don't need to know.'

Kath sighed and looked at herself in the two-way mirror, then realised the duty solicitor was in there and may be watching her. She tucked her hair behind one ear and turned back to Suki. 'If my witness decides not to say anything—and she might because of certain circumstances that have arisen we did not see coming—I basically don't have anything.'

Kath's mobile rang. Ruth.

'Hey, what's up?'

'Just heard from Todd. Marvin apparently told him where we were yesterday and what we were doing.' Silence.

Kath frowned. 'And?'

'Todd wants a look at the guy that killed his little girl.'

'Crap.' Kath rubbed her eyes and then remembered she was wearing mascara and stopped. 'That's a really bad idea. I don't want him back in the hospital.'

'That's kind of what I said,' Ruth replied. 'I did ask if he'd talked over that particular chestnut with Dr Taylor. Apparently, they've had a falling out and Todd doesn't really care what anyone else thinks.'

Kath heard a commotion outside the door. 'Okay, I'll call him. Gotta go.'

As she replaced her phone in her trouser pocket, Danny entered the room, flanked by two uniformed officers. He smiled at Kath and then Suki who gestured for him to sit opposite her.

'Ladies. What a glorious morning.'

Yeah right, thought Kath. *Glorious for only one of us.* The two PCs positioned themselves against the wall.

'This is Dr Lapido,' Kath said, stepping back from the table. 'She would like to talk to you about Daisy.'

'About my journey, you mean. My Becoming.' Danny nodded. 'I'm always happy to talk about that.' Kath started the audio and video equipment. There was a knock at the door. It opened slowly and the desk sergeant pushed his head through and gestured to Kath.

'There's someone at the desk to see you.' The sergeant looked at Danny and then back at Kath. He mouthed 'Todd' at her and she left the room and followed him through to the front desk.

Todd looked well, if a little pale. Kath took his hand.

'I really don't think this is a good idea, and protocol dictates that I—'

He removed his hand a little too quickly from hers. 'I think I deserve to see him, don't you?'

In the few seconds of silence that fell between them, all sorts of thoughts and possible tragic scenarios filled Kath's head. Her heart couldn't disagree with him; maybe she would want that too in his position. But her police officer head was ringing with the sound of alarm bells and the seven kinds of wrong that could turn the situation on its head and possibly end her career.

Her heart won. 'Okay. But it will be brief and you will not do anything stupid. That's a requirement, not a request. I'm thinking about your welfare here.' *And my job*, her brain chorused.

'Thank you.' He followed her through to the adjacent room to the interview room where the mirror allowed them to see Suki and Danny. Kath closed the door quietly, nodding to the duty solicitor who looked weary and fed up even at the early hour. He might have been forty or sixty but it looked as if the job had taken a toll on his face. If he knew who Todd was, he gave no sign of recognition. Todd pressed himself against the glass, then moved back slightly as his breath fogged his view. Danny was facing the mirror, admiring himself as he talked, flicking his blonde fringe from his eyes and touching the corner of his mouth, checking what was left of his lipstick from the night before. Kath flicked the switch that turned off the sound. She was not about to let Todd hear Danny's words. They watched for a minute in silence.

'He's quite beautiful.' Todd's statement took her by surprise.

'Todd, I have to tell you I'm breaking a whole lot of rules by letting you in here. Don't make me regret my decision.' Kath was hoping the solicitor was too disinterested to give a damn about what she was doing. She glanced over at him, but he was staring through the glass with a bored expression on his face.

'I appreciate everything you've done for me,' Todd said, never taking his eyes from the young man that had taken the life of his child. 'Has he said anything yet?'

Suki was writing on her pad, making the odd comment. Danny was relaxed, his body forming an open pose, smiling, nodding.

'What I'm about to tell you stays between us, okay?' She wanted to tell the solicitor to go and get himself a coffee but she had broken enough rules since she'd walked into the station and just had to hope he really didn't care what she was about to impart. Todd nodded and she continued.

'He has effectively denied murder on the grounds Daisy is still alive within him. He has become her; she has become him... it's so complicated. That's why I asked for the psych evaluation.' She paused. 'We are looking at the possibility of not being able to move forward as we wanted. It may be that Dr Lapido will determine he is not fit to stand trial.'

Todd turned to her and she continued. 'There are all kinds of personality disorders that may allow him to...' She didn't want to say the words 'get away with it' and fought for something else to clarify the situation. 'We just may not be able to go where we had hoped to go with the case.'

Todd turned back to look at Danny. 'It's freaky... so fucking freaky.'

Kath frowned, not really understanding where he was going with his thoughts.

'He has her smile,' Todd said simply. 'He has Daisy's smile.' He took a sharp inhalation and put a hand to his chest. Kath moved closer to the door, ready to get medical assistance if needed. *"Please don't let him fall"*, Kath prayed silently to all the gods she didn't believe in. She wanted to push, to ask about Miranda, but she was genuinely afraid.

'Miranda told me everything about that day.'

Kath offered up a silent thank you to the previously disavowed gods and stayed quiet.

'But even though she told me he did it, that she had no part in it, it's only her words told to me only.' He turned to face her, arms now by his sides. 'And I will tell her to say nothing. And this will all be over. Right?'

He had voiced what Kath was going to say. She could have Miranda charged but if she refused to speak, to give a statement, then the evidence, the actual physical, irrefutable evidence, was non-existent. Even though they had Danny's saliva on Daisy's cheek, it did not say he killed her.

'It's not a good result for my first cold case.' Kath tried to lighten the mood but knew she was probably coming across as crass and selfish. Todd didn't acknowledge her comment and she was grateful to let it disappear into the ether.

Suddenly, Danny waved at Todd as if he knew he was there, and Todd recoiled as if he had been shot.

'He can't see me, can he?'

Kath took hold of his upper arms. 'Of course not. I think you should leave now.'

The issue of his housekeeper being related to the person in the next room was still invading her thoughts, and she needed to wrap up this situation and get Todd out of there.

'Come on.' She moved him towards the door and he let her, following her through as she passed him to push open the door to reception. She had a desperate thought that he might try to burst into the room where Danny was but he remained straight ahead and they moved outside to the car park.

'Go home,' she said. 'Get some rest. I'll come by later.'

He nodded, got into his car and pulled away.

Danny was being taken back to the cells as Kath moved into the interview room. Suki sat back in her chair and folded her arms under her breasts. Kath turned off the audio and video recorders.

'Bat shit crazy?'

Suki laughed. 'There are no stations where you can stop and hop on board his train of thought.'

'So, what do you recommend?'

Suki gathered her pad and pen and returned them to her briefcase. 'I suggest a secure unit until a judge looks at the tape and I've submitted my report. But, in my opinion, he's not fit to stand trial.'

'Great,' said Kath under her breath.

Suki stood and Kath walked her out to the front desk.

'I'll make some calls, Kath. I think there may be a bed at Heston Grange. I can arrange for him to be transferred there for the time being. Is that okay with you?'

Kath tried to place the name. 'Worcestershire? Herefordshire?'

Suki nodded. 'On the border, Leominster way. Out in the sticks. Was a kind of stately home at one point. I believe the upkeep was too much and so it was sold and turned into a psychiatric hospital. It's a good place.'

The two women shook hands and Kath went back down to the custody sergeant to let him know what was going on. Frustration rumbled inside her but there was nothing else to be done until the judge had made the ruling. A text came through from Ruth. She and Marvin were on their way to Todd's house. Mrs Tinkerson was already there. Kath didn't envy Ruth that conversation but she knew Ruth would handle it. She walked out to her car and glanced up as the fat raindrops fell on her face and mingled with the tears that had been waiting to fall.

| 39 |

'Turn that frown upside down, Marvin. He's probably shot off to Malinsgate to see Kath.' Ruth pulled the car into Todd's driveway. She felt the wave of disappointment coming off the young man as he noted the absence of Todd's car. She wanted to ruffle his hair in a motherly way as they got out of the car and stood at the front door but she felt it would be mean. Marvin worked hard on teasing his short hair into a moussed boyband style and Ruth felt he wouldn't appreciate her gesture. Mrs Tinkerson opened the door, resignation on her face as she admitted the two detectives.

'Is that your car out front, Mrs Tinkerson? I was expecting your bicycle.' Ruth tried a safe comment for opening. God, the woman was hard work.

They followed her into the kitchen. 'If it looks like rain, I come in my husband's car.' At the mention of the weather status, raindrops bounced off the patio.

'I think she just made it rain,' Ruth leaned over and whispered in Marvin's ear, and he grinned. Mrs Tinkerson wheeled round quickly, and Ruth felt like a schoolgirl caught passing a dubious note in front of the strictest teacher.

'Mr Prospero is not—'

'It's not him we've come to see. It's you. Please have a seat.'

The housekeeper pursed her thin lips and sat on the edge of the seat, brushing a few cat hairs from the table top into her palm, pushing them into her apron pocket. Marvin remained standing and moved towards the back door. Ruth had gone over the conversation in her head countless times since Byron had given them the news but she couldn't seem to find an easy way to impart the knowledge.

'This may be difficult to hear but it's about your daughter Harriet.'

'Detective, I would prefer if you just came out and say what you have to say. I am used to plain speaking.' Mrs Tinkerson said with an impatient sigh.

Ruth nodded, relieved she could just offload the information. 'I'm afraid she has passed away.'

There was no reaction in the face of the housekeeper but Ruth detected her hands moving inside her apron pocket. 'She was dead to me the first time she put that poison into her body.'

Okay, thought Ruth. *No need for the softly, softly approach.*

'She died of a drug overdose in Worcester but... she had a son. You have a grandson.'

Still no reaction. Ruth ploughed on.

'His father is also dead. The child was put into foster care when he was still a baby.'

Marvin looked over to Ruth. He was standing behind Mrs Tinkerson with a somewhat perplexed look on his face. In his experience people usually showed more emotion when finding out such news.

'There's no easy way to say this, Mrs Tinkerson, but your grandson is Danny Halstead, the killer of Daisy Prospero.'

Ida stopped the car across the driveway, seeing two cars already there. Miranda leaned across and kissed her on the cheek.

'Thank you for last night. I'll ring you later.'

Ida nodded and watched her walk to Todd's front door and let herself in with her key. They had spent the evening talking through everything that had happened in both their lives over the past ten years, talking into the early hours until Miranda finally couldn't contain the yawns and went to get some sleep in her old room. Ida had already made the bed up in the hope she would visit and her heart was warmed by Miranda's presence and the rekindling of the closeness they had always had. She had no idea how their future lives would intertwine but she held fast to the strong bond they had and knew she had to let her foster daughter work her way through the revelations of the past few days. She pulled away and Miranda turned to wave.

Miranda closed the door and heard the voices coming from the kitchen, wondering where Todd was and feeling anxious, eager to speak with him. She had texted him earlier in the morning and he had sent back a reply that said he had things to do and would see her later.

She went into the kitchen to find Marvin filling the kettle and Ruth and Mrs Tinkerson sitting at the table. 'What's happening?' She looked from face to face, trying to gauge the mood.

Ruth stood. 'Miranda, could you give us a minute, please?' She gestured into the interior of the house.

'Um...okay.' Her hands plucked at her skirt. Mrs Tinkerson glared at her but said nothing. Miranda left the room and went upstairs to get a shower and a change of clothes. Ruth remained standing.

'Can I get you some tea, Mrs Tinkerson?' Marvin asked as he grabbed a couple of mugs from the back of the worktop. She rose so swiftly her chair pushed into Marvin's legs and he yelped.

'I do not need tea and sympathy.' Her lips set themselves back into their straight line as she stopped talking. Her hands came out of her apron pocket and a fine mist of cat hair floated above the table.

'I'm sure this is a shock for you, Mrs—'

'There is no shock, Detective. Only resignation. A bad seed from a bad apple. That is no surprise to me. Now, if you'll excuse me, I have cleaning to do and beds to make.' She moved quickly out of the room and they heard her climbing the stairs.

Marvin rubbed his legs. 'Christ, she's hard. I was expecting more of a reaction.'

'We all have different ways of coping with news like that,' said Ruth. She turned to the door as she heard tyres on the driveway.

'That could be Todd. We really need to bring him up to speed.' Marvin set the coffee machine to run, knowing it was Todd's preferred beverage, and joined Ruth at the kitchen doorway.

Todd gave a weak smile as he entered the house. 'Is that the coffee machine I hear, Marvin?' Todd joined them in the kitchen, glancing upstairs as he passed the staircase, hearing the shower running and the footsteps of who he assumed was Mrs Tinkerson.

'How are you feeling?' Marvin was the first out of the gate and Ruth let him lead. Todd opened the back door, pulled a cigarette from the packet on the edge of the worktop and lit it, drawing the smoke deep into his body and releasing it to blend with the raindrops that were becoming heavier.

'I've just come face to face, almost, with Daisy's killer. But I'm weirdly okay.'

Marvin's face held enough anxiety for the both of them. The more he got to know him, the more impressed he became, and he thought Todd had the biggest heart of anyone he had ever known.

Ruth's phone rang and the noise broke the mood. She gestured to Marvin that she would take it somewhere else in the house.

'That's probably DCI Fortune filling her in on what just happened.' He smoked quietly as Marvin, desperate to know what had transpired but eager not to appear eager, prepared coffee for the three of them whether anyone really wanted it or not.

'Were you here looking for me?' He flicked his cigarette butt onto the patio and watched the rain extinguish the ember. Marvin heard Ruth still talking to Kath and took an executive decision.

'Actually, no. We had some new information relating to Mrs Tinkerson.' Marvin passed a mug to Todd who took it, put it down, lit another cigarette and picked up the mug again.

'I don't want to sound like a doctor or anything'—Marvin gestured to the second cigarette—'but should you be doing that after your scare?'

'Don't concern yourself. I'm fine. Are you going to tell me what you're doing here?' He sipped his coffee and waited.

Marvin's heart was beating double time. 'Danny is Mrs Tinkerson's grandson.'

As the words left Marvin's mouth, they heard the front door open and close softly and then the sound of a car starting and pulling away.

Todd looked at Marvin. 'Was that her?'

Marvin nodded. 'Think so.' He went through the conversation he and Ruth had just had. Todd's eyes widened and he shook his head.

'I had no idea about her daughter. She never mentioned anything to me. Only, I think, a brother somewhere in Solihull, I think.' He drained his mug and aimed his latest butt into the rain.

'What strange connections these are. We've both lost a daughter. I've gained another daughter and she has gained a grandchild that killed my child.'

Ruth appeared in the doorway.

'I've just filled him in on the situation so far,' Marvin confessed.

'Looks like Danny will be going to a secure unit if Dr Lapido can arrange it.' She waved her phone at them. 'Kath is heading back to Madeley.'

Todd moved past Ruth as they heard footsteps coming down the stairs. As Miranda hit the bottom step, Todd folded her into his arms.

'I think we're done here,' said Ruth quietly to Marvin. They moved to the front door. Miranda's face was buried in Todd's chest. He turned his head slowly, not wishing to move his daughter from his embrace.

'Thank you. Again.'

'No problem,' said Ruth. 'We'll leave you two to talk. You've got our numbers if you need anything.'

Back at the Madeley station, the team sat at their various desks, munching on sandwiches and pasta salads Shirl had bought from the Tesco store up the road. The mood was flat, each member lost in their own thoughts. Kath had spoken to Lenny after pulling into the car park, updating him on the situation. He had made all the right noises but seemed distracted. He'd said he would be round later with Chinese food. Kath had a feeling there was something needing to be said, but she moved it to the back of her mind for later. Halfway through her egg mayonnaise sandwich, her phone rang, making them all jump. Kath made affirmative noises, trying to disguise a mouthful of food. She hung up and pushed the other sandwich away from her.

'That was Suki. She's confirmed a place at Heston Grange for Danny. I'll contact Worcester and ask them to collect him from here.'

'What about all the evidence?' Shirl's vowels wound their way around lettuce and pasta as she gestured towards the evidence bags still on the table.

'Leave it there for the moment. It may just have to stay here. I am doubting the CPS will want any part of this circus.'

'It feels a bit like we've blown it.' Marvin voiced what they were all thinking, and Kath knew she had to muster her own attitude to pull the team back together. A fractured and demoralised team was no good for anyone.

'It wasn't us,' Kath said, spinning in her chair to look everyone in the eye. 'Circumstances dictated the way this has panned out. We could not have foreseen what would come to light when we started on this case.'

Ruth nodded, gathering her empty food wrapper and hunting like a search dog for any more rubbish on the other desks. 'I suppose we thought—well, I think I did a bit—this would be less frustrating than an alive case.' There was a collective mumble of agreement, and she went on, tidying as she went round the room. 'I kind of had this vision everything would come together, bad guys found, prosecuted, in prison, families getting justice after perhaps a really, really long time... and I guess it all feels a bit flat.' She grabbed Kath's other sandwich and threw it in the bin.

'Hey! I was going to have that tomorrow.'

If Ruth had worn glasses, she would have tilted her head and looked over the top of them. 'And you wouldn't just be cosying up to Lenny in bed, you'd be having a three-way with E. coli.'

'Neat freak,' Kath muttered, smiling to herself. She picked up a sheaf of papers and then threw them back onto the desk. She stood. 'Fuck it. Everyone, go home. Take the rest of the day and the night to wind down, get rid of all this shit we've been carrying around. Meet back here fresh in the morning and we'll... well, I guess tidy this and put it to bed, get the loose threads cut off. I'm going to stop talking now, except for checking in with Malinsgate for the transfer. Go.'

She pointed to the door and picked up the office phone. As she confirmed what would happen, Marvin and Shirl went out together. Byron shut down what he had been working on and Ruth met him at the door.

'Have you felt good doing this so far?'

'Yeah.' He nodded and slung his canvas bag across his body. 'It doesn't feel like it's not a victory, you know?'

Ruth nodded. 'I think there's a few too many negatives in that sentence but I get what you're saying. It's because you're not used to this setup... this environment. We're old and cynical, you're young and fresh. Don't lose the magic. See you tomorrow.'

He patted her shoulder and went down the stairs. Ruth pottered about the office, watering the plants, wiping the desks with the flimsy wet wipes all offices seemed to have and usually left the tag unsealed so that the first two wipes just dried out. Kath was now speaking to her opposite number in Worcester, lots of head nodding and thanks. As Ruth finally picked up her bag and pulled out her car keys, Kath stood.

'All done. He'll actually be collected this afternoon sometime.' They locked the office and walked out to their cars.

'Home to Lenny, is it?' Ruth got in her car and left the door open for an answer.

Kath screwed her face up and shrugged. 'I think there's something off with him but can't put my finger on it.'

'Undress in the car and step through the door naked—that'll focus his interest.'

Kath laughed and relaxed. 'How the hell do you think up these things?'

Ruth raised her eyebrow and shut the car door. 'You haven't...?'

Ruth waved and pulled away, leaving Kath wondering if she could actually get out of her bra and blouse without the airbag going off.

| 40 |

Kath had thought better of undressing on the driveway, as Lenny was not at her cottage when she pulled up. She went inside and put the heating on, had a shower and put on her usual jogging bottoms and an oversized T-shirt, then thought better of it and opted for a pair of silky pyjamas and matching long robe in a pale grey. Lenny entered the kitchen carrying a small carrier bag with the food.

'Not much there for the two of us.' She kissed him on the lips and he half-responded, his lips brushing hers in an almost dismissive gesture.

'Wasn't very hungry but thought you might be,' he said, pulling the foil containers from the bag.

She stopped his hands and turned him to her. 'What's the matter?'

His eyes looked around the room, everywhere but at her face. 'It's Susan. She called me. She thinks she wants us to try again.'

Kath's hands fell away from him, and the smell of the food suddenly brought on nausea and a tightness in her body. *Not now*, she said to herself. *Not now everything is just falling into place for us.*

'Okay... how do you feel about that?' *Please say you hate the idea; please say you're not leaving me.* Snatches of dialogue ran through her brain and she tried hard to shut out her inner voice.

'It's not what I want,' he said, and she sighed inwardly. 'But it was hard, you know?'

Kath nodded and tried to be supportive, stroking his arm, a half-smile playing around the corners of her mouth.

'She was crying, and I knew it was just a reaction to her being on her own. I think the kids might have been talking to her... I get the impression they might have tried to persuade her.' He seemed lost in the memory of his afternoon but snapped back to the present. He pulled Kath close to him. She buried her face in his chest and smelt the essence of him and knew, as much as she had sympathy for his wife, she wanted to fight for her man. He had always been hers and it was her time now. She had never been the kind of woman that diffused difficult romantic situations by leading men into her bedroom and abandoning herself to sexual union. But she wanted to feel him close to her now, to cement their relationship. She stroked his face, pushed the food to one side and took his hand, pulling him gently upstairs.

The sex was intense and short-lived. There was no humour, no laughter. As Lenny's breathing softened into a light sleep, Kath went into the bathroom. Her silk apparel lay in a heap at the side of the bed, and she had grabbed her jogging bottoms and T-shirt and moved into the bathroom to get dressed so as not to disturb him. She smiled at herself in the mirror, tucking her blonde hair behind her ears and wondering if it was time for a new style; a whole new look. She had to pull the drawstring tighter now on her joggers as she looked down and realised the weight was dropping off her again. But now it was okay. She could go back to how she was. She didn't need the comfort and disguise of the fat around her breasts and belly and hips. She needed to hold the lipstick in her hands and make the decision to call Sal and end this. Maybe there was no need to confess to Lenny. As long as she fully embraced her crime herself, there was no need for anyone else to know. No need for any pain to be inflicted. She had kept it all within her for so many years. Now, she could let it go.

She bent to the cupboard under the sink, moved the toilet rolls and fell back in horror, twisting her torso and banging her ankle against the porcelain base of the toilet as she saw the lipstick was not in its usual upright position, nestled behind the rolls. It was on its side, the gold case glowing bright as a beacon, calling her to caress it. *He's found it*, she thought and looked over at the new roll on the holder and knew he had replaced it and had found her secret. She tried to work out when he had found it. But he hadn't said anything; hadn't asked her what it was or why it was there. She picked up the tube and pushed herself to her feet. She was glad they had not eaten the food. Her belly felt raw and unpleasant. She sat on the toilet seat, turning over the lipstick tube in her hands which was now clammy and warm and knew she had to feel it all again. It was the only way now to get rid of it, with Sal's help.

October 17, 1997

First, there was recognition. Reginald Miller's eyes widened as a memory fought its way to the front of his brain. Then his mouth curled into what he would have thought of as a smile but the woman before him saw as a toothy grimace, the fine downy hair of old age settling in the lines of his lower face. Then, as the woman lifted the rock, there was fear and resignation. Murmured words of past experiences assaulted his ears like clashing cymbals and Reginald knew, with absolute certainty, he would not see another day dawn.

He crumpled with the first blow like a marionette with each string severed one at a time in a slow sequence. He moaned and pulled a withered hand close to the wound, trying to cradle his face as blood seeped through his fingers. His eyes were shut tight as if he knew there would be more to come. The streetlight from the alleyway behind the kitchen illuminated the body on the floor, blood now pooling black against the worn linoleum. His survival instinct kicked in and he tried to pull himself underneath one of the kitchen chairs. Kath put down the rock and pulled his legs towards her. He was not going to be spared. She had started down a path from which there was no backing out, and her initial revulsion at what she was actually doing had dissipated and now there was just determination to rid the world of paedophile Reginald Miller. No more would he press his mother's lipstick to the faces of little girls with one hand as his other found its way underneath their dresses. No more dancing and twirling in tiny white pants stained with urine. And now his pants and trousers were stained, the dampness spreading like the blood. It had to be over now. It was the third blow that killed him but she didn't know.

Many blows later, his face was a meat puzzle—eyes, nose and lips rearranged by the rock. Kath took a step back and breathed slowly. No going back now. She placed the rock inside the plastic bag and then inside the shoulder bag she had brought with her. The lights were still off all through the house. He hadn't bothered to put them on as he'd come downstairs when he'd heard the back door being opened. He had never moved the key from under the rusted milk bottle holder by the back door.

She did a slow turn as the rock nestled against her hip, checking there was nothing obvious out of place in the grimy kitchen. She listened for any noises outside but it was all quiet at two thirty-seven in the morning.

She took off her latex gloves, slick with blood, and added them to the bag. Then, she snapped on a new pair. It just made sense to be careful even though she was not at all worried about her DNA or fingerprints being found in the property. She would more than likely be first on the scene once the incident was reported. And anyway, if not first, it would be her team—well, her DI's team—who would be called to investigate. And she was a big part of that team.

Detective Sergeant Kath Fortune closed the door behind her and checked the few feet across the garden to the back gate. She moved quickly, her thin frame squeezing out of the gate, into the alleyway, the gate stiff with age and rot. The alley was narrow; trees and shrubs lined the one side hiding the outskirts of the churchyard and the other side was all high fences shielding the back gardens for which she was thankful. One house two doors down had an upstairs light on but the curtains were drawn, and Kath gave a cursory glance, then proceeded to the end of the alley and onto the road that ran through the estate.

She went along with the banter when she had to face the body, her colleagues all knowing exactly what Reg Miller had done to many victims yet never being able to make a case stick. Victims, some into their forties, could not bring themselves to dredge up the past. Younger ones were too traumatised and parents were unwilling to put them through any more pain. He had been attacked before by vigilante groups but the police had defended him against the violence as was their duty of care to every member of the public. But privately, all the coppers hated him for what he was and what he did.

The irony of it was that Kath had been the one to interview the woman two doors down who'd told her she had seen a skinny figure with a shoulder bag slung across their body walking down the alleyway away from Reg's place at about two in the morning. The woman had sworn it was a woman; Kath had not pressed her or tried to sway her in any way, just taken the statement and reported back. When the murder board went up in the office, the DI had written that the possible person of interest was a skinny woman with a shoulder bag and dark clothing. Kath had decided at that point exactly what she would do as an extra measure of protection. She piled on the weight quickly and knew she would have to get over the ribbing from her colleagues and the sometimes unkind remarks she would overhear. But it would be worth it and she would bear it.

Two months later, she'd rented a log cabin in a remote corner of Wales, took the rock with her and, in the dead of night in another country, dropped the murder weapon carefully into the deepest part of the river.

The killer of Reginald Miller was never found and nobody really cared. He was packed up in a box and marked as a cold case, perhaps one day to be re-opened. But it wasn't a priority and it would disappear from everyone's radar as more important cases took over the lives of the officers.

Kath exhaled and placed the tube on the edge of the wash basin. She could hear Lenny snoring and allowed herself a smile as she pulled herself off the toilet seat and looked again in the mirror. She slipped the lipstick into her pocket and went downstairs, suddenly feeling ravenous. She tore off the cardboard lid of one of the containers, still slightly warm, and began picking out the mushrooms from the chow mein and popping them into her mouth. She flicked on the kettle and, as she passed the bin, let the lipstick tube plop gently into the plastic liner.

| 41 |

Her mobile woke both of them, Lenny rousing with a start and Kath swinging her legs onto the floor as she answered. She stood quickly, her naked body provoking an admiring glance from Lenny. She turned to look at him as she listened, open-mouthed at what was being said to her.

He mouthed, 'What?' and sat up, pulling on his shirt from where he had thrown it on the end of the bed last night.

'Right, thanks. No, it's okay. I'm used to being woken up early, don't apologise. I'm glad I know. How did—' She paused as the voice on the other end interrupted her. She wiped a hand across her eyes, listening to yet another aspect of the case she could not have even imagined.

'No, I'll deal with all that when I get in. Cheers.' She hung up and sat back down on the bed. Lenny scooted over and put his arms around her.

'Tell me.'

She hung her head and laughed. 'You won't fucking believe it.' She turned to him and wriggled herself from his embrace, standing and putting her hands on hips. She had to laugh; it was all so bloody ridiculous.

'A dog walker found a body in the woods about'—she looked at the clock on her bedside table—'forty minutes ago. It's Danny Halstead and he's very fucking dead.'

Kath dressed quickly and texted everyone to get to the office as soon as possible. She slurped a coffee with Lenny, not wanting to just rush out of the house after the night they'd had. Lenny looked tired but seemed in better spirits. He said he was going to speak to Susan again and affirm his decision to end their marriage. At least one thing was going in Kath's favour.

Kath was the first in the office. The others arrived one by one and tried to make sense of Kath's one-sided telephone conversation as she ascertained exactly what had happened so she could relay the information. She grabbed her cigarettes and went outside with her mobile.

'Good morning, DCI Fortune. I take it you've heard the news.'

Kath blew smoke into the trees, the leaves already beginning to turn as the summer was laying waste to an early autumn.

'It was you, wasn't it?' She tried to keep the tremor from her voice.

'I can't confirm or deny anything but I don't like child killers on my patch.' She paused but received no response from Kath. 'From what I knew of him and the information I had been given, there was no way you'd get a conviction. This solution ties everything up for all concerned.'

'Dammit, Sal, you didn't give me a fighting chance. I just needed more time—'

'No.' Sal's voice was hard and business like. She was all about problems and solutions in the simplest manner possible. 'We both know this would have dragged with no clear result in sight. You now have an ending. Move on and get over it.'

Kath stood and smoked and kicked twigs and dirt and stones with the toe of her boot like a petulant child who saw no way of getting what she wanted.

Sal finally broke the silence. 'Anything else come to mind you want to discuss?'

Kath aimed the spent butt into the road and a passing motorist gave her the finger as it landed on his bonnet. Her bladder threatened to let her down and she squeezed all the muscles as she fought to get the words out.

'I think I may be calling you on the other number quite soon, yes.'

'I look forward to that call.' Sal hung up and Kath was left at the roadside wondering what had happened to her life.

Marvin was pacing the office with Shirl glaring at him every time he passed her desk.

'It's not going to make her come up those stairs any faster, so bloody sit down.' Ruth pointed at him and he sat just as Kath appeared in the office. He leaned forward, desperate to stand again but too afraid of the comeback.

'So, there we are.' Kath threw her smokes and lighter onto her desk and perched on the end, looking at all the expectant faces.

'Early yesterday evening, two "police officers" and someone purporting to be a "psychiatrist"'—she held up her hands and made the quote marks sign—'came to fetch Danny and take him to Heston Grange. The custody sergeant checked their IDs and the paperwork and it looked in order. The two men and one female escorted Danny to their vehicle—a private ambulance by all accounts—and off they went. Danny's body was found early this morning by a dog walker in woodland near Pershore. One shot to the head.'

'Sal?' Ruth didn't need to ask but felt she had to voice what everyone was thinking.

Kath smiled but it didn't reach her eyes. 'She cannot confirm or deny her involvement. I've spoken to Mary Amos. She's setting up a live investigation at the Worcester end and we may need to send her some of our investigation notes, as he was officially in our custody until he was... taken.'

Shirl lay almost horizontal in her chair and put her feet on the edge of her desk. 'Maybe it's the best solution. We were never gonna get him to court, were we?'

'That's kind of what Sal said,' Kath replied. She sat in her chair, spread her legs and rested her elbows on her knees, looking across at everyone in turn.

'I'm going to phone Todd and see if I can pop round and tell him the news. And Miranda, as I guess she'll be there. Ruth, take Marvin and go and tell Mrs Tinkerson her grandson is dead. Shirl, gather all our evidence and put it in the box with the original case files. Check if I've missed anything.' Shirl nodded. She had always been the one to cover Kath's back in case she ran off with an idea and maybe hadn't stopped to think through a process.

Byron peered from the side of one of his monitors. 'Me?'

'Sorry, Byron.' Kath stood and rubbed her hand across her eyes which were not fringed with mascara this morning. 'I guess I've called you in for nothing, but... you are a part of this team and I didn't want to tell you by phone when I'd called everyone else in. Is that okay?'

He nodded and smiled. 'Actually, I had an idea for developing some new software for the next case... there will be a next case, won't there?'

All eyes turned to Kath. She stood in the middle of the room, commanding her team as she had always done. It was time to put this one to bed and move forward.

'Yes, Byron, there will be a next case. And I'd like you to choose it.' Now Byron was the one being stared at. He blushed and pushed his curtain of hair over his shoulder, pulling it all forward and round so it all lay over the one side.

'I'd really like that. Thank you.'

Ruth stood. 'I know this doesn't seem like a victory and we haven't had the ending we were hoping for but I think we all deserve a round of applause. We've done good work here.' She started to clap and the team stood and clapped with her.

Todd and Miranda sat together on the sofa as Kath explained exactly what had gone on with Danny. She left out the details of who may have been responsible. Todd put his arm around his daughter and hugged her to him as she cried softly. Kath said they would not be involved in the new active investigation and they should put it behind them and move on with their lives. Todd told her an envelope had been waiting for him on the doormat when he got up. Mrs Tinkerson had written him a brief note resigning from her position and expressing, in her own terse way, her appreciation of their ten-year relationship as boss and housekeeper.

As Kath walked out to her car under a cloudy sky, followed by Todd, a car pulled up and a tall middle-aged man in ripped jeans and T-shirt got out. Todd and the man embraced, and Kath waved and moved off, leaving Todd to the next stage of his life.

'Miranda, I'd like you to meet Scottie, my bandmate and long-time friend.' She shook the hand offered and looked into the brown eyes of Hark's lead guitarist.

'Scottie, this is my daughter.'

'Oh... what? I mean, wow...'

Todd laughed and slapped him on the back. 'Let's get coffee and I'll tell you what's been going on in my life since we last spoke.'

Miranda wandered around the house, upstairs and down, tidying, cleaning, leaving Todd and Scottie to catch up. He'd explained to her that they had a phone call once or twice a year and Scottie had texted Todd unexpectedly to ask if he could come and see him.

Now, she stood just outside the slightly open door of Todd's study and listened as they played guitars together—an acoustic version of one of their greatest hits. The sound warmed her, and she crushed the yellow duster in her fist and wrapped her arms around her body. The sound was light and sweet, and she felt, at last, that she was really home.

| 42 |

Kath stood looking up at the stars. There was no light pollution and the brightness enveloped her. She moved to the bottom of the garden, barely making out the silhouettes of the cows in the far meadow. She tapped the number into her phone and waited for the connection. A number she had been made to promise to memorise, never to be written anywhere.

Sal answered on the second ring. 'So, you're ready?'

Kath nodded, aware no one could see her do it but it confirmed in her own mind and body that she was about to do the thing that would set her free. 'Yes. I'm ready.'

'I won't bother you with details, names etc. You need to know as little as possible for your own protection.'

Kath nodded again and waited.

'He's already serving a seventeen-year sentence for murder. From the details you gave me, it will be an airtight confession. He will get time added on and he'll never see the light of day. His family will be adequately compensated for his gesture, as was promised to him. Any questions?'

Kath's breath disappeared into the breezy night. 'His cold case is sitting in my boxes of files at the office, so...'

'Up to you,' Sal said. 'You can pass the files to the Worcester police if you want or tie it up from your end, although I recommend the former.'

They both took in the silence for a moment.

'Thank you doesn't seem enough.'

Sal laughed. 'You saved my fucking life. This is something I can do for you. Until next time, babe.'

Kath hugged the phone to her chest. A cow suddenly bellowed into the night and Kath copied the sound back at it, then laughed long and hard as the tears rolled down her cheeks.

About The Author

Julia Vaughan

Julia Vaughan, author of Daisy Chain, is a Medical Secretary living in Shropshire with her husband and 2 cats. As a youngster, she wanted to be Destiny Angel or one of Charlie's Angels. Neither came to pass. Julia completed a degree from Worcester University in English & Literary Studies with Associated Drama and has been writing crime and mystery fiction for years, with the odd short story published. She's happiest when watching Columbo, Law & Order and Midsomer Murders. Daisy Chain is Julia's debut full-length novel.

Grave Issue

DCI Kath Fortune - Book 2

Who killed Abraham and Esther Downing in the 1970s?

What is the significance of the seven tiny skeletons unearthed in the garden of the Downing's cottage?

And why does no-one care?

As DCI Kath Fortune and her Cold Case team dive deep into their second investigation they come up against a wall of silence surrounding the reclusive couple. With Kath trying to piece together the clues and keep her personal and professional relationships on track, her past comes back to haunt her and time is running out on all counts.

Grave Issue is out now

The Rapunzel Murders

DCI Kath Fortune - Book 3

Three dead girls
A wild country estate
Whispers of witchcraft

Deep in the Shropshire countryside the Quartermaine estate, with its wild woods, has always been a source of myths and legends. But when the bodies of three young girls are found in the folly, DCI Kath Fortune and her cold case team need answers.

Psychic Lane Petreus is called on to help discover the secrets that the matriarch of the manor is determined to keep hidden but when Lane's life is threatened, Kath must use all the means at her disposal to save Lane and solve the case.

The Rapunzel Murders is out 19th September 2024 in ebook and paperback

Printed in Great Britain
by Amazon

47188549R00169